avenged

DARK ROAD SERIES

KRYS FENNER

avenged

DARK ROAD SERIES #3

Published by

TWO REALMS PUBLISHING LLC

HTTPS://TWO-REALMS-PUBLISHING-LLC.COM/

Cover and Interior Design: We Got You Covered Book Design

Editor: Jamie Morris

Printed in the United States of America

To my family and friends—thank you so much for your patience and support. Without it, this book would not have been possible.

"O spare me, that I may recover strength, before I go hence, and be no more."

– Psalms 39:13, New King James Bible

"UNDERWATER"

Straight ahead, the ledge calls my name;
Today, tomorrow, it's always the same.
The road shakes, yet remains unchanged,
Like the beat of an empty heart I cannot claim.

I try to escape, but I cannot get free;
Its hold is stronger than I'd like to believe.
With every step, its grip tightens in my chest,
Until dust is all that's left.

Written by: Bella Kynaston

prologue

Gervasio pulled a pack of cigarettes from the pocket of his jeans, slipped one of the cancer sticks from the box and popped it between his lips. Lighting it, he glanced at the clock. How long had Ileana been out? Shouldn't she have come to by now? He didn't hit her that hard. Right? He needed her conscious. She was the only one who could tell him who had Giovanna.

Ileana's eyes fluttered open. She blinked a few times.

His gaze followed hers as it dropped to her oh-so-creamy thighs and settled on the black-and-blue marks that had developed in the last thirty minutes. It's what she got for fighting him. Her daughter, Giovanna, was going to be his one and only. She would grow into the woman he would marry. The woman who would carry on his line. All Ileana had to do was give her blessing. But the bitch wouldn't do that. Well, she would now. And if she continued to fight him, he'd make her beg for death.

Gervasio took another drag and exhaled a cloud of smoke. "About time you came to."

Ileana lifted her head for a moment, then blinked again and glanced toward her wrists.

Extension cords hadn't been his preferred option, but they were what was at

1

hand. As long as the knots held, he didn't care what he used.

Ileana looked over her shoulder toward the bedroom. Probably remembering what they'd done in there, Gervasio thought, his spine tingling at the remembered sting of the scratches up and down his back and chest. It had certainly been fun. Definitely something he'd have to do again—just not with Ileana.

Gervasio lowered his gaze to the ripped denim skirt Ileana still had on. Then again, maybe he could make an exception.

But not until the woman told him where she'd hidden Giovanna.

"What ..." Ileana paused. "What do you want?"

"It's simple, really. You tell me where Giovanna is, and I promise this will go easy." Of course, he'd still have to kill her, but he would make it quicker and less painful than if she didn't cooperate. Or else he'd have to see what other goodies he could find to use on her.

"*¡Foda-se! Nunca vou te dizer onde ela está.*"

Fuck him? Gervasio shook his head. It was hard to believe she was the mother of the woman he would one day marry. "Well, that is just rude. There is no need for that kind of language. As for the rest, I have no idea what you said. You know I don't speak Portuguese."

"Then I'll say it more clearly. *Nunca te diré dónde está ella.*" Ileana spit out the words and tugged on the cords that tied her wrists to the chair.

"*¿Nunca? ¿De verdad? Ya lo veremos.*" Gervasio dragged on his cigarette as he closed the distance between them, then pressed the lit end against her knee. "Never?" That word was not in his vocabulary. Ileana would sing like a siren by the time he was through.

The smell of burnt pork filled his nostrils as he held the cigarette ember in place. The woman had yet to cry out. Yet. He waited patiently. She could only hold in the scream for so long. The pain would eventually get to her. He'd witnessed enough *interrogations* to know that she would break—no matter her level of tolerance. Yeah, Ileana may have married Juan, but no way she'd ever been subjected to anything like this before.

Lifting the cigarette from her skin, Gervasio crouched down on his haunches. He took another drag and blew the smoke into her face. "Why don't we try this again? Where is Giovanna?"

This time, Ileana spit in his face. "*¡Vá para o inferno!*"

Go to hell? Oh, this bitch was asking for it. Rising to his feet, Gervasio backhanded her across the cheek. The chair rocked from the power of his strike. Ileana blinked and tears rolled down her cheeks. But crying wasn't the answer he was looking for.

"Tell me where the fuck she is!"

When she didn't respond, he took one last pull off his cigarette, then tossed it to the floor and ground it out with his boot heel. "Fine. Have it your way."

Shoving the dead butt into his jeans pocket, he nodded, then turned toward the kitchen. He was bound to find something— a knife with a good blade would do the trick. Gervasio started tugging open drawers. He'd never been inside the boss's house before, so he wasn't sure.... Ah, yes. Perfect. The eight-inch blade gleaming up at him from the drawer beside the sink would work beautifully. He hated the idea of carving up that gorgeous face, but she hadn't given him a choice. Gervasio yanked another drawer open. Hmm. What was this? A hammer? No. Wooden. A mallet. It would work. He'd just removed the tool from the drawer, when a noise in the living room caught his attention. He darted out of the kitchen.

"What the hell?" Somehow, Ileana had managed to free her hands. Gervasio grabbed her and struggled to shove her back against the chair. Ileana yanked at his restraining arm and tried to loosen his grip. Shit, she was strong!

As she slapped him across the face with her free hand, something sharp ripped across his cheek. He ignored the pain, and moved to tighten his hold on the woman, but she struck again, digging in and dragging the jagged object from his forehead down to his upper lip. He yowled and stumbled back, giving Ileana the chance to scramble to her feet and stumble toward the bedroom, the chair still tied to one ankle.

"You bitch!" Gervasio launched himself at her and tackled her to the ground. Grabbing her hair, he slammed her head into the hardwood floor. She kicked at him, and the heel of her free foot slammed into his shin. The shooting pain pissed him off even more. He clapped his hands on either side of her ears, then flipped her over with such force that the chair cracked. Straddling her, he wrapped his hands around her throat.

"All you had to do was welcome me into your family! Agree to let Giovanna be mine!"

Her hazel eyes widened as she clawed at his arms. Her mouth opened, but no sound came out.

"Say she's mine!" Tightening his grip around her neck, his thumbs crossed over one another. So, what if Giovanna was only two months old? He'd known from the first day he saw that gorgeous baby that she was meant to be his one day. All this woman had to do was give her blessing. Just say okay. Then, when the time came, he'd take Juan's place and Giovanna would be by his side. Juan had given his approval. Why couldn't Ileana? Why couldn't she just say yes? Just fucking say yes!

The fight in Ileana faded. Her fingers went limp and her arms fell away from Gervasio's wrists. As he watched, her life disappeared from her once bright eyes.

Gervasio blinked and let go of her neck. He gripped the back of his head. Shit. What the hell had he done? He stood and dug his cell phone out of his pocket. Pacing from one side of the living room to the other, he dialed the one person who could help.

one

Gervasio eyed the papers in his hands. How had he been so blind to the connection that stared him in the face? And how had he so badly misjudged the one person he had ever truly trusted? He should've had the man investigated when they first met. Some of the trouble he currently found himself in would never have occurred. He most certainly would have taken a different approach with his girl.

He would never forget how he and she crossed paths at the Fourth of July party last year. Her features had turned and turned in his mind, until recognition hit. It had been many years, but once he saw the resemblance to her beautiful mother, he knew. He'd been a mere teenager when he'd met Ileana Castell. Not that she ever introduced herself as a Castell. Instead, she spoke of herself as Ileana Costa. That woman was exquisite. A pure gem that shone, even in death.

And Ileana Costa had tasted divine, too. But, despite his relentless torture, she had refused to tell him where she'd hidden her daughter. When he left her, in the center of a scene made to appear as if she had taken her own life, he knew no more of her daughter's whereabouts than when he'd first entered the house. Then, by happy coincidence, years later, he ran into the girl at a Fourth of July party. A sweet, rich aroma radiated from her skin. As beautiful as her mother, the girl tasted even lovelier. If things had ended differently, he wouldn't be in hiding, right now. Instead, he and Giovanna would be married, and she'd be carrying his son. As it should be.

But events had not gone precisely to plan, and now he *was* in hiding. Thankfully, Gervasio had a list of names. It was the reason he sat in a warehouse, concealed from the police, who scoured the city for any clue of his whereabouts. He was also keeping himself out of sight of his enemies—as well as giving himself much-needed time to hatch his plan for revenge. His girl's entire family—including the woman Giovanna now called mother, who had left Rescate County for safety's sake—would pay for keeping them apart. This time, nothing would be left to chance. He'd take everything into his own hands.

Unfortunately, to get to all the names on his hit list, he would have to use every person who remained loyal to him—and there was a diminishing number of those. For starters, his own brother had betrayed him, along with his girl's scheming brother.

Gervasio dragged a finger down the sheet of paper as he scanned the words written clear as day. It seemed that Swifty, Gervasio's former right-hand man, who was also known as Luis Hernandez, had actually been born Sabio Costa. This made him a blood brother to Gervasio's girl, Giovanna Costa, who was now known as Bella Kynaston.

Getting to Swifty would be easy. All Gervasio had to do was grab the guy's baby sister and hold her hostage—which, anyway, fit in with his plans quite nicely. Getting to his own brother, Cristobal, would be slightly more of a challenge. Then again, if the rumors were true, Cristobal had befriended Swifty, meaning chances were good he could entice them to rescue his own sweet Giovanna, now known as Bella, together. Then he could make short work of killing both Cristobal and Swifty, lessening his remaining problems significantly.

Tapping his chin, Gervasio glanced around the abandoned warehouse. It would take time, but he had the capability to properly execute a full-on plan of destruction. He'd consider the sacrifice of this property a small price to pay for the satisfaction.

He rubbed the jagged scar on his face. It served as a reminder of where he'd been—and exactly where he intended to go. He felt himself grinning at the thought of the two plans he'd formulated. What was most pleasing was that both ended the same way: with bodies on the floor.

Jeremiah hefted Bell's suitcase out of the trunk. It was strange to bring her things home to his house without her, but he'd pick her up from the recovery center soon enough. Bella, who had completed the first two levels of treatment in the hospital, was now being seen on an outpatient basis at Luna Hills Recovery. "Intensive therapy," Bell called it—explaining, when he asked, that she'd be doing a lot of talking as doctors got to the root of her addiction.

God, he hated to think of how close he came to losing her forever. During the worst minutes of his life, he had witnessed her heart giving out completely. By God's will, it hadn't been her time to go. The way they had gotten to that moment, though? It left a lot of unanswered questions. There were a number of things he wanted to ask since she started on her journey to recovery. But, on reflection, he wasn't sure he was ready to handle the truth.

Sure, the video had proven Bella hadn't attempted to take her own life, but why were the letters in her handwriting. She must have written them herself, right? If so, when? Then there was the pill bottle, marked with two sets of fingerprints, one of which was Bell's. How had her prints ended up on the bottle? If he hadn't overheard his father mention that her hands had never left the arms of the chair, Jeremiah would've assumed she'd picked up the bottle herself, and taken the pills.

He shuddered. Yeah. He wasn't sure which scared him more, the questions or the answers.

Jeremiah closed the front door and set the suitcase on the floor. Down the hall, he saw his sister standing outside her bedroom, arms crossed. As he headed towards her, he heard their parents offering suggestions to one another from inside Amanda's room.

"I don't think we have a choice. We'll have to take out Mandy's bed and exchange it for a couple of twin beds."

Jeremiah poked his head into the room, just in time to see their mother, Christine, point toward the middle of Amanda's headboard and say, "We can add a nightstand between them." Their father leaned back against the dresser. "Yeah, but that won't give her any place to put her clothes. Unless Amanda cleans out a couple of drawers and slims her closet down."

"How long have they been discussing this?" Jeremiah asked his sister. She hadn't been thrilled with the idea of sharing a room with Bella to begin with. Now, their parents were discussing how to rearrange her bedroom as if she had no say in the matter.

"A few minutes. I tried helping and got pushed aside. God, I can't wait to turn eighteen."

Jeremiah raised an eyebrow at the comment, which Mandy had been making more and more since the first of the year. He wondered, was she planning to jump right up and move out when she turned eighteen in April, even though there'd still be a good month and a half of school before she graduated? He hoped not.

But that was months away. Now, he stepped into Amanda's bedroom and cleared his throat. "Some food for thought. Have you considered how uncomfortable this will make Bella?"

"Of course, we have, but where else can she stay?" His mother made her way across the room and paused, staring into Amanda's packed closet.

Jeremiah sighed. "I don't think rearranging Mandy's room will make things better. Bella won't just feel like she's inconvenienced the family, generally. Now, she's going to worry about the situation Mandy's been put in."

He glanced at Mandy, who rolled her eyes, but didn't say anything.

"Do you have another idea, son?" his father asked.

"She could move into my room. And before you go all parental, hear me out." Jeremiah paused. He'd seen how nervous Bell had been all morning after visiting her father's grave. Then she'd begun twisting the hem of her blouse tighter and tighter the closer they got to the recovery center. So much had happened to her in such a short period of time: Her rapist had left her pregnant; then Bell lost the baby. Her father had been killed and her mother had disappeared. She needed someplace peaceful to stay—somewhere she wouldn't be subjected to the tension of sharing a room with his already restless, on-edge sister.

His mother sat on Amanda's bed. "We're listening."

"If she stays in my room, she'll have her own space, and so will Mandy. You guys just finished the basement, so I can stay down there. The more peace and calm Bell has, the less of a chance she'll relapse. At least that's how I see it."

"You may be right." His mother sighed and glanced around the room.

With his mother's agreement, Jeremiah turned to his father. "Dad?"

His father nodded. "It's a good plan. I'm just concerned for her. No matter where she sleeps, the situation will not be easy on her—especially with Gervasio Rodriguez still out there somewhere."

What? Didn't his father believe the guy had left town? Surely, he couldn't be stupid enough to come after Bell again?

His mother voiced his question. "You think he'll come looking for her?"

"I do. Both of them. We'll have to be more vigilant than ever."

"Both? Both of whom?" Jeremiah hated it when his parents had silent conversations right in front of him. When neither his father nor mother responded, he arched an eyebrow at his sister. Maybe she had some idea of what the hell his parents meant, but the blank look on her face told him she was just as confused as he was.

His mother stood up and patted his shoulder. "Come on. Let's go get your room ready for Bella, then we can get you set up downstairs."

Juan followed the path behind the cabin. The heat and wisps of steam radiating from the fire pit indicated a fire had recently been extinguished. Although neither his son nor his son's companion were in the small building, he assumed at least one of them was close by.

Passing another stand of trees, he confirmed his opinion of the place, which hadn't altered since he'd first found the safe house. It was well isolated, difficult to find without directions. And, once, it had belonged to him. A fact Sabio likely hadn't learned. Still, he had to give his son credit. His boy had grown into a smart young man—even if Juan, himself, had had next to nothing to do with that outcome.

A branch snapped beneath his foot. Juan growled at the noise giving his position away.

Slipping behind a nearby tree, he surveyed his surroundings. No movement caught his eye. It didn't appear his misstep had attracted attention. Satisfied that he remained unnoticed, Juan left the cover of the tree and continued on his way, hoping he would find Sabio soon. With his enemy out there, he certainly did not want to be caught off guard.

Click.

The sound of a pistol being cocked behind him was unmistakable. Without hesitation, Juan lifted his hands into the air. "I am unarmed."

"Dad?"

"*Sí.*" Relieved to hear his son's voice, Juan turned, expecting Sabio to lower the gun. But the weapon remained pointed at him. Inwardly, he groaned. His son's response probably had to do with their last meeting. Unfortunately, it had not gone well.

Sabio's next words affirmed Juan's thought. "What the hell are you doing here? Didn't you get the picture last time? I don't want, nor do I need your help."

"I understand you are upset with me. While you have reason, would you please disengage your weapon?"

His son smirked, returned the safety to its rightful position, and tucked the gun into his waistband. "What? Don't trust my aim?"

"I am quite certain you have learned to fire that weapon appropriately, otherwise you should not carry it."

"No thanks to you, but, yeah, I did. Now, what're you doing here?"

"I have seen your sister and—"

"Are you shitting me? You tell me not to contact her, and you have the balls to go see her? What'd you do? Hold out your hand and say, 'Sorry I disappeared, but I'm your father.'"

Juan pinched the bridge of his nose. Of course, he had not introduced himself to his daughter at all. Nor did he intend to ever do so. The less she knew of his existence, the better her own life would be. "No, my son. I watched her from a distance, as I asked you to do. She was in the cemetery mourning the man she called father. I believe she spotted me, but I suspect she thought I was Gervasio, which is why I am here."

Sabio's face softened somewhat. "Okay. You have my attention, so speak."

"You have access to information that I do not and which I believe can be useful, if we choose to work together."

Raising his eyebrows, Sabio asked, "And why would I do that? It isn't like you've given me any reason to trust you. The one time I needed you most to help my sister, you left me hanging. No response, no call ... nothing. Gigi nearly died because of it." He shoved his hands into his jeans pockets.

Linking his own hands behind his back, Juan nodded. His son made a fair assessment of the situation. Thus far, Sabio had done all the work. He needed to prove his worth to his son. "I apologize. I carefully weighed all the options and concluded you and your sister were safest if I maintained my distance. That included our communications as well. Much time had passed when I realized the error of my decision."

"I take it that you have a plan, then?"

"I do. You are quite apt with computers and other electronic resources. I, on the other hand, am an excellent shooter. If Gervasio has done all this to seek me out, then I should be the one doing the, shall we say, ground work." Juan carefully offered only the essentials of what he deemed important. Although his son was brilliant, he was only eighteen years of age. On the other hand, perhaps his son's youth had caused Juan to underestimate him.

"I fail to see how your ability with a weapon in any way proves I can trust you. And for all the great shot you claim to be, you haven't exactly protected us. Gervasio found Gigi, and now she's dealing with something no one should ever have to—especially not at the age of sixteen."

Juan held back a smile. Ileana would have seen the humor in how much their son took after her. Before Sabio, Ileana had been the only person to ever call him on his crap. Now, their son was filling her shoes. Clearly, only one thing would convince Sabio he could be trusted.

"You are correct. And I must live with the choices I made that allowed for those events to occur in Giovanna's life. The only way I know how to make things right is to do what I should have many years ago. Go to the desk in the bedroom. There is a false bottom in the center drawer. Inside is a file. That should be sufficient evidence for you to trust me in this endeavor."

"You must think I'm a real idiot. I found that file a long time ago. So, yes, I'm fully aware of your skills. The question is, why should I tell you anything about what I learn about Gervasio's whereabouts?"

"Because it is best if I deal with him before your sister makes any attempts at revenge. My hands are already dirty. Taking him out will not wash my sins away, but it will prevent you or your sister from collecting any sins of your own—at least on Gervasio's account. Is not that a good enough reason?" Juan's question came out in a snarl.

Sabio dragged a hand down his face, thought for a moment, then nodded slowly. "I can't argue with that. For now, we'll work together."

Bella rolled over to her side. She opened an eye and glanced at the clock on the nightstand. Midnight. Had she really only been in bed for two hours? She buried her nose into the pillow. Miah's scent lingered. His natural musk should've done the trick. It should've been enough to give her the peace she always felt around him. But tonight nothing quieted the whirlwind in her brain.

It was like a tornado had set up shop in her head and was tossing around everything that had occurred within the last few weeks. The discovery of her father's death, the loss of her baby, her mother taking off—not to mention the court decision that landed her here, in the Detrone house. The Detrones had been really nice, and in particular she was grateful to be allowed to stay in Miah's room, rather than share a room with Amanda. Being alone gave her time to think. But thinking wouldn't help her get a full night's sleep.

She eased out of bed, tiptoed over, and pressed her ear to the door, listening for any noise to indicate someone was still up. She'd give anything, she thought, just to overhear one of the Detrones talking to her mother. The only call to her mother she'd made herself had been declined. Her one consolation had been brief conversations with both of her grandmothers. Thankfully, neither of them knew everything that had occurred. A small blessing in disguise. She smiled a little. Maybe it was one of Alex's silver linings.

Bella cracked Miah's bedroom door. All seemed quiet. She slipped out and padded down the hall toward the kitchen—and the basement door.

What if Miah had already passed out? He looked exhausted at dinner. Not that she'd paid much attention to anything happening at the dinner table. Instead, her earlier conversation with the psychiatrist had consumed most of her thoughts. They'd discussed a plan: no immediate return to school, twenty to twenty-five hours a week at the facility on an outpatient basis, and a lot of freaking therapy. She'd have to talk herself blue if she intended to get better. Not like anyone would actually listen.

Now, having tiptoed down the basements stairs, Bella bit her bottom lip and stared at the back of Miah's head. God, what was she doing? She couldn't run to Miah every time sleep refused to come. She had to learn to depend on herself. She was all she had, really. Without saying a word, she pivoted on her foot and turned back toward the stairs.

"Bell? You okay?"

Damn. Offering the hint of a smile, she faced him. She should probably be honest, but whatever words she might use to describe her feelings failed her at the moment. So, she only said, "Yeah. Go back to sleep. I didn't mean to wake you."

"You didn't." Miah rolled over, lifted the covers, and patted the spot beside him.

It was all the invitation she needed. Crawling into the bed, Bella said, "I'm sorry. I just ... this is ... I don't know ... strange. But when I'm with you ..." Bella propped up on her elbow. "It's you, Miah. Your presence gives me a little bit of peace. You have to know that."

"I do, but I didn't think my parents would go for us sharing a bed. I hoped my room would be enough." Miah reached up and tucked a loose strand of hair behind her ear.

"Don't get me wrong, it helps, and I appreciate it, but...."

He sat up and climbed out of the bed. "Come on. I can't have you sleeping down here."

"Then what do we do?"

"I have an idea." Miah grinned.

t w o

Sheriff Jamar Detrone crossed his arms and eyed the remains that had been discovered thus far. The cabin, situated on a good acre of land, had been abandoned long ago. But, at some point, the grounds behind the house had been designated as a burial site—for at least seven people, most of them now nothing but bone. Jamar wondered, had Simms known what they would find here when his team came looking?

Several weeks ago, he'd had both Rodney Harrison and Detective Nathan Simms arrested. While the two of them had revealed a lot of information, unfortunately, most of what the pair coughed up were things the sheriff and his force already knew. However, Simms's last tip had led them to this piece of property, owned by a mystery man named "Gerald Ross." But when they tried to trace Ross, they hit a dead end. It seemed to Jamar that "Ross" was just another one of Gervasio Rodriguez's aliases—but they had yet to get hard evidence to corroborate his hunch.

The sheriff sighed. How many aliases could the guy have? And what else did he have hidden?

His thoughts were interrupted by one of the forensics guys calling out, "We've got another one."

"Christ." Walking over to the newly dug site, Jamar eyed the latest remains, which gave him the feeling of bugs crawling all over him. It was a big, muscular body, but its abdominal cavity was not only caved in, the skin had been flayed from the muscle, and the eyes bulged from blackened sockets. Though the body looked bad, it was much more recent than the others they'd discovered.

Detective Russell stepped up beside Jamar and glanced at the latest find. "Holy shit."

"This isn't the worst we've seen, today."

"No, it's not that." Russell knelt beside the open grave. "I think this is one of the last recruits for the Grim Reapers, a soldier that served under Bronco."

Had this all been Gervasio's handiwork? The guy had taken over the Grim Reapers in his early twenties. But until they had proof that Gerald Ross was one of his aliases…. Jamar shook his head. "If that's the case, I'd sure like to know what led to his death. We need to get a forensic anthropologist out here. Only way to make certain every set of remains gets identified."

"There's a good one up in Albuquerque," Russell offered. "I'll put a call in and see if she can make the trip."

Why hadn't Russell ever been promoted to Sergeant? The man obviously knew how to do his job and do it well. Jamar hadn't discussed the prospect of promotion with the detective, although he wasn't sure why. Could be because Russell hadn't bothered with the sergeant's exam. According to his file, the guy had received excellent reviews, but didn't seem all that ambitious. More information was needed before he could make a final decision. Now, all he said was, "Keep me posted."

Then Jamar gestured to the body. "And this guy? Who do you think it is?"

"Rolando 'Bárbaro' Gomez. His nickname literally means 'cruel.' His record supports it, too. We've collared him at least three times on assault charges."

Jamar rubbed his chin. Despite speculation on the reliability of Bella's testimony—speculation based on her more recent behavior—he'd never doubted her. And this guy, what was left of him, along with Russell's intel, made him think. "Kind of sounds how Bella described her second attacker." He said this hesitantly, as all the evidence they had pointed to the kid they'd arrested. What if they were wrong, though?

As Detective Russell stood, brushing dirt from his hands, he voiced Jamar's concerns. "But the evidence all points to Petar Jacobs. Unless…. You can't possibly think Simms had anything to do with this. Do you?"

"Simms was taking bribes and hindering prosecution regarding several incidents involving Gervasio Rodriguez. What's to say he wouldn't tamper with evidence?"

"I would have staked my career on Simms being straight—that is, if you hadn't already proven me wrong once. It's just ... I thought I knew him."

"I know. It's hard to see one of our own turn. But we'll do what we've done before—follow the evidence. Why don't you go back to Gabriella Caprise and see if she's willing to talk now. I'll get Ali to pull the tapes from the evidence locker." Simms had spilled about kickbacks he's taken for helping Rodriguez out in certain situations, but he'd never admitted to actually tampering with evidence. But if he had....

Six months since Bella had been raped, and they were still piecing evidence together. Well, nothing for it but to keep on pushing at the leads they had. If he planned to pay a visit to Simms, he needed to make sure he went in with more than a few guesses. Hard proof would be required, including pictures of everything that had been discovered at the house Simms had so kindly directed them to.

Bella checked her watch. Her first group session had dispersed a few minutes early, giving her some time to herself to digest what happened. She hadn't really listened to a word any of the other girls in her group said and had quickly declined when they offered her the chance to speak. She'd repeated her story enough for a lifetime. If she could help it, she'd never utter another word on the matter.

She glanced from one end of the hall to the other. It looked empty, but was she truly alone? The counselors and psychiatrists were a bunch of buttinskis. They might as well have cameras built into the backs of their heads. Rumor had it that, even when they weren't around, they always knew what was going on.

But even if they were watching on some hidden cameras, all they would see was Bella exploring the hallways, learning the lay of the land. Though she'd have plenty of time for that. As her psychiatrist explained, she would begin with intensive outpatient treatment for a couple of weeks. Then they'd reassess and generate a plan based on her rate of recovery. They'd talked about how things could go at great length. Well, actually, it was her doctor who had done most of the talking. She'd only half-listened. All she cared about was getting out of the room.

Unfortunately, she'd been moved from one room of torture to another. In every single one of these "therapy rooms," they expected her to get in touch with her feelings. She'd avoided sharing her emotions thus far. But how long could she avoid letting people in? Becoming an open book had never been part of her personal plan, but it seemed to be the most important feature of their plans.

Bella paused mid-stride and eyed the door to the chapel. She'd barely glanced at the place during her initial visit a couple days earlier. But now something caused her to linger. Cautiously, she eased into the doorway and peered inside, where rows of empty pews gave way to an altar that stood front and center. From there, she imagined, the pastor addressed the congregation.

But that wasn't what captured her attention. What called out to her was the piano, which sat just behind the altar. She glanced over her shoulder, eying the hallway. Still no one to be seen. Biting her bottom lip, Bella stepped inside and slipped down the aisle.

After peeking back again and assuring herself there was no one around, she inhaled deeply, then climbed up to the altar platform and headed directly for the piano. She regarded the ivory keys, but hesitated to touch them. How long had it been since she played? When was the last time she'd sung? Was it when she was with David?

Drawn by the urge to sing, she sat on the bench. Her fingers naturally conformed to the keys, and her feet easily located the pedals. Much time might have passed, but her body hadn't forgotten how to play. Before her heart had the chance to catch up, her brain selected a song, which her fingers began to play.

It was "Broken" by Lifehouse, and the title was fitting for how she felt. Her body had physically healed. She'd recovered from the last attempt on her life, but everything that transpired and led to that event consumed her soul. There had been no time for her to mourn the loss of a child she didn't want. Hell, she'd barely processed the loss of her father. Her heart remained in a million pieces—yet everyone seemed to believe she could jump through hoops and rebuild the life she'd once had.

As the first verse of "Broken" fluttered through her lips like an old memory, she realized that her life was the broken clock the song spoke of. If only her world had stopped completely. She was beyond damaged. Her heart only continued to beat because she had Miah to hold onto. But even with him by her side, she was barely able to breathe through the pain.

Tears trickled down her cheeks as the chorus poured out from her heart.

"Bella?"

Caught red handed, she pulled her fingers from the keys and quickly wiped the tears from her face. No one needed to know how bad the pain was.

Her gaze shifted to her psychiatrist. "Is my ride here?"

"Yes. What were you doing?"

"Nothing." She got to her feet and jumped off the platform, hoping her doctor wouldn't push her. She gave a backwards glance at the piano. It felt nice to connect to the instrument. It pulled some of the heartache out of her. Like a freshly cut vein, her heart bled with the words of the song.

"Well, for 'nothing,' that was certainly something." When Bella didn't respond, her doctor continued. "You know you can tell me anything and it goes nowhere. Right?"

The woman had repeated this same sentence at every session Bella'd attended. Maybe she thought if she said it enough, Bella would finally believe it. Now, almost convinced, Bella fidgeted with the hem of her t-shirt. No, she decided. It would be too much to share what the piano meant to her. This woman couldn't be fully trusted, no matter how much she tried to convince Bella otherwise. So, shrugging, Bella only said, "I was just fooling around."

"Okay. If that's what you want to go with, I'll accept it. For now."

"Um, well, okay. I'll see you tomorrow." Bella stepped past her psychiatrist and headed for the hall. What the hell did she mean, "for now"? Could it mean she wouldn't accept the answer in the future? Or that she'd seen enough to know better? Had her doctor been listening long enough to realize how significant the piano was to her?

The most she'd ever revealed to anyone about the piano was to tell them how she learned to play as a kid. While her mother had some idea of how important the instrument was, even she didn't know why. Only one person had ever known the real reason, but he wasn't around anymore. He'd been ripped away from her in the worst way possible.

Exiting the building, she spotted Mrs. Detrone's van. Tugging the door open, Bella hopped in. After greeting Mrs. Detrone, Bella peeked at the back seat to find the twins fast asleep in their car seats. Usually, Miah's three-year-old sister, Natasha, came along for the ride, too. She normally talked Bella's ear off, although most of what the little girl said was complete nonsense. What would it be like to have her innocence again?

"Where's Nat?" Bella asked Miah's mom.

"She's on a play date. We're picking her up on the way home."

"Oh." After buckling her seatbelt, Bella stared out the window. It was rare for her to have the chance to speak with Mrs. Detrone without anyone else around. Some time ago, the woman had told Bella that they shared a piece of Bella's new reality: they'd both been raped.

"Is everything okay? You look a little distracted," Mrs. Detrone said.

Bella hadn't spoken in group therapy, but maybe she could talk to Miah's mother. Those girls were a bunch of strangers, but this woman had not only taken her in, but also happened to be her favorite author. If she couldn't trust her, then who could she trust?

Bella glanced over. "Today was my first group session."

"I see."

"Did you go through therapy? After … it … happened, I mean." God, Bella still had a hard time choking out the word "rape." It was an awful word used to describe an awful act. She'd like to get hold of the bastard who put the word in her world and strangle it out of him.

"I did. It wasn't easy, though. So don't beat yourself up if you aren't ready to talk to the other girls about the rape. We all deal with things in our own way and our own time. How I handled my rape won't be the same way you handle yours."

Sounded like something her psychiatrist would say. Had the two women talked? It made sense that they would, but since Mrs. Detrone had never talked about her rape with her own children, why would she discuss it with a complete stranger to her?

"How did you deal with it?"

"I got angry. I took self-defense classes. My therapy had to be geared toward those feelings. Just like your therapy is set up to work for you. Look, when you're in the group setting, don't focus on the rape. Focus on recovery. Let the other girls tell you how they're recovering. If you give that your attention, I promise, it'll make a huge difference."

"You think so?" Bella asked to be polite. But the thing that Mrs. Detrone had said that really made an impact was talking about taking self-defense classes. Now that was an idea.

Eyeing the three-story house, Amanda parked the Dodge in front of the fountain that was the centerpiece of the Warren family residence's circular drive. "I can't believe I'm doing this," she hissed into her cell phone.

"You don't have to go through with this," Vick responded.

A few weeks earlier she and Vick decided to share the letter each had received from Bella. When Vick read Bella's request that Amanda protect the guys Bella cared about, Amanda and Vick had argued. While Bella's concern for himself and Jeremiah made perfect sense to Vick, he took issue with Bella expecting Amanda to provide support for David Warren. Not after all the guy had done.

Now, Amanda countered, "It may be easy for you to disregard Bella, but she isn't sleeping in the room across from yours."

"Okay, fine. Do whatever. I don't care." Vick's sarcasm was evident to Amanda, even with their iffy cell connection.

"Stop being such a jackass," she said. Then, frustrated by his lack of regard for anyone other than himself, Amanda hung up. Jerk deserved a taste of his own medicine. She silenced her cell. God, why couldn't he just have been supportive? Dismissing her annoyance with Vick, she climbed out of the car, headed up the stairs to the massive front door, and knocked.

Would a butler answer? If she was lucky that'd be exactly what happened. If David's twin sister, Heather, answered, she'd probably get the door slammed in her face. And she really had no desire to kick the door down. She could punch Heather again, of course. Although, that might not be the best approach.

An older man in a black suit opened the door. He definitely looked like a butler! "May I help you?" he asked.

"Um, yeah. I'm here to see David Warren. He in?"

"Yes. May I tell him who is calling?"

"Amanda Detrone." Then, before she could be denied entry, she stepped across the threshold into the foyer.

"Madam! I beg your pardon!"

Down a long hallway, Amanda saw Heather step out of the kitchen, her hands wrapped around a mug. "It's okay, Geoffrey," the girl called out. "Let her in."

"Of course, madam." The butler closed the door behind Amanda, bowed, and excused himself.

Talk about weird. Never in a million years had she imagined Heather would come to her aid. "So ... explanation?" Amanda said to Heather, once David's sister got close enough that they could talk without yelling.

"I could say the same thing. Except I know why you're here."

"You do?" Amanda raised an eyebrow. Vick wouldn't have revealed the request Bella'd made of her. Could Bella have told Heather, herself? No way.

Heather laughed. "I see by your confusion you don't have the whole picture."

"No point in disagreeing. Obviously, I'm missing something here."

Heather took a folded piece of paper from her back pocket and handed it to Amanda. "Let's just say I intervened on my brother's behalf. He was already heartbroken from his breakup with Bella. Her suicide note, or whatever it is, was the last thing he needed to read."

Unsure what to think or do, Amanda stared at the paper in her hands.

"Go ahead and read it," Heather said. "I have."

Inhaling deeply, Amanda unfolded the letter and revealed Bella's words to David.

David,

I tried many times to be completely honest with you. Tell you how I really felt and everything I was going through. I'm sorry I couldn't find the courage until now.

That may not hold a lot of weight, but this is my last chance. Please understand none of what I'm about to say is a reflection on you. You're a great guy and you deserve to be happy. You deserve a girl who can truly love you.

I wish at some point I loved you like you did me. It would've been easier on both of us, but what remained of my heart belonged to another. I cared about you as a friend, so I tried in some small way to love you. Except there was nothing left of my shattered heart to give away. I finally understand it will never be whole again.

You had every right to question me about Jeremiah.

I never fully let him go. While I suppose a part of me hoped he would want me back one day, I know that will never happen. I'm too far broken to deserve anyone, including you. The small semblance of existence you gave me can't stop the pain I struggle with every day.

I don't want you to hurt, but I don't want to hurt anymore either. With time, and me out of the way, you'll be free to move on. I know there's a girl out there who will cherish and protect your heart at all costs. Not like me.

In the beginning, you won't think you need someone to lean on, but until you heal, I've asked a friend to check on you. It's important you continue moving forward. I'm sorry for everything I haven't done. I hope one day you can forgive me.

Always,
Bella

Oh, boy, Amanda thought. She was in way over her head. Her only salvation, David, hadn't read the letter. But how much of what Bella wrote had she said in the last conversation the two shared? "Has David said anything about what happened when they broke up?" she asked Heather.

"No. He refuses to talk about it. I can tell you though, whatever went down, it was bad."

"How do you know that?"

"David has anger issues, but nothing like what I saw today at soccer practice. And now he's in the gym working out—hard. Not a good sign." Heather took the letter back and returned it to her pocket.

"I have to at least try. I owe Bella that much."

Heather shrugged. "Don't say I didn't warn you. Gym is down the hall. First door on your left."

David grunted as he pressed the weights above his head, and sweat rolled down his face. He'd already done one set of twenty-five reps, but his body didn't ache yet. So, he added another ten pounds to each side of the bar for a total of 230 pounds. That should do it. Every part of his body needed to burn as he pounded out another five reps.

The rumor mill at school had been grinding non-stop the last six weeks. Initially, everyone thought Bella attempted suicide. Then people thought someone tried to kill her. Either way, everything was all about her. Bella, Bella, Bella, non-fucking-stop. The girl he loved, who never loved him back. He couldn't keep himself from thinking about her. David lifted the weights one last time and returned them to their anchors. Slowly, he sat up and grabbed a towel to wipe his face.

He'd released a lot of the anger he'd been holding in since their break-up at soccer practice. Rightfully, Coach Yager called him out, saying, "Soccer is no place for lack of control. Get your shit together. I need my captain out there."

Their first game was in a couple of weeks. If he couldn't be the captain his team needed, he'd lose his position—which felt like all he had left. Bella was a complication that could ruin him. But this was his senior year, and he planned to be remembered after he graduated. So, he came to the gym to sweat all of her shit out of his system.

David stood and crossed the room to do some pull-ups. Just then, he heard a soft knock, followed by a squeak as the door opened.

"Go away Heather. I'm not in the mood." Without turning, David placed his hands on the pull-up bar.

"Hello? No way could I ever be mistaken for your sister."

Startled, he turned, and his gaze landed on the caramel-skinned beauty in the doorway. Amanda? What was she doing there?

Before he could ask, she said, "I came by to see how you were doing."

"As you can see, I'm fine." The word didn't match how he felt, but the last thing he wanted was a friend of Bella's in his business. He tightened his grip on the pull-up bar and hoisted himself with the satisfying strength of his curled arms. Silently, he started counting off the repetitions.

When his lack of interest didn't seem to discourage Amanda, David dropped to the floor and turned to glare at her. "Can't you see I'm in the middle of a workout?"

"I'm not blind, nor am I deaf. I could hear your grunts all the way down the hall. I mean, is it really necessary to do all that? Or are you purposely trying to kill yourself?"

"Whatever I'm doing, it's my business, not yours. So, get the hell out." He walked over to the bench where he'd left his towel, scooped it up, and wiped the sweat from his face.

Amanda threw her hands in the air. "Fine. Whatever. I tried. I did what she asked. No worries. I can show—"

"What do you mean, you did what she asked?"

"Exactly what I said."

"Which is what? What did she ask?"

Amanda seemed to soften. "Look," she said, "I don't know what Bella thought would happen, but she wanted me to check on you. Maybe she didn't love you, but she does care. I wouldn't be here if she didn't."

"Good for her. Doesn't change what happened. Doesn't change how I feel. Doesn't change the fact that she led me on."

Amanda frowned. "I'm not going to defend her and say what she did was right. It was pretty screwed up, but she's been through a lot—and it's messed her up, you know?"

"And here I thought you weren't going to defend her." David shook his head. "Weren't you saying you could show yourself out? Please do." David stepped back to the pull-up bar and began counting his reps again, as Amanda pulled the door closed behind her.

Bella eyed Dr. Shah. A dark-skinned, older woman, who wore her salt-and-pepper hair swept into a little bun, the woman's tidy appearance reminded Bella of her mother. It was only her third day at Luna Hills, and she already had a new doctor. Evidently, someone thought this doctor fit her needs better than her previous doctor—even though her father had chosen the other one before he died.

Sighing, Bella responded to Dr. Shah's question. "I don't really know a lot about my biological parents. Just that my mother died of a drug overdose, and my father was a drug lord."

"Well, that's quite a dramatic summary, Bella. What about your adoptive parents? What can you tell me about them?"

Dr. Shah leaned back in her chair, draped one leg over the other, and laced her fingers together around her knee.

"My dad was DeWei Kynaston. You might have known him. He was a counselor at the local detention center. His father died while they were in China, which is where his mother was from. He stayed there until college, which is where he met my mother." Without warning, Bella felt tears rolling down her cheeks. Struggling to continue, she added, "Now, my father is dead and my mother's left me. You must have known that, right?"

Dr. Shah didn't respond to Bella's accusation. Instead, she said, "That's an awful lot for a sixteen-year-old to deal with."

"Yeah, well, I didn't have a choice." Bella swiped at her tears. She glanced around the room. The walls were painted a soft peach. Several prints with inspirational words were hung around the room. Like her last doctor's office, this one was meant to evoke warm fuzzies and loosen the tongue. Not likely, these days.

"The choice is in how you handle what has happened. Do you talk about how much you miss your father? Or how upset you are with your mother?"

Bella was startled. How had the doctor deduced those facts from what she'd just said? "I don't talk about them at all."

"Then that is where we'll start."

"Why?" None of her parents, biological or adoptive, had anything to do with her addiction. Right? It was her problem, wasn't it? Wasn't that why her father had chosen the other lady in the first place? To deal with Bella's real issues? But, Bella reflected, he'd had no idea about the pills at the time. If he had known, would he have selected another doctor? Like the one who sat in front of her?

Dr. Shah already seemed smarter. She was right. Bella missed her father deeply. He'd been a great man and had cared so much for her. And she'd repaid him by getting him killed. Remembering how her father had chased after her, more tears trickled down her cheeks. Even when she'd acted like she hated him, he still saved her. She missed him so much.

"I want you to understand something. You're here for us to get to the root of your addiction, and there are a number of factors to take into consideration. Sometimes, addictions are genetic. Many are psychological or emotional. Knowing what we do of your biological parents, we understand that you have a genetic predisposition, but with what has happened in the past six months, we know you have some psychological problems, too. Working with this knowledge, we can help you find a way to face the addiction."

"I could get better?"

Dr. Shah leaned forward. "You'll have to learn to handle your problems differently. But, in essence, yes, you could get better."

"I want to ... for him."

"He's important to you, and he's a good place to start. Talk to me more about DeWei."

"I didn't know what to expect. But for a second, I thought I was getting through to him." Amanda rolled onto her side and curled up against Vick. She'd driven around town for a little while after David practically kicked her out of his parents' house. How had she read the situation so wrong? Easy. She hardly knew the guy she'd been charged with looking after.

Vick ran his fingers through her dark brown locks. "You going to try again?"

"I feel like I have to. Not so much because Bella asked me to, but because I've seen him. He's not just hurt, he's devastated. I just ... I wish I had more to go on."

"Have you thought about talking to Bella? See what she's willing to tell you about their last conversation?"

"I thought about that all afternoon." Amanda reached across Vick's chest and laced their hands together. Theoretically, it would be simple to talk to her brother's girlfriend, now that they lived in the same house. But Amanda already knew the conversation would be tough going. And Bella had so many things to deal with already, it seemed wrong to add to the pile.

"But you won't."

"You know me so well."

Vick leaned down and kissed her forehead. "I know you believe you should be able to handle this by yourself."

"That's not entirely true. I mean, I do think I can take care of this, but it isn't just that. She's dealing with so much, and she's doing it alone. We've all kind of abandoned her."

"Except Jeremiah."

"Yeah, but I wonder if that's only because he hasn't read his letter." Lord, she prayed he never planned to. Especially if Bella's words were anything like those she'd written to David. It broke her heart. Bella had taken advantage of David's feelings for her, understanding quite well how badly he'd be hurt in the end. So,

Bella asked her to check on him. But until Heather had shoved the Bella's note into her hand, Amanda hadn't known how hard it would be.

"Jeremiah never read his letter?"

"No. And he's not the only one."

Vick shifted his head and raised an eyebrow. "What're you talking about?"

"Heather got to the letter Bella sent to David first. He has no idea it exists. I'm not sure he ever will."

"I'm kind of surprised. I never pegged Heather as someone to be protective of her brother—or anyone else, for that matter."

"I'm beginning to think the whole bitchiness act is a farce," Amanda said. The girl was probably as lonely as her brother. Amanda had noticed that no one else had been home—except the butler. From what she could tell, Heather and David's parents weren't homebodies, to say the least. Thankfully, she had grown up quite differently. With a houseful of siblings and parents who regularly demonstrated their love for the whole clan.

Amanda stared at her boyfriend's fingers. One day she'd have to tell him, but right then was not the time.

"You may be right. But what about David. Any ideas on what you're going to do?"

Her choices were limited. "Be supportive. Show up at his soccer games. Acknowledge him at school. Keep trying. It's all I can do, until the wall breaks."

"You really are an amazing girl. One of the many reasons I love you, even if I was a dick earlier."

"You said 'dick'! My virgin ears."

"Shut up." Vick tugged her closer and kissed her lips. Her mouth parted, and his tongue touched hers. With one hand wrapped around her back, he pressed his chest into hers, sliding his other hand down her spine until it cupped her ass. Then, he ground his hips against hers and rolled her onto her back.

Amanda moaned into his mouth and deepened the kiss. They were the only ones at his parents' house. Knowing they had an hour before anyone arrived home, she slipped her hands beneath his shirt and clung to his bare back, while she swiveled her hips against his. Releasing the kiss, she gazed up and saw his chocolate brown eyes shining with desire. Their minds had synched—and they both had only one thing banging around their brains.

three

"Where's Bell?" Jeremiah scanned the full room. They'd arrived at this family night event at her treatment center less than ten minutes ago, and she'd already successfully disappeared. Either not hearing his question, or ignoring it, his mother and Dr. Shah walked off together. When Bell mentioned the event to his parents the night before, she hadn't been too excited about their attendance. She'd even had a nightmare, last night, but refused to tell him what it was about. He suspected it had something to do with her treatment, though.

Jeremiah sighed. When would things return to normal for them? Since there was no immediate answer to that question, he glanced around again. Bell couldn't have gone far.

Pushing through the crowd, he paused every few feet to see if he could spot her talking with a new friend here at the center. Her old friends had kind of turned their backs on her, he'd noticed. This was something he needed to discuss with them. He suspected that those letters they'd each received had something to do with it, but whatever it was that was causing them to keep their distance had to be put aside.

Looking out a side door, he glanced down the hall. He remembered that during the tour he'd taken with Bell on her first day she'd shown a tiny bit of interest in the chapel—well, not the chapel, but the instrument inside the chapel. Heading towards the chapel on a hunch, Jeremiah wondered how long it had been since the last time he and Bell had played the piano together? How long had it been since she had sung or played at all? Music was so much a part of her life, it would be a shame if she never regained her passion for it.

Then, just steps away from the chapel, he heard it—the voice of an angel belting out emotions like nothing he'd ever heard. His hunch had paid off. It was Bell. Standing in the doorway, he listened, as her fingers skillfully moved from one chord to the next, her voice melding perfectly with the notes. He recognized the song, "My Immortal," by Evanescence. One verse passed her lips, and it stopped him in his tracks. So much loss and loneliness came through her words—and she was singing without inhibition.

Every word she sang broke his heart. As if she'd been left to fight alone. The way she'd always been. No one by her side. No one to comfort her. No one to tell her it would all be okay. She wasn't supposed to feel that way. And yet he'd done the same thing all of her friends had done, in a way. Although his motives were good, he hadn't been there for her, lately. Instead, he'd maintained his distance with the hope that it would give her the chance to focus on her recovery. Had it been the wrong thing to do? Had he made the wrong choice again?

Dammit. In the hospital, he'd promised her father he'd take care of her. DeWei knew he wasn't going to make it, and he had spoken to Jeremiah as if he were Bell's future. Now, it was time he acted like the man her father had believed him to be.

Jeremiah entered the chapel and padded along the carpeted aisle, pausing at the edge of the front pew. Up close, he could see she was crying.

Bell finished the song. Sniffling, she swiped tears from her cheekbones. Her gaze landed on him for a second before she looked away. "Sorry I disappeared."

"It's okay." Jeremiah brushed a hand across the top of his head. What was he doing here? Besides standing around like a complete idiot. He shoved his hands in his jeans pockets. What the hell was he supposed to say? An apology would be a good start. Part of him wanted to run; the other part wanted to embrace her and never let go. "I haven't heard you sing in a while. It was beautiful."

"Thank you. I probably should have stayed. Your parents came to show their support, but, I don't know ... seems wrong somehow it isn't my parents out there. I didn't think I could hang out as if everything were normal, you know?"

His mom, at least, had seemed okay with wherever she thought Bell had gone. Perhaps at some point his parents would come looking for them, but for now they had one another. "No worries. I figured you probably had a reason, but I had to be sure you were all right."

"Not positive I'm all right, but I'm here."

"Good, I'm glad. You mind if I come up?" Jeremiah swallowed. Courage had never been his strong suit. Stupidity and promises, sure. But with a little push, maybe those could add up to courage. He didn't know.

"I guess not."

Cautiously, he approached the piano and sat on the bench beside her. "I feel like I owe you an apology."

"What? Why?"

"I haven't exactly been a very good boyfriend. Hell, not really even a friend. I've kind of bailed on you. I know I lie in the bed and hold you at night, but there's probably a lot more I could do. Sneaking in at night doesn't seem like enough." The words just tumbled out of him. God must've helped him find the right thing to say. Maybe he would live up to the promise he'd made to DeWei, after all.

"I disagree. Sleeping with me at night, it may not seem like a lot to you, but it makes a bigger difference than you can imagine. Things may not be where you or I would like them to be, but I'm going for one day at a time."

Jeremiah stared at the ivory keys. A single key sounded like noise, not music. Several notes, though, worked together to make music. He looked at Bell. Like a chord, they had to work together.

"Do you want to know why I hid in here?" she asked.

He nodded, grateful she was including him in her inner life.

"Music allows me to express myself. A lot of times, I don't think I can find the right words anymore, but the songs ... they give me the right words. Dr. Shah believes music could be cathartic for me."

Jeremiah grasped Bell's hand and laced his fingers through hers. "I think she's right. Could be good for both of us."

"Maybe." A small smile played on Bell's lips.

"Would you play something else?"

Voicemail, again! Gervasio growled at the phone. Where the hell were all of his people? Neither of his inside men had answered, and *Mamá Gallina* had disappeared on him, too. He had other connections—but they were a last resort. Still, it was absolutely imperative that he discover what was going on.

He'd memorized the New York number a long time ago. Even back then, he'd been smart enough to protect himself. If he went down for the murder of Ileana Costa, he would have proof of a co-conspirator. To this day, though, the murder had not come to light. Thus, the association remained intact. Gervasio dialed and pressed the burner phone to his ear.

The man answered after two rings. "It has been quite some time, El Silbón."

"*Sí.* I call when needed." Upon their first meeting, his comrade had nicknamed Gervasio after The Whistler, a figure of Hispanic myth. According to legend, the young man killed his father so he could eat his organs. After the young man's death, the only warning anyone got of his ghostly presence was the eerie whistle he emitted. Gervasio neither whistled, nor had he been born in the region where the tale was commonly known. Still, he felt the name fit him aptly.

"As always, I am at your service. What can I do for you?"

"I need information."

On the other end of the line, the man snickered, before he asked, "Can you be more specific?"

"*Mamá Gallina*, Santa Maria, Jorge. Why they not answer phone?"

"So, you haven't heard?"

"I not call if I know answer. Tell me where they go." This was the reason he used the New Yorker as little as possible. The man treated him as if he were stupid. Unfortunately, he also knew way too much for his own good. They were more alike than either would ever admit.

"All three have been arrested," the man said. "In fact, at least two of them have finagled a deal with the county prosecutor. They also provided insight into some of your identities. And I believe one of your more useful properties was discovered in the process."

Gervasio snarled. This could not have happened. His personal body farm could not have been located. But if it had? The New Yorker never lied to him. Never. It was the reason he still trusted the man.

Choking back his anger, Gervasio asked about another soldier. "What of Verdugo?"

"You know, I have always admired how coldhearted executioners must be. No one ever truly considers them evil. They are simply doing their job. Though, I suppose, if they were viewed as devilish monsters, then they too would have to go into hiding."

"We talk again soon," Gervasio said, abruptly. Why did the New Yorker have to speak in riddles? So many words used to get to one simple point. But the news was good. Things worked in his favor if Bronco had truly gone into hiding.

A broad smile crossed his lips. He hung up the phone and tucked it into the pocket of his black jeans. Quickly, he collected a few key items to hide his face. There was a job to do.

"Nope. Jeremiah didn't say anything." Amanda frowned. She had no idea why her brother called this meeting. He'd been quieter since the family night session he attended Wednesday night with their parents. Something happened that night, but he refused to share whatever it was. Of course, she had her own issues to deal with. Amanda had spent the past four afternoons at David's soccer practice, but she'd had no luck breaking down his walls.

"You don't think it could have anything to do with our letters?" Vick raised his eyebrows at Amanda as he asked.

"I hope not. Because I'll be damned if I'm saying two words about mine unless he's read his," Alex said, striding into the room and hopping up on the teacher's desk.

Amanda tucked her chin in her hand. The last she'd heard, Jeremiah's letter remained in police custody as evidence—taken before her brother had the chance to read it. Her father had had to produce a warrant before Amanda would release the letter Bella addressed to her, though—and by then, she'd made a copy of it. Although she'd mentioned the letter David received to Vick, she hadn't uttered one word about that letter to her father. Unless Jamar planned to beat the knowledge out of her, she would never tell him of its existence.

"You live with him. How's it possible you don't know what's going on?" Sarresh crossed her arms.

Amanda sighed. She should've expected the question, but still, it bothered her that her cousin even asked. "Because I'm not up his ass, and I have my own life. Besides, you're related to him, too. Why don't you know?"

"It's not exactly like we talk. He kind of hates me," Sarresh said, with a snort.

Alex raised an eyebrow. "He doesn't talk to me, either, really. Not now."

"And Jeremiah and I don't hang out much anymore," Vick added, with a glance at Amanda.

Truth be told, Amanda knew that none of them talked with her brother the way they used to. She offered a tiny smile to her boyfriend. "You know, most of his time's been spent with Bella. Even before she woke up, he was at the hospital, like, all the time. He's not blind. He's gotta have noticed we kind of cut our ties with her. And, like Vick said, maybe he called us together because of the letters. Maybe he thinks we've abandoned Bella because of what she wrote to us."

"We all agreed not to discuss our letters, but what if how we reacted to them ..."

Alex cut Vick off. "And exactly how've we reacted? Like normal people would? If that's what he wants to talk about, I'm not staying." The girl hopped down from the desk.

Sarresh jumped to her feet. "If she's going, so am I!"

"Guys come on. Shouldn't we at least hear him out?" Who was Amanda kidding? She wanted to follow right after them. But she had to live with Jeremiah. And Bella's letter to her asked her to look out for her brother. Although, with Bella in the house, that no longer seemed to be required. Still.... Amanda eyed both girls as they paused mid-step. All she could do was convince them to stay. Anything beyond that would be up to her brother.

In retrospect, he should've been prepared for the fallout. But Jeremiah hadn't anticipated that Alex and Sarresh would be yelling at each other when he got there. Nor did he expect his sister to be in the middle of the two girls, looking like she was ready to rip the hair out of someone's head. He hadn't been positive whose—until she glared at him. Obviously, he'd been clueless before he arrived at the meeting he'd scheduled himself.

Which was exactly why he now stood outside the elevator on the first floor of the police station. He had to do what he should've done before he pulled Bell's friends together—read the letter she'd written to him.

He shoved his hands into his pockets and rocked back and forth. None of them had told him what their letters contained. They all had insisted, though, that, if he wanted them to give Bell a true second chance, he had to read his. Jeremiah eyed the front door. But they would never know if he walked out without reading a single word. Just then, the elevator doors slid open.

Jeremiah made a choice. He stepped into the elevator and pushed the button for the third floor. He was committed. Regardless of what the letter said, he would not turn his back on Bell. She needed him too much. Besides, he had promised her father, on the man's death bed, that he would stay by Bella's side.

Which reminded him of the way, unwittingly, he had obtained the reassurance Bell would need to believe her father had forgiven her. The hateful words she'd said wouldn't haunt her if Jeremiah had anything to do with it. The topic had only come up once, but he knew when it came up again, he could show her what DeWei said.

With a *ding*, The elevator doors slid open, and Jeremiah stepped into the squad room and headed for his father's office. A couple of the detectives nodded their acknowledgement. He approached Detective Russell's desk. It was the last desk between him and his destination.

"Jeremiah? What are you doing here?" Detective Russell closed the file he was reading.

"I came by to talk to my dad."

"I'm sorry, but you just missed him. He probably won't be back for a while. Something I can help you with?"

Jeremiah sighed. As he dragged his hand across the top of his head, he noticed his hair had to be cut down. How had he let it get this long? Not that it was the topic at hand. That topic was whether or not he could trust this guy with his request. Not wanting to back down now, he decided to give it a shot. "Maybe. There's a letter you guys have that was addressed to me. From Bella's case. It's evidence, but I was hoping I could read it."

"I thought your dad let you read it before it got turned over."

Jeremiah shook his head. "He gave me the chance, but I didn't take it." He dropped his head. He hadn't read the damn thing back then because he refused to believe Bell had made an attempt to take her own life. Now, he questioned everything he once thought about her.

Detective Russell tucked the file in a drawer. "I don't see why not. Have a seat and I'll go get it." Russell stood and gestured to the chair.

"Thanks, I appreciate it." Jeremiah wasn't sure if he felt more relieved or anxious. He wiped his hands on his jeans. *God, give me strength.*

It shouldn't take long for Russell to return with the letter. The station only had three floors, plus a basement, but waiting felt like it was going to kill him. His nerves were racked as he contemplated the outcome. What if, after he read it, his entire perspective changed? No. Wouldn't happen. His feelings for Bell couldn't be altered. Not by a letter. Right?

Jeremiah bent over and put his head in his hands.

"All right, son, here it is. Now, this is in an evidence bag so you ... whoa. You okay?"

Jeremiah popped up out of the chair. "Yeah. I just ... I'd like to read it."

"Okay. Let's go to one of the interview rooms."

Jeremiah followed Detective Russell across the squad to an empty interview room, where the man laid the evidence bag containing the letter on the table.

Jeremiah eyed the letter. It was so small, but its contents were potentially so huge. His gaze shifted from the note to Detective Russell. "Do you mind if I have some privacy? I promise I won't take it out of the bag."

"Sure. I'll be right outside." With that Russell shut the door.

Bella belted out the final verse of "Heavy in Your Arms," by Florence and the Machine. Her fingers pounded away at the ivory keys as she echoed one single word: *heavy.* To outside eyes, things would appear better—at least in a small way. Inside, though, she felt lifeless—she was in a relationship that grasped at tiny straws of love. Miah carried so much of what remained of her heart. Yet, the last two days had shown her exactly how much her love weighed him down. She worked to put the puzzle pieces back together. Could she be pieced together in the right way before he gave up? Aside from Miah, she had no clue what she truly needed. Fear gripped her heart as she sang the last few lines of the song. She could just feel abandonment greedily waiting for her.

Bella slid off the bench, sighing heavily and headed toward the platform stairs, but stopped, before stepping down. There, at the front of the altar, was an open Bible on a stand. Had it been there the last time she'd visited the chapel? She couldn't remember. She also couldn't remember how long it had been since she'd read even a passage from the book. Three months? Four?

She eyed the Bible suspiciously. Had it been left there on purpose? For her?

That was stupid. Who would do that?

Hanging her head, she headed toward the stairs—but almost like the book was a magnet, she somehow managed to bump into the stand, and actually knocked the Bible to the floor.

Shit. As Bella crouched down to pick the Bible off the floor, she saw it had fallen open to the Book of Psalms. Her father's favorite book. It brought back one of the last good memories she had of DeWei, the last teen session she'd attended. Her father's words echoed in her mind. He'd spoken about how the broken were pieced together by God's loving hand. How His love helped many to battle their personal demons.

The memory broke the dam inside of her, releasing all she'd held onto for months. Falling to her knees, Bella cried in great heaves. Amid her sobs, she screamed at the Bible as if it were the object of all her anguish, then grabbed the book and tossed it across the room.

"Bell!" Feet thudded over the carpet, and a pair of strong arms wrapped around her.

She collapsed against Jeremiah's body, wailing. There was so much loss to mourn: her unborn child, her father, her mother, her friends.... Her child had been ripped from her body; her father would never return; her mother had disappeared without a word; her friends had turned their back on her. Yes, she knew she'd hurt them, but they'd hurt her too. Where had God been to protect her from the pain? He left her before the rape. Rightfully she blamed Him for everything that followed. Why would He speak to her now? He hadn't saved her. Miah was the one who had been there for her. Miah was by her side through the coma. Miah stayed by her side as she recovered. Miah loved her despite all the tragic events and the drama those events had caused. Now, it was Miah who held her tightly, Miah who said, "It's okay Bell. I got you." It was Miah's hand that caressed Bella's cheek and wiped away the tears.

Bella lifted her eyes to his face. She shivered. *Is it possible?* Could God have saved her by bringing Miah into her life? How had she never realized this before?

"Bell, you okay?"

"I think so."

Neither of them had said much since leaving Luna Hills. Had her outpouring of emotion been too much for him? Jeremiah had only been this cold and distant with her once before. Dear God, she couldn't handle another break-up. If that happened, where would she live? Her mother had made Miah's parents her temporary guardians.

Bella tugged the ends of her hair over her shoulder. Breaking the silence, she said, "I'm sorry about back there."

"I suppose it was going to happen sooner or later. I mean it isn't like you could write your feelings down for the rest of your life."

"Write down my feelings? What? What do you mean?"

Then she understood. Miah must have read the note she'd written him months ago. She looked out the window.

"You had to know I'd eventually read your letter. It's not like you ever planned to talk to me about it. Did you know I defended you to our friends, to my dad? I told him no way you'd ever do anything to hurt yourself."

Catching herself before any idiotic words tumbled free, Bella clamped her lips tight. What could she say? He'd already made up his mind—he'd decided to be angry, to feel hurt. Perhaps she shouldn't be surprised. Although the origin of the pills the surly man used in his attempt to kill her had never been made public, Jamar knew. But surely, he would never have shared that information with Jeremiah.

Bella glanced at Miah, again. His expression was grim. Finding no words to defend herself, she turned back to look out the window.

"Nothing to say? Really? That's just great Bell! You can't even tell me why? I deserve at least that." Jeremiah's voice was low, but vibrating with anger.

Staring at the buildings blurring by, Bella sighed. "What's there to explain? I said it all in my letter."

"Bullshit! You reminiscence a hell of a lot, then you yank the rug from under my feet. 'Find somebody to love, somebody to make you happy.' Like you didn't do any of that?"

Bella turned to glare at him. Miah had a lot of nerve to question how she said goodbye. "Excuse me if I didn't want you to mourn me. I'll try to care a little less."

"That was you caring? You were going to kill yourself!"

"You just don't get it. None of you understand how bad it was for me. The pain doesn't heal. It doesn't go away. It's there every day, haunting me. Some days I can't breathe it's so bad; others, it's all I can do not to take a blade to my wrist. The pills helped for a little while, but I had to take more and more to numb the ache. Then they stopped working. All I could think about was sparing myself and the baby more misery. So, I made a choice. If you think for one second I don't still struggle with this, then you need to wake the hell up." Tears rolled down her cheeks.

Miah was quiet for a moment. Then, in a soft voice, he asked, "You still think about it? About suicide?"

The words had tumbled out before she could stop them. But they had been true. There were moments when the urge was so strong ... but something always prevented her from trying again. Wiping the tears away, Bella bit the inside of her cheek.

"Sometimes."

"Like when?" Miah gripped the steering wheel so hard his knuckles turned white.

In the thick silence that followed his question, Bella said, "After I found out about my dad, and my mom left; it didn't feel like I had anything left worth fighting for."

"You have me, your friends; you have a home."

"A home? No I don't. Or have you forgotten my mother abandoned me. And my friends? What a joke. They were done with me before the ink dried. As for you ... until two days ago we've been estranged. We were more like roommates than people in a real relationship."

"Roommates? I sleep in the same bed as you every night. I called our friends together to try to convince them to give you the support you need. When people at school say you attempted suicide because you faked the rape allegations, I defend you. I got my parents to give you your own space instead of you having to share with Amanda, to make our house as much of a home as possible for you. I can't imagine in what world a roommate would do all that."

Miah swung the car wide and pulled into the driveway. He shut off the ignition and climbed out.

Bella jumped out and followed after him. Maybe *roommate* wasn't exactly accurate. Everything he'd done reflected what kind of guy he was, though. A really good guy. But still.... "That doesn't make the situation any more comfortable. Yes, we share a bed, but only because it was the one thing you could do. You got our friends together because you felt like an ass. As for the people at school, I don't give a shit what they think. It doesn't change what happened. And the house ... nothing will ever make this a home to me. It's a place to lay my head. Nothing more."

"How can you say that?" Miah stopped in the open doorway.

Shaking her head, Bella started past him. He grabbed her arm, but she yanked free and said, "With a father who always brings work home with him and a mother who lies to her children, it's quite easy."

"What the hell are you talking about?"

"Ask them. It isn't my place to tell." Angry tears rolled down her cheeks. Bella stormed down the hallway and slammed their bedroom door shut. She hadn't mean to reveal all she had, but the dam had been ready to burst.

Jeremiah rolled over and stared up at the ceiling, thinking about Bell in the room above him. How could she have planned to take her own life? How could she say goodbye forever? In a letter for him to read after the fact? When he'd read the letter, he hadn't just been angry, he'd been hurt—yet thankful, too. Whatever happened that night, she'd made it through.

For her to admit she still thought about suicide though? He had no clue what to make of that. What would stop her from trying again? It was all too much.

How many times could he and Bell do this dance? Were they destined to fight like this for the rest of their lives? It wasn't as if all the time they'd shared together had been bad, though. A small smile crept onto Jeremiah's lips. The beginning of her letter mentioned the first time they met. What a beautiful day that had been. She was as much an angel then as she was now. Her presence still knocked him off his feet.

But that breakdown at Luna Hills. She hadn't offered an explanation, and he hadn't requested one. Jeremiah sighed. Maybe he should have. The situation caught him entirely off guard. He'd gone to the recovery center intending to discuss the letter. All his anger dissipated, though, the second he stepped into the chapel and spotted Bella curled into a fetal position on the floor. The way she cried, it was as if she'd never stop. In that instant, his heart had broken, and he'd rushed to her side forgetting all about the letter.

Thinking of how vulnerable she had been, Jeremiah made a decision. He jumped out of bed and took the basement stairs two at a time. Slipping into the hall, he padded along the carpeted floor to his room, where Bella was sleeping. He inhaled deeply and opened the door.

Bell looked up. She wasn't asleep. Exhaling, he crossed the room and climbed into the bed. "I'm sorry."

"Me, too." She laced her fingers through his and squeezed.

He'd hoped for more from her, but that was a start. Relationships, he knew, only survived if both people worked on it together. Whatever move he made next, it had to get them going in the right direction, or their relationship would die.

Jeremiah reached up to sweep her hair to the side, then pressed a tender kiss on the scar that was a reminder of how it all began. "I shouldn't have—"

"I was scared."

"What?" Did he hear her correctly? Did she just admit to an emotion?

"Part of me wanted to tell you what was in the letter, but ... I was afraid of how you'd react if you knew."

Jeremiah pulled Bell tight and buried his nose in her hair. "Why would you hide?"

"You're all I have left. If I lose you.... I have no hope without you."

Jeremiah rested his forehead against hers. He had to show her how much hope there was. She had to know how much he yearned for her touch, her love. He couldn't live without her. But the letter had revealed how easily he could lose her, and it frightened him.

He looked into her eyes. She held his gaze. All his fear got pushed aside as the love they had for one another filled his soul. He kissed her deeply. The feel of her breasts pressed against his chest, the soft dip in her low back, the natural curve of her hips turned him on. He desired her completely. His heart raced. He was hard, but they were not prepared to take that step.

Their lips parted, both panting.

"Bell."

"Miah." Bell whispered his name, and it spoke volumes.

He nuzzled her, breathing in her natural lavender scent. "I've really missed you."

"Me, too. I need you with me. I want you with me. I want us. I love you." She reached up, cupped his cheek, and brushed a soft kiss on his lips.

Finally, everything felt right in his world.

Jeremiah stretched and eyed the clock on his nightstand. 11:30. He listened carefully. Had his parents finally gone to bed? The twins had been fidgety this evening, keeping him downstairs and away from Bella's bed. He tiptoed up the stairs and cracked the door. No light. No noise. The coast was clear.

He slipped down the hall, quietly opened the door, and stepped inside—to find Bella sitting up in the bed with a Bible open in her lap, tears rolling down her cheeks.

Jeremiah settled beside her and placed a hand over hers. "Hey. You okay?"

"No." Bella moved the Bible aside and curled against him. Burying her face into his chest, she started to cry.

Arms wrapped around her, he rubbed circles on her back, as he had in the past to help soothe her emotions. What could've possibly caused this? He glanced at the Bible and saw she had been reading the Book of Psalms. What could she have read there to bring her to tears?

Jeremiah continued to rub her back and kissed her forehead.

She looked up at him. "I'm sorry."

"Hey, no. You don't have to apologize. If you need to cry, cry. If you want to talk, then talk. Whatever you need, I'll be here. I'll always be right here." She had to understand nothing could make him walk away—not again. He'd go to the moon and back to keep her by his side.

Bella sniffled, but tears continued to run down her face. "Really?"

"Really." Even as he wondered what he could do to wipe all doubt from her mind, Jeremiah realized … it was time he showed her the video. He'd held onto it for months, waiting for the right moment. Her father told him he'd know. And DeWei had been right. He did know. The moment was now.

Jeremiah brushed the tears from her cheeks and gripped her hand. "Come with me?"

"Now?"

"Yes. I know it's late, but I promise it'll be worth it."

At the stoplight, Jeremiah glanced at his girlfriend. Expecting a battle, he hadn't given her any details about where they were headed. This was a big step, one he was attempting to prepare for—unfortunately, he didn't know just how Bella'd respond. Also, if his parents found out they'd left the house after midnight, they were both in huge trouble. The grounding would be worth it, though, if things worked out the way he hoped. Anyway, there was no turning back, now.

Jeremiah pulled into the church parking lot, eased the car into a spot, and shut off the engine. "You ready?"

"No. No." Bella's hazel eyes widened and her body stiffened.

How could he convince her it was time? How could he show her she could do what she feared most? "You can go back in there. I have faith in you."

"No."

"What'll it take to get you to go inside?"

Jeremiah could see Bell was on the brink of a panic attack. He had to have a backup plan.

"Nothing will make me go back in there. I can't believe you even brought me here."

"Book of Psalms. Why were you reading it?"

Bell rubbed up her arms, then rubbed at her sternum, as her breathing became ragged. Tears rolled down her cheeks. In a tiny voice, she said, "I can't. I'm not strong enough. Please, please … take me home."

There was only one thing he could do. Saying, "Then I'll bear the weight," Jeremiah pulled the keys from the ignition, walked to the passenger side, and opened the door. Then, in three slow, gentle movements, he lifted her out of the car.

He was surprised to receive no resistance. Instead of stiffening, as he pulled her close Bell's body curled into him, her head nestling perfectly against his chest. He pressed a feather kiss to her forehead. "Don't worry. I got you."

Knowing the pastor left the door open all night so everyone had access to God's house, he carried Bell across the parking lot to the side door. He maneuvered her so he could turn the handle, then glanced down. Despite all the jostling, Bell's eyes remained firmly closed—but the incipient panic attack seemed to have passed off without becoming full blown.

Carrying her up the dimly lit aisle, he remembered how DeWei had wisely suggested that, when the time was right, Jeremiah bring her back to this piano—apparently, this church's piano was where it had all begun. He knew that, whatever else happened tonight, seated at the piano, which was the one connection she still had to her father, she was going to find some peace.

Satisfied this had been the right decision, he lowered Bell onto the bench. He removed his arm from beneath the crook of her knees and stood up straight. How long would it take for her to trust the situation? Though he'd like to be home before his parents woke up and realized they were gone, he'd wait however long he had to. For her, he'd do practically anything.

Her eyes fluttered open. Looking at the white and black keys before her, she blinked tears free from the corners of her eyes.

"This is where you need to be." Jeremiah settled onto the bench beside her.

More tears trickled down her cheeks, as she placed her hands on the keys. Then, unexpectedly, she started to recite a Bible verse: "As for me, I will call upon God; and the LORD shall save me. Evening, and morning, and at noon, will I pray, and cry aloud: and he shall hear my voice. He hath delivered my soul in peace from the battle *that was* against me: for there were many with me."

"Is that ... ?" It was Psalms 55:16-18. Jeremiah knew that particular passage had been the lesson for the last teen Bible study session they'd attended together. He'd sat beside her as they soaked up the words and discussed their meaning. *Broken, but made whole.* No wonder she'd broken down.

Bella stared at Jeremiah's phone. On the screen, she saw her father lying in a hospital bed, hooked up to several machines. Holding back tears, she glanced at Miah. "What the hell is this?"

"I spoke with DeWei before he passed. He had some things to say to you, so he asked me to record him."

"I don't ..." It made no sense. Why would her father record a video for her when he'd been fighting for his life? All his energy should have been focused on himself. But it wasn't. It seemed he'd put her first, like he always had.

Her finger hovered over the play button. Why was it so hard to depress the damn button? What if all he said was to look after her mother? Or what if he pointed out every single one of her faults? He might say he thought she was a failure. After all, they'd never spoken after that last fight. Bella sighed. She wasn't even sure what they'd been arguing about.

She looked to Miah. He'd been nothing but supportive. Even now, he waited patiently, encouraging her to do what she had to. If she told him she couldn't watch the video, he'd probably be okay with it. He'd tell her she could try another time. It was just the kind of guy he was. How had she come to deserve him? He loved her in ways she never thought she needed.

Staring into his warm, emerald green eyes, she took a small piece of his courage and pushed the button. Her father's voice came over the small speaker.

"Is it on?"

He sounded weak, but clear. It was awful seeing him look so pale. It was all Bella could do not to throw herself on the ground sobbing. But she didn't. She listened to the last words she'd ever hear her father speak.

"Yes, sir. We're recording."

"Very good. Maylin, my Cinderella, there is much I wish to say to you. I feel it is important you know I love you. And I forgive you. I do not want you to blame yourself for anything that happened a couple of days ago. You must know I understand your words were said out of anger. I do not believe you hate me. Though I am concerned you truly hate yourself. I had been convinced I was doing the right thing by giving you space. Perhaps if I had followed my instinct, we would not be here."

Her father paused and wiped at his face. Though he seemed to try to hide it, he winced as if in pain. The camera shifted slightly to the right.

Jeremiah's voice filled the silence. *"Dr. Kynaston? You okay? Do you need me to get the doctor?"*

"No. I do not have long, and I must get this out. Keep going."

"Okay. If you're sure, we're still recording."

The camera returned to its original position.

"As I was saying, do not blame yourself. A lot of bad things happened to you, but they do not define you. You are still the same wonderful girl I raised. She is inside of you somewhere. You simply have to find her again. I have faith you can do that. I have faith because God still walks beside you. You just … you just have to let Him in. Let Him carry your burden. You do not have to carry the weight alone. I love you, my Cinderella. And while I wish we could have one more dance, know I will cherish the ones we did have. And I will always watch over you. It is just what fathers do."

"Anything else?"

DeWei shook his head to dismiss the camera. *"No. I am done. You should return to her side. She will soon need you more than ever."*

"Dr. Kynaston …" The video cut off.

Tears trickled down Bella's cheeks. She shut her eyes. Despite her horrible last words to her father, he'd still loved her. Those words, she hadn't spoken them out of anger, but out of pure spite. Well, not all of what she'd said. The second part had been the simple truth: She hated herself. And she still hated herself. She hated who she'd become. She hated her desire to be numb. She hated the crap that was always in her head. She hated her life.

A crack had been made in her soul the day she was raped. The foundation of her beliefs fractured the day their home had been vandalized and she'd been assaulted. And what little remained had disintegrated the day her father and child died.

Now, she sobbed … for the loss of her father … for the loss of her unborn child … for the loss of her purity. Most importantly, she cried for the loss of her faith. She cried because she'd been left alone in this world.

Taking the phone from her hands, Miah tucked her against his chest. "I'm right here. I'm not going anywhere," he said.

Those words. They meant more than she could ever say. They were so close to what her father had said in his parting words, that God was there with her. That

He'd always been beside her. Miah, too, had been by her side—for months now. Her boyfriend wasn't a god, she knew, but he had been brought to her by God. As if God was preparing her for the pain she'd been bound to face.

And if she'd never met Miah? Then there would have been no one to stop her from committing suicide. She wouldn't be here. Bella clung to Miah, crying now for the loss that could've been. The weight of her pain had to be lifted. No longer could she carry it. *God, please! Please take it! I can't do this anymore!*

Then, as if in answer to her prayers, Bella felt, in her heart, another pair of arms embracing her, and a voice she'd nearly forgotten whispering in her mind. With that, the pain she'd be in for so long eased. The weight on her soul released. Her entire body calmed, and the tears streaming down her face slowed. Slowly, she opened her eyes. Her father was right. God had returned to her. With or without Miah, she would never again be alone.

"You okay?" Miah pressed a tender kiss to her forehead.

Quietly, she nodded. The world felt a little lighter. She splayed her fingers across the keyboard. Bella glanced at her boyfriend. "My father told you to bring me here, didn't he?"

"Yes. He said I'd know when the time was right."

"This is where I learned to play the piano. My father, he got one of the ladies here to teach me. I came every day after school. I would sit and practice whenever he was here. I played my first recital here. The song I sang that day, it was for him."

"What song is that?"

A small smile tugged on the corners of her lips. Lifting her gaze to the ceiling, she realized this was a way she could tell her father how much she loved him. Bella depressed the chords she'd learned years ago and began to play their song, "Cinderella," by Steven Curtis Chapman, with the lyrics slightly altered, as they had been, to reflect her as Cinderella, dancing with her father. She'd been ten when she learned the song, six years ago. Now, the first verse fell from her lips as if no time at all had passed.

As she sang the second verse, she remembered the last good days she and her father had had together, like the night of Homecoming. Had that been the last time they danced? Yes, but it was a dance she would cherish for the rest of her life. One beautiful memory among thousands she had of her father.

She repeated the chorus, tears thickening her throat. He had to know. He had to know how much she loved him. How much she missed him. How much she'd give for one more dance. This was her chance to make things right. For him to know everything he meant to her.

Getting out the third verse was hard. It spoke about things she'd never get to experience, now: Her father walking her down the aisle. Her father being there for the birth of her first child. Jeremiah's hand on her shoulder helped her through, helped her to know that her father would always be with her. He was in her head. He was in her heart. He was a part of the woman she would become.

She poured all she had into the final chorus. This was their song. This was one of the many ways he would always be with her. She would always be his Cinderella. As she sang the final note, Bella glanced at the ceiling one last time. For you, Bàba.

Happy tears prickled the corner of her eyes. She swiped at her face and looked to Miah. "Thank you," she said.

four

"Are you nervous?"

"What makes you ask that?" Bella arched an eyebrow.

Miah pointed at the bag lunch still clutched in her hand—and then to the locker she'd just closed. "If last night wasn't an indicator, then that would be."

"Oh." She looked at the lunch bag and giggled, nervously. Miah was right. Last night, she had tossed and turned. Even his presence hadn't lulled her to sleep like it usually did. Now, Bella unlocked her locker, put her lunch away, and shut the door again.

Miah slid his hand in hers and squeezed. "It's okay. You can do this."

"I keep thinking about what everyone's going to say."

"I thought you didn't care."

"I don't, but that doesn't mean I want to hear it."

It would probably be just like before. People murmuring as she made her way down the hall. Students calling her names.

It was her first day back at school. Her psychiatrist, having concluded that Bella's breakdown over the last two days was actually a breakthrough, decided it would be okay for Bella to return to school two or three days a week and work her way up to the full five.

Bella was less than thrilled by this idea. But here she was.

Miah brushed a hand over the top of his buzz cut. Yesterday, he shaved it down. Not quite bald, but a rather sexy close cut. "You've got nothing to worry about. I'll walk with you between classes. Mom talked to Principal Owen, and he's asked my teachers to make an exception if I'm late."

"Seems like an awful lot of trouble. It's only a few days out of the week to start. I ..." The sentence dropped off, as she considered her previous experience. She hadn't really handled the situation last time. The pills she'd been taking helped a little bit, at least allowed her to pretend to cope. But things had to be different this time around.

Bella stopped mid-step and tenderly kissed Miah on the lips.

"Not that I'm complaining, but what was that for?"

She felt herself smiling. Although the kiss was for so much more than she had time to share, she could at least say, "For being here. I can't tell you how much it means to me."

"I wouldn't be anywhere else." Miah hugged her to his chest and pressed a kiss to her forehead.

The beat of his heart brought her a welcomed peace—it was one of the many things she loved about lying in his arms at night. Hearing his heart, a warm calm coursed through her body.

"Whore." Keith muttered, as he walked by.

Miah released his grip on Bella and moved to chase after the guy, but Bella grasped his arm and held him back. "Let it go. He isn't worth it." Keith was a friend of David's. Miah couldn't fight all of David's friends on Bella's behalf.

"He shouldn't have called you that."

"And getting into it with him won't change that he did." Miah could rush off and play hero, but it wouldn't help. It would only make the situation worse. Thankfully, her boyfriend appeared to realize it too.

Draping an arm around her shoulder, Miah pressed another feather kiss into her hair. "He gets one reprieve. Next time, he won't be so lucky."

"Okay." She understood. Guys had their macho tendencies. But hopefully there wouldn't be a next time. Bella leaned her head against Miah, and they walked toward her first class.

What a way to begin the week.

David glanced at the other students gathered around their lockers. Something was going on. Usually the rumor mill didn't buzz this early. He hated catching whatever it was they had to say. It hardly mattered anymore. He grabbed the last book he needed and closed his locker.

"Man, have I got news." Keith propped himself against the lockers.

Inwardly, David groaned. It was too early in the morning for his friend's antics. If he could, he'd shove Keith into an unused locker, just so he'd never have to hear the guy's drama again. "Unless it has to do with soccer, I don't want to know."

"Your ex-girlfriend has returned."

What? David leaned his forehead against his locker. Bella had come back to school? Not that he expected to be forewarned, but knowing ahead of time would have made this a little easier. Or maybe not. He pounded his head lightly against the locker. "Great."

"Don't worry man, I got your back."

"What're you talking about?"

"I told her she was a whore."

David looked up to see a wide grin spread across Keith's face. He glowered at his best friend. He played on the field with Keith. Whatever the guy had to say next, if he was smart, he'd tread carefully. "You did what?"

"It wasn't direct, or anything. I just sort of said it as I walked by her and that guy."

"What guy?" David's hand balled into a fist. Jeremiah? He and Bella had been inseparable at the beginning of the year. Then the dumbass dumped her and ... well, David preferred not to dwell too much on the aftermath.

As if he couldn't spill it fast enough, Keith said, "The one she was hanging all over. That Jeremiah guy. The one she left you for."

In one swift move, David knocked Keith to the floor.

"What the hell, man?"

"Leave Bella alone." Before he could be dragged to the principal's office for getting in yet another fight, David turned to leave. A bunch of students had already gathered around them, but David growled, and they parted like the Red

Sea. He stormed off and headed straight for the gym. Having energy to burn had never been good for him. Blowing off his first class would be better than bursting into another unexpected explosion.

Clumping toward the gym, he wondered what had just happened. He and Bella weren't even together, and he still acted like a lovesick fool. David dragged a hand down his face. He'd actually punched Keith. Maybe he could claim temporary insanity. So, what if he'd been irritated by every word his friend mumbled. The fact remained that Bella was his ex-girlfriend, and people would talk about her. God, he had to get that girl out of his head.

Distracted by his thoughts, David wasn't paying any attention to where he was going, and he bumped into a girl in the hallway, knocking her books to the ground.

"Oh shit. I'm—"

"A jackass." The girl got down and proceeded to collect her belongings.

Whoa. That was a bit harsh, David thought. It wasn't as if he did it on purpose. David picked up the notebook nearest him. "Here, let me help."

"Thanks, but I think I can handle it," she said sarcastically, snatching the notebook from him and gathering the last of her things.

Forgetting everything else, David stared at the girl. She was like no one he'd ever met. Her dark auburn hair contrasted with her pale skin; she was tall, maybe around five-ten, and gorgeous as hell. She didn't so much as look at him as pierce his soul with her steel gray eyes. She wore a dark gray t-shirt with *Rock'n'Roll* written across it in sparkles, a pair of black, skintight jeans, and boots to match. Who was she?

"I'm … um … really sorry. You must be new. I'm David."

"And you're … um … kind of in the way. Now, if you don't mind." She stepped around him.

Suddenly desperate, David grabbed her arm. "Wait. Can I at least get your name?"

"My name is none of your damn business. Now, you have two seconds to release me before I make you howl like a dog."

"Warren." Coach Yager called out from the gym.

Dammit! He let go of his mystery girl. "I *am* going to find out who you are," he said, defiantly.

"Don't bet your ass on it," she said, and walked away.

A wide grin spread across his face. She was definitely something. David grabbed his books and jogged over to the gym. "What's going on Coach?"

"I should ask you the same thing. Why is it I just got notice of another fight?" Shaking his head, Coach Yager headed toward his office.

David followed. How could the coach have heard? Not more than five minutes had passed. Probably a teacher texted the coach. "It wasn't that big of a deal." David shrugged.

"I hope to hell not. Our season is only beginning. The last thing we need is for you to be suspended again—or benched."

"Benched?"

"Yes, son. Benched. Your grades aren't the only thing that impacts your eligibility. Your behavior does, too. So, no more fights. We clear?" Coach Yager stopped in front of his office door and paused with his hand on the knob.

Soccer was all David had, left. He refused to jeopardize his only hope of getting out of this small-ass town his parents insisted they live in. His twin had to suffer through another year—but that was her own fault. It certainly didn't mean he had to stay.

David nodded. "You have my word."

"Good. Now, hit the weights, and I'll take care of your first period class."

The police had deserted the house. They probably believed the evidence they required had all been collected. Juan wasn't sure, though. He studied the bedroom that belonged to Gervasio Rodriguez. The room was almost bare. He crossed to the dresser and rifled through the contents of the top drawer. Just clothes.

Juan moved on to the second drawer. More clothes. Sighing, he kneeled down to open the final drawer. *There has to be something*, he thought. Except it came up empty, too. Angrily, he shoved the drawer shut—and it rattled. *It's possible.* Slowly, he pulled the bottom drawer entirely out of the dresser. And sure enough. There it was. A thin piece of wood laid across the bottom of the drawer.

Juan gently pushed on the wood. It wiggled. Pulling out his knife, he placed the blade in the tiny opening beside the wood panel and lifted it. Beneath, was a lock box.

He removed the box and replaced the panel, then shoved the drawer back into position. In case the police came back, everything had to look exactly the way it had.

Juan's phone vibrated. "Have you found something?" he asked.

"A warehouse. Under one of his aliases—one we hadn't heard of before."

Juan was pleased. His son had done well. "Any other locations under the same name?"

"No. Cristobal is checking on other names, but it looks good. And there's been some low-level activity at the warehouse. Not enough to cause suspicion to most."

Juan peered out the window, glancing up and down the alley. No one. "Very well. Text me the address. I shall go there now."

The line disconnected. Juan hadn't expected more than a quick exchange with his son, but the abrupt end of the call stung for a brief second. Giving it no more thought, Juan shoved the phone in his pocket and slithered out the window. He had work to do.

Thy r back.

David's sister texted him during his workout to let him know their parents were home. He groaned. He hated it when their parents were around. The months until graduation couldn't go fast enough. For now, though, hiding out in the gym would only work for so long. He tucked his cell phone into his jeans pocket. If luck was on his side, his parents would be nowhere around when he got in. If luck wasn't on his side ... well, he'd be in for one of his father's lectures. Surely, he'd have done something to upset his parents. Even if they'd been gone for a month.

David walked past the equipment he'd been using and let the gym door bang behind him.

"Finally! I thought you'd never be done."

Christ. How long had she been waiting? Although she was a dark-haired beauty, Amanda annoyed the shit out of him—almost as much as his own sister did. "Now is not the time."

"Come on. I've been here for an hour. You can at least talk to me." Amanda got to her feet and slid a backpack strap over her shoulder.

"Yeah, well, you could've warned me Bella was coming back to school today. But, no, I had to find out from Keith."

"I'm sorry about that. I was on my way to tell you when he *fell* into the lockers. Nice hit by the way."

"Have you lost your mind? I'm this close to getting benched for the season, and you're praising me?" Surely, she couldn't be that stupid. David clenched his hands. He had to get away. He pivoted and headed toward the exit.

She followed. "Sorry. Maybe a compliment wasn't the way to go. I'm not good at these things."

"No shit."

"Hey! You don't have to be a jackass. I'm just trying to do what Bella asked me to. Not like she gave me instructions or anything. Whatever, I won't keep chasing you. I'm done." Amanda stopped in the middle of the hallway.

David kept walking. He didn't care what she did. If anything, it was a relief that she wouldn't be following him anymore.

Then, the word "instructions" echoed in his brain. David paused mid-step and turned around. "What're you talking about?"

"Just what I said. I give up."

"Not that. The 'instructions' part. How, exactly, did Bella give you instructions?" He hadn't given much thought to her showing up at his parents' house and mentioning Bella's request that she check on him. But now?

Amanda stood staring at him with a deer-in-the-headlight look in her wide green eyes. "That's, um, kind of the point. She didn't. Give me instructions, I mean."

David stepped toward her. "Then why did you say that?"

"Because ... I just meant it would've been nice if she'd pointed me in some kind of direction." Amanda backed up a couple of steps.

David grabbed her arm, and her green eyes widened even more. He growled. "Tell me what the hell you're talking about, Amanda."

"Fine! I meant in her letter. My letter. She wrote us all letters. Happy?!"

"Who's 'us?'" He hadn't gotten a letter from Bella. Why not? Or had she sent out letters after she and he'd broken up? No way. From what he'd heard, there hadn't been time for her to write any damned letters between the time he'd left and when that guy'd tried to kill her.

"All of us. Her friends, family, the people she cared about."

"Did she write me one?"

"Yes."

David released her arm and slapped her across the face. Prying answers out of her was like pulling teeth. Her one-word reply pissed him off even more. "Tell me where the hell it is!"

Shocked by the blow, Amanda gasped and rubbed her cheek. "Get the hell away from me," she said, glowering at him.

"Amanda, I'm ..." What had he done? He stumbled backwards. What kind of man had he become? He'd reacted the way his father would.

Amanda headed for the exit. She stopped at the door and glanced over her shoulder. "Really, I should tell you to go screw yourself, but I try to keep my promises. Your sister has your letter."

"Thank—"

"Save it. I'm considering my promise kept." With that, she shoved open the door and stomped through it.

"Ow." Sitting on the kitchen table, her feet dangled over the edge. Amanda winced as Vick pressed the bag of ice to the bright red welt on her cheek. Thankfully, Jeremiah had been too preoccupied to notice it, and he hadn't even asked why she wanted him to drop her off at Vick's. Which was for the best, because, although Amanda and Vick had been dating for months, they still hadn't officially told anyone. Especially not Jeremiah.

"Will you please tell me how this happened?"

"Can you not act all like my boyfriend if I do?"

Shaking his head, Vick crossed his arms. "I'm going with no."

"Then please, just let it go." It was exactly what she planned to do. She'd poked the beast, and this was how she'd been rewarded. Nothing else to do but avoid the beast, in the future.

"You have a welt on your face. How do you expect me to let that go?"

"Pretend it isn't there."

Vick pulled the bag of ice away from his girlfriend's cheek. "If it isn't there, then you don't need this."

"That isn't fair."

"Then tell me what happened." He offered her the bag of ice in exchange for the truth.

With a sigh, Amanda grabbed the icepack. Some days Vick's pigheadedness matched her own. "Fine. I told you I was going to stay after school to catch up with David. Right?"

"Yeah."

"Well, I inadvertently mentioned the letters. He might've gotten a little angry when I tried to string him along him with my answers. And, um, he might have smacked me." Actually, Amanda was making light of it now, but David had downright scared the shit out of her. No guy had ever frightened her before—but that guy, he had demons in those blue eyes.

Steam practically poured from Vick's ears. "He did what?"

"Nothing. He did nothing. See, I've forgotten about it already." She attempted to smile and failed. Her cheek muscles were too sore to cooperate.

"Bullshit."

Amanda giggled, then winced. Vick rarely cussed, but she was always tickled when the words uncontrollably tumbled out of his mouth. "Ow. Don't make me laugh. It hurts."

"I'd apologize, but I'm a tad annoyed. I can't believe Jeremiah let the guy get away with this."

"He doesn't know." And there went the dog's breakfast.

"Wait, wasn't he there when David hit you?"

"No, he was waiting outside for me."

Vick propped himself against the kitchen counter and glared at her. "Dammit Amanda!"

"I didn't think it would get out of hand." She almost mumbled something about his second cussword. Two in less than five minutes was a rarity, but she thought better of it. "Listen, babe, I know you're upset about this, but can you please, please, let this go?"

"Amanda, you know I love you. That's why I can't let this go. I'll talk to Jeremiah tomorrow at school. Okay?" Vick wedged himself between her legs.

Lightly, he brushed a kiss against her forehead.

"Okay."

Doing up his jeans, David checked himself in the mirror. He dragged a hand through his short, blue-black locks and brushed them into place. Despite his parents' return, last evening had ended quietly. Instead, of dealing with his father, though, he'd contended with his own emotional demons. His guilt over slapping Amanda tormented him the entire night. He'd only slept about three hours. It hadn't been the first time he'd hit anyone, of course, but he knew he'd crossed a line. For the first time, he felt he had treated someone the way his father treated people—as if they had no feelings and were only there for his convenience. Hardly the type of man David wanted to emulate.

David grabbed his backpack and headed downstairs. His sister sat alone at the kitchen island and spooned a piece of grapefruit in her mouth. With a barely audible sigh, he stepped into the room and dropped his backpack by the table.

Tension was high between the them. Yesterday, when he'd gotten home, he went straight upstairs and ransacked her room, searching for the letter. Although he hadn't hit Heather, he threatened her enough that, at one point, she cowered from him. Just as if he'd been their father.

David scowled. When had he turned into a man he despised?

Heather finished the grapefruit and set down her spoon. "Chef left you a vegetarian omelet on the stove. There's some turkey bacon, too."

"Thanks." *Yuck, vegetarian.* Their parents had definitely returned. Chef only made omelets without meat when his mother was around. David grabbed his omelet and bacon and carried his plate to the island.

Heather drained the last of her juice and lifted her gaze to him. "I'm sorry I kept the letter from you."

"It's okay. I get why you did it. You were trying to protect me." He offered his twin a slice of bacon. Seeing how little his sister had eaten, he figured their mother had gone off on one of her weight rants. The woman was borderline anorexic, herself. And she was trying to make Heather bone-thin, too, even shipping her off to fat camp before they moved to Rescate County.

Hesitantly, Heather accepted the bacon, chewing quickly, almost like she didn't want anyone to notice. "Yeah. Just don't tell people I care, otherwise I'll start a rumor about you talking in your sleep."

"That would be one interesting rumor." David smiled.

Grinning back at her brother, Heather hopped off the stool and placed her dirty dishes in the sink. "It would be. Now, if you'll excuse me, I've got to join mother for a couple of hours at the gym, followed by a day at the spa."

"No school?"

"Not today, anyway." Heather snickered. "By the way, father wants you to stop in his office before you leave."

The morning had begun so smoothly. He should've known the request would come at some point. David lowered his fork and glanced at his sister. "Thanks for the warning."

"Hey, twins have to stick together." She nodded and disappeared down the hall.

Each of them had their own struggles with their parents. If Heather gained an ounce over 115 pounds, their mother called her fat. The woman yelled at the staff and his sister for a week last summer, when Heather pushed 140 pounds. That was one of the few times he'd ever comforted his twin.

David looked over his plate. He hated wasting food that had been prepared for him, but the longer he sat there, the more nervous he felt. He gathered up his dishes, trashed the food, and set the dishes in the sink. Snagging his backpack, he made his way to the one room in the house he prayed would be empty.

But it wasn't. The door to his father's office was open. Pausing, David mentally collected himself, and then walked in.

"Those reports should've been on my desk two days ago. You have an hour to get them to me or you're fired. It's that simple." Their father gestured, and David followed the silent instructions, closing the door behind him and sitting in a chair in front of his father's desk. Patiently he waited for his father to finish the call. Only then was it okay for him to speak.

"You wanted to see me."

His father leaned back and steepled his fingers. "I received an interesting call last night."

"Oh?"

"Yes. Principal Owen reached out to your mother and me to express his concern. He said you've been in two fights this year already. And he'd heard a rumor of a third. If you end up in one more fight this year, he says he'll have no choice but to expel you."

This was bad. His father, the hypocrite, abhorred violence—unless he was the one administering it. David swallowed. The man unnerved him more than he dared admit. "It wasn't a fight, Dad. Keith and I had a ... a disagreement."

David's father stood, walked around the desk, and backhanded David. "I don't give a shit what you call it. I expect better. You're a Warren. Do you understand?"

"Yes, sir."

"Good. Now get the hell out of my office."

Leave it alone. Let it go. Amanda's words had tumbled around in Vick's brain for the last twenty-four hours. And he had fully intended to do as his girlfriend asked ... until he spotted the person who was, if not his main concern, at least causing Vick additional annoyance.

Pushing through the throng of students, Vick reached out and slammed Jeremiah's locker shut. "Why didn't you stay with your sister yesterday afternoon?"

"What the hell, man?"

"Answer the question."

"Not that it's any of your business, but I spent some quality time with Bell, before I took her to the center." Jeremiah opened his locker and grabbed another book.

"Let me get this straight. You left your sister to play footsy with your girlfriend?"

"I wouldn't put it that way, but ... what's the big deal? Amanda's fine."

"Unbelievable. You're either blind or so selfish you don't care about the shiner she got."

Jeremiah stared at Vick. "What're you talking about? She doesn't have a black eye."

"If you weren't so busy ogling Bella yesterday, you would have noticed the welt on Amanda's face—or all the make-up she gunked on today to cover the shit up."

"This is my sister we're talking about. She'd tell me if something happened."

Crossing his arms, Vick smirked. Apparently, Jeremiah was dumber than he looked. "You really believe that's true?"

"Yeah, I do. Amanda and I tell each other everything."

Vick grinned. "That's bullshit, and I know it. For a fact." Although they hadn't shown their letters to anyone else, he and Amanda had shared their letters from Bella with one another. Of course, he hadn't shared the *entire* letter with Amanda. Not the part where Bella said, *If you truly love Amanda, be honest with her about Taryn. She deserves to know all of you and that includes your past, present, and future.* No, he hadn't shared that.

Jeremiah had paused for a moment, likely to prepare his next barb: "Unlike you, I haven't turned my back on my sister. Then again, I guess blood is thicker than water."

Jeremiah impugning Vick's relationship with Bella, the girl he called "sister," was the last straw. His fist balled up and seemed to thrust forward of its own volition, landing a punch against Jeremiah's jaw and knocking him back into the lockers.

"I didn't turn my back on her!"

"Bullshit!" Jeremiah slugged Vick in the face with a right hook, causing him to stumble. But Vick regained his footing and busted Jeremiah in the nose. Blood spurted everywhere, and his knuckles throbbed, but he only wanted to pound the guy who used to be his friend, over and over again.

Jeremiah got in first, though, striking Vick with an uppercut; then crouching low and sweeping his leg toward Vick's ankle, which, theoretically should've thrown Vick to the floor, but a pair of arms slipped beneath his and yanked him back before Jeremiah could connect.

Vick struggled against the grip the arms held him in. Then Principal Owen stepped between Vick and Jeremiah. He looked from one to the other. Turning to the two teachers holding them apart, he said, "Take them both to the nurse. I'll go call their parents."

five

Bella clutched her books while she waited outside the classroom for Miah to come and escort her to her next class. The new routine comforted her, assuring her of her boyfriend's support.

Just then, one of her classmates pushed past her. "Freak," he muttered.

Trying to brush it off, Bella remembered the names people had called her before. *Slut* and *whore* were just the beginning of it. She'd also been labeled, *psychotic whacko, demented weirdo, certifiable.* The term *freak* didn't even phase her.

But where was Miah? Bella glanced at her watch. Maybe he stopped at his locker for a notebook or something. Chewing the inside of her cheek, she peered down the hall. Lots of students gathered around lockers or dilly-dallying toward their next classes. The sixty-second warning rang. Bella knew Miah wouldn't have bailed on her if he could have helped it. Something happened. She had to find out what.

As the last students cleared the hallway, Bella headed for the administrative office. On her way, she recalled the day she'd gone there to meet the new student she'd been assigned to guide. It had been Jeremiah. Smiling briefly to herself, she pushed the office door open and stepped inside.

The plump administrative assistant stood. "Well, look who's returned."

"Hey, Mrs. Brown, is Principal Owen in?"

The woman hadn't even gotten her mouth open, when Principal Owen stepped in. "Bella? Is everything okay?"

"I'm not sure. Jeremiah is supposed to walk me to every class, but he didn't show at the end of last period. Have you … Principal Owen?"

The man's face had shifted from concern to frustration. "He's being escorted to the nurse's office."

"What? Is he all right?"

"Aside from a few scrapes and bruises, he's fine." The principal walked past her toward his office.

Scrapes and bruises? Did he get into it with David again? "Principal Owen? Was he fighting?"

The man paused and said gruffly, "You should get to class."

"Please? Please tell me." Things had just started to improve—both for Miah and between the two of them. Another suspension wasn't something he needed on his record, especially if it involved her … again.

The principal sighed and rubbed at his nose. "He got in a fight with Victor Hilliard."

"What? But they're friends." At least they used to be. Vick had stopped talking to her, but she didn't actually know if Miah had still been hanging out with Vick before she moved in.

"I promise you, it was Victor Hilliard."

Bella thought quickly. "I know you probably want to call their parents, but before you do, can I please go talk to Jeremiah and Vick? Figure out what happened."

"I don't know, Bella …"

"Please, Principal Owen. I know Mrs. Detrone has told you some of what's going on, but that doesn't mean it's everything. Please, let me help if I can." Guys butt heads on stupid things all the time, but it hardly ever ended with fists. And not between those two. If punches were thrown, then the fight pretty much certainly revolved around her.

The principal folded his arms across his chest. "One condition. Whatever you find out, you share with me. I promise you it won't leave my office. Do we have an accord?"

"Yes, sir." Not sure she'd want to share whatever she learned with Principal Owen, but seeing it as her only choice, Bella left the administrative office and walked quickly toward the nurse's office. If Vick and Miah had fought over her, then it was her place to intervene.

Stopping in front of the nurse's office, Bella stared at the door. It had been just over two weeks since she'd been released from the hospital, and there she stood, trying to help someone else. Suddenly, she wanted to be anywhere else and felt the longing to be numb that accompanied the impulse. Then she remembered she wasn't alone. *God help me*, she said, quietly, and almost instantly feeling strengthened, she entered the nurse's office.

There they were, the two nimrods, both of whom she loved in different ways, sitting on cots across from one another. Each held an icepack to his face.

Bella glanced around. Apparently, the nurse had stepped out, which absolutely worked in her own favor. Plastering a warm smile on her face, she moved between the two cots and folded her hands in front of her, a welcoming technique she'd learned from her father. "What happened?" she asked, quietly.

"He started it," Miah and Vick said simultaneously, pointing at one another.

Calmly, Bella raised a hand to silence them both. First, she turned her attention to her boyfriend. Hopefully, Vick wouldn't interrupt. "Let's try this again. Miah, what happened?"

"I'm not entirely sure. All I know is he came up to my locker and yelled at me about some invisible mark on Amanda's face. Which I didn't see at all. Did you?"

"Yes. But Mandy wouldn't tell me how she got it when I asked her last night." Bella had actually noticed it when Amanda was in the car. Maybe if she'd asked about it then, this whole fight could have been prevented. But, still, how had Miah missed the mark?

Vick smirked. "And here you thought I was lying."

"Which brings me to you, Vick. You seem to know how it happened. So, care to fill in the blanks?" Bella turned her attention the guy who long ago labeled himself her brother. Although lately, he'd been acting more like an ex-friend.

"Amanda was doing what you asked. She kept checking on David. I'm not clear on all the details, but yesterday, after school, she let it slip about the letter you wrote him—and then he got angry and hit her."

Jeremiah's mouth dropped open. "What?"

"Oh, boy." Any sense of having the upper hand left Bella. She dropped onto the edge of the cot Miah occupied. Why hadn't Amanda told her this last night? No! Why on earth had Amanda followed through on the request in the letter?

Lowering his icepack, Vick said, "I've tried to talk her out of keeping an eye on him, but she wouldn't listen to me."

"And what? You thought punching me would help? Great plan." Jeremiah shook his head and snickered.

Bella started to feel an anxiety attack coming on. But this was not the time to panic, nor would pills help in the situation. Despite the way Amanda treated her, she'd been a true friend. Half nodding to herself, Bella decided it was time she repaid the favor.

She lifted her gaze to Vick, one of the people who'd left her. He should've stayed, should have remained a part of her support group. She felt sad, but this wasn't about him, right now. It was about taking the burden off of Amanda. "You can tell your girlfriend I'll handle David."

"Girlfriend?" Jeremiah asked, looking puzzled, as he glanced from Vick to Bella.

Vick shook his head. "Now's not the time. Ask your sister if you want to know anything more, okay?"

Miah scowled, but returned to the main topic of discussion. "Bell, if you're going to talk to David, I'll be with you."

As much as the idea of having Miah by her side comforted her, it wouldn't do much good if she had to worry about another fistfight breaking out.

Bella stood up and sighed. "No. He's my problem. I need to handle it alone."

"And what's to stop him from hitting you, too?"

"He won't." She hoped this was true. The only time he'd gotten angry enough with her to punch something was when they broke up. Instead of swinging at her, though, he put a hole in the wall. Still, under the circumstances, that was perhaps something best kept to herself.

Vick returned the icepack to his cheek. "I'm with Jeremiah on this. I don't think you should talk to him by yourself. But if I couldn't stop Amanda, I don't stand a chance in hell of stopping you."

"You're right. You can't. And neither can you, Miah." Refusing to say another word on the matter, Bella pivoted on her heel and grabbed up her books.

Miah hopped off the cot. "Wait, where're you going?"

"I have to go talk to Principal Owen. Once I explain what happened, hopefully, he won't suspend either one of you." Giving Miah a brief smile, Bella pressed a tender kiss to his lips.

"Thank you." Miah dropped his forehead against hers.

Bella squeezed his hand and walked away. She paused at the door and glanced at Vick. "Those letters were never meant to be sent."

"What?"

"Just thought you should know."

After Bella left, Vick glanced at Jeremiah. "Do you know what she meant by that?"

Jeremiah slowly shook his head. "I'm not sure."

That was a half-ass answer if he ever heard one. Vick raised an eyebrow and waited.

"I mean, I don't have the whole picture."

Vick sighed. "Well, friend, how 'bout you tell me what you do know?"

"She attempted suicide at least once. I don't know exactly when. I just know it was sometime before that guy tried to kill her."

Vick was shocked to hear it said in such a matter-of-fact way. "How much time?" Based on the letters, they all assumed Bella had tried to kill herself. But now he had confirmation.

"A matter of days. She hasn't told me everything about the suicide attempt, but from what she has said ... I think the pills the guy used, I think they were hers."

So, her first attempt had failed somehow, and then something prevented a second. She must have written the letters before the first time.

"You guys seem better, Jere. Have you forgiven her?"

"I have. But it hasn't been easy." Jeremiah paused and sat down on the cot again. "We got into a fight on the way back to the house, Friday. I went to bed that night like usual, but all I could think about was what it would be like without her. I can't imagine being without her again. We both want to fix things, so we're going to give it our best."

Vick considered what Jeremiah was saying. He didn't want to lose Bella either. Before the letters, they'd acknowledged how hard things were for Bella, but obviously, things were worse than they thought. How could he, of all people, have missed how bad it had gotten for her? Vick groaned. God, he was such an ass.

"I'm sorry I punched you."

"I probably would've done the same thing in your shoes." Jeremiah shrugged off the apology.

Vick stood and held out his hand in a gesture of peace. Maybe they weren't the friends they once were, but it didn't mean they couldn't try. "We cool?"

"We're cool." Jeremiah accepted the proffered hand.

"Thanks, man."

"So, you're dating my sister, huh?"

"Uh, yeah. You don't seem as surprised as I thought you'd be. Not sure how Bella knew." Uneasy, Vick felt a grin crawl across his puss.

Jeremiah chuckled. "I knew Amanda was dating somebody, just not who. The real question is, do our parents know?"

"Well ... Amanda doesn't know this, but ... I asked your parents' permission before I took her out. But, like I said, Amanda has no idea. So, how about we keep it between us?"

Snickering, Jeremiah zipped his lips. "I never heard a thing."

"Have you heard from your dad, yet?"

Crikey, Cristobal had begun to get on his nerves. Since last night, the guy had asked that question every five freaking minutes. If his father didn't report in soon, they'd have a body on their hands—because he'd strangle Cristobal, himself.

Luis glanced at the guy. "Has my phone gone off, yet?"

"No."

"Then I haven't heard from him." He turned back to the adoption papers in front of him. The last conversation he had had with his father got him thinking. How had Gervasio discovered who Bella was in the first place? Luis had carefully hidden all the photographs and letters he received from Juan, and Gervasio never visited that house. Even if the man had snuck in and located the materials, none of Juan's letters identified Bella as his daughter.

Cristobal paced the room. "I hate this waiting."

"Then make yourself useful. Go get us some food."

Luis turned his attention to the next section. He had no idea what he was looking for; he simply wanted to find something that gave him an idea how Gervasio found out the truth.

Muttering, Cristobal stomped back to the bedroom he was using. He returned with socks and shoes, which he shoved on before leaving—slamming the door behind him.

It took every ounce of control Luis had to keep from shouting. The kid was so annoying. Luis inhaled and released a deep breath. "I have the patience of a tiger."

"New motto?" Slowly, Juan eased the door shut.

Luis spun around to face his father. The man must have purposely waited for Cristobal to leave before slipping in. "I'll need to repeat it a few more times."

"Please let me know if it helps."

"I'm sure I'll find out the next time you chase down a lead." He couldn't help but grin. Then Luis got serious. "I'm going to assume if you're here that you did not find Gervasio."

"You are correct. Gervasio had occupied the warehouse, but has not returned in the last twenty-four hours, and I do not believe he plans to. However, I did find something of interest in his home."

"When did you go to his house?" Luis sat up so quickly he nearly fell out of his chair. His father was a wanted man. Why would he do something so reckless?

"Yesterday afternoon. It is where I was when you phoned."

He jumped to his feet. "Are you trying to get caught?" His heart thudded in his chest. Surprise, surprise. He actually cared about the father he barely knew.

"It was not a concern. The home was unoccupied, and there were no police to see me. As well, I remained hidden from sight. I have been trained well."

Juan set a rather odd-looking, shallow lockbox on the desk. "It was well hidden."

"You don't say." Luis eyed the unusual lock and whistled. Where had Gervasio obtained such a thing? He heard of this particular security measure, but had not seen one in person. It not only required an accurate pass code, it had an embedded fingerprint scanner—and, he knew from his research, it was lined with a microscopic incendiary device. If the improper code or print was used, the box and anything inside it would be immediately destroyed.

"I am positive you can successfully open this box. With it so protected, it must contain information of great value to Gervasio."

His father had a lot of faith in his skills. Luis crossed his arms and lifted his gaze to Juan. "It won't be easy. And it'll take time. I'll have to crack the numbers first, then find a way to get a copy of Gervasio's print in order to access it."

"My confidence in you does not waver. For now, I take my leave. I will comb through the warehouse for a clue to Gervasio's current whereabouts. I shall contact you if I locate anything. In the meantime, I have a gift for you."

"What?" Luis raised an eyebrow. Since when did his father give him gifts?

Juan removed a small piece of paper from the inside pocket of his coat. He handed it to his son. "For when you meet with your sister. Your mother was a good friend to the woman who adopted Giovanna—I mean Bella. This should be all the proof she needs to believe what you tell her is true."

"I ..." Luis stared at the photograph in his hands. It was a picture of all four of them, evidently taken not long before his and Bella's mother, Ileana, died. He had no words to respond. When the door closed, he looked up in time to see his father leave.

Aurora kneed the punching bag one last time. She had to keep her legs strong—in case he found her. Thankfully, this town was large enough for her to hide and hide well. All she had to do was blend in and not draw unnecessary attention to herself.

Glancing around, she saw she was alone. Good. She preferred to shower in the gym locker room rather than the motel, which was disgusting, but cheap. Just to be on the safe side, she'd taken two rooms for an extended stay. She'd had plenty of cash to handle the cost of the rooms, plus, a little for the woman at the front desk person, who would likely keep her mouth shut about the transaction.

Tugging off her gloves, Aurora opened the locker and grabbed a towel, along with her travel bag. The kit contained everything she needed. A nice, warm shower would be absolute heaven. Softly, she shut the locker.

Then, *Bam!* Aurora jumped. What the hell? Quietly, she padded to the end of the aisle and glanced around the empty locker room.

Bam!

This time, she could tell the sound came from the gym. Quickly, she yanked off her sneakers and tiptoed to the locker room door and cracked it open ever so slightly.

Peeking into the gym, she almost gasped. It was the guy who'd knocked into her. What did he say his name was? David? Yeah. That was it.

Not realizing he was putting on a show, he got up from the bench press and snagged a hand towel to wipe his face. No shirt. Only shorts that clung to his well-formed body. Her eyes trailed down his back, from top to bottom. Gorgeous blue-black hair. Strong, sturdy neck. Tattoos that molded perfectly to his back muscles. Nice round ass. Thick, long legs.

Dear God, he's exquisite. With a deep breath, she eased the door closed. For the last day, his piercing blue eyes had haunted her. But she had to do what she had to do. If she was lucky, he'd be done and gone before she got out of the shower. Not that luck had ever been on her side.

I expect better. You're a Warren.

As his father's words played over and over in his head, David wanted to throw one of the free weights onto the rack on front of him. But he knew it wouldn't actually make him feel better. If nothing else, though, he supposed the past twenty-four hours had provided a much-needed wake-up call. David grabbed hold of a fifty-pound dumbbell and hoisted it over his head to work his triceps. Whether his parents intended to stay around for a while or not, he had to get his anger under control. This latest thing with Amanda made him realize how bad it had gotten.

He wanted to talk to someone about it. His mother wouldn't be much help, though. She'd simply insist there was absolutely nothing wrong with him. Maybe his twin? Heather used to be someone he could talk to. But lately, not so much.

David brought the dumbbell over his head and returned it the rack. Then he saw that he wasn't alone. Slack-jawed, he stared at the red-headed beauty walking towards him from the locker room. She'd stopped him in his tracks the day before, when they literally ran into one another. Now, he saw he'd been right: She was drop-dead gorgeous.

Dark auburn locks slicked back. Muscular curves that formed a perfect hourglass figure. Black boots with silver buckles on the side. Ripped black jeans hugging lean, stellar legs. White t-shirt bearing the word *Disturbed* scrawled above a skull.

Thumbs hooked in her front pockets, she walked purposefully toward the gym door. Afraid he'd lose his chance, David jumped in front of the door to block her exit.

"Hi."

"You really know how to piss a girl off."

A sly grin tugged on the corners of his lips and he crossed his arms. "I'll make you a deal. Tell me your name and I'll step aside."

She popped out a hip and folded her own arms. "How about you move or I make you scream like a girl?"

"I don't believe you can … "

"You don't know me, so don't act like you do. Now move the hell out of my way." With stormy gray eyes, she glared at him and got in his face.

The girl moved so close he could have pressed his lips to hers, and desire burned so hot in his body, he felt his blood would boil. For a split second, he thought she wanted him to wrap his arms around her and kiss her. Then, just as quickly, whatever he'd seen in those gray orbs of hers was gone. David gripped the back of his neck. "I don't understand why you won't give me your name."

"Because it's safer if you don't know." She said, and took a step back.

Her words confused him. But there was something about this girl. David stepped aside. "I'm not giving up," he said.

"You should. In fact, you should forget I even exist." And with that, she left the gym.

Jeremiah stroked Bell's back with one hand and threaded the fingers of his other hand through hers. The feel of her curled against his bare chest made his body hum. Kissing her forehead, he allowed her natural lavender scent to fill his nostrils. Slowly, Jeremiah released the breath. "You smell like heaven."

"I think you're exaggerating."

"Maybe, but there is definitely something magical about you." She'd proven this earlier, for sure. He wasn't sure exactly how she did it, but Bell said something to Principal Owen that made the man change his mind about suspending him and Vick. Instead, they got in-school detention for the week. Whatever magic she'd done had saved their asses.

"Well, that wasn't magic today, if that's what you mean. And, seriously, Miah, I'd prefer not to be put in that position again, if that's okay with you."

Her statement slapped the joy off his face. On the way home from school, he'd asked what happened, but she'd shut him down. Now, he really wanted to know. "Bell, what did you tell the principal?"

Instead of answering, she shuddered. Uncertain how to read her reaction, Jeremiah moved his hand to her head and dragged his fingers gently through her dark tresses. Her hair was luxuriously soft, almost like silk. His body stirred. Her touch had always charged him in wonderful ways, but lately the sensation of any part of her against his skin awakened pure desire in him. It was still too soon to act on those urges, though. He knew that.

Bell shifted her face and laid her chin on his chest. She stared up at him with a sad look in her hazel brown eyes. "I told him that I caused a situation, and the two of you got into a fight over the result."

"And he accepted that?"

"No. But I told him enough to satisfy him."

"Well, you got us out of a lot of trouble. Do you know how amazing you are?" Jeremiah tucked a finger beneath her chin and pulled her to him until their lips touched.

"I wanted to protect you."

He rolled Bell onto her back and angled his body atop hers. Staring into her wide eyes, he caressed her cheek and kissed her deeply. Their tongues swirled in a battle of longing. He thrust his hands through her satin hair, and she gripped his back, her breasts pressing into his chest. Warmth spread through his body. Lust couldn't consume him ... not yet. As much as he yearned to have more of her, they weren't ready. He'd simply have to maintain control. Or struggle with control.

Slowly their lips parted. Jeremiah dropped his head into the crook of her neck and pressed a tender kiss to her shoulder. "You protect me just by being here."

"Thank you."

"For what?" Jeremiah lifted his head and eyed Bell.

She surprised him with her answer: "Loving me, even when sometimes ... I'm not sure I deserve it. I know you'll argue with me, but I need you to know, it's how I feel."

She was absolutely right. He would've argued with her. She deserved the world. And if he had anything to do with it, he'd be the one to give it to her.

Jeremiah sighed. "Okay."

"Okay?"

"Okay." He kissed the tip of her nose and rolled over to his back, tugging her along with him.

A small smile crept onto Bell's face. She curled up to Jeremiah and rested her head on his chest. "Okay."

six

Bella stared out the window at the black VW Beetle that had spent the last two weeks in the driveway. Her mother left the keys with the Detrones, but it wasn't as if Bella'd been allowed to drive it.

With a sigh, she glanced at her homework. This was a home-school day, and her tutor left about ten minutes ago. Although the girl who tutored her was fairly nice, Bella hated being stuck inside the Detrones' house—no matter how much Miah tried to make it feel like home.

Well, whether she wanted to or not, she had work to do. With all the time she'd spent in the hospital, she had to play catch-up. Bella dragged herself across the kitchen and sat in the breakfast nook. Next on the list was Shakespeare. Almost anything would have been better than Shakespeare, which was so tiring to read. But she was amused by the play that had been assigned: *Romeo and Juliet* seemed appropriate for someone who'd attempted suicide.

Bella snagged her notebook and flipped it open to a blank page. There, she scribbled a few words that rattled around in her brain.

One more, two more, no more;
Some days feel like a chore.
The world I no longer see,
Blinded by all the pain inside of me.

Then, she lifted her gaze toward the window. She'd give anything for a small piece of home—a letter or a call from her mother, something to remind her she had family, that she wasn't completely alone.

"You look like you could use a getaway." Miah's mother appeared in the doorway.

"I suppose, but it isn't like I can do anything about it."

The woman disappeared down the hall. When she returned, she had a set of keys in her hand. She sat across from Bella. "You have to understand, trust is a two-way street. We want you to trust us as much as we trust you."

"I'm not sure what to say to that. I mean ... I feel like I've misplaced my trust too many times. I'm trying to find a way to trust again. I'm just ... I'm not sure how."

"Nothing happens overnight. Be patient. I promise it'll happen." Miah's mom reached across the table, turned over one of Bella's hands, and folded it around the keys.

Bella glanced down. They were her keys. Her gaze snapped back to Jeremiah's mom. Could she be saying what Bella thought? "Are you giving me permission?"

"More like a little trust."

Bella bit the inside of her lip. Such a small gesture, yet it gave her more than she'd dared ask for. In that moment, she was reminded of a print on the wall of her psychiatrist's office, which said, *Be not afraid to speak; someone will listen.*

"Mrs. Detrone? Did you ever get over it?" Their common history was the reason her mother arranged for Bella to stay with the Detrones. But how would living with Miah's mom help if they never spoke about the fact that each of them had been raped?

"There is no getting over it. You just learn to accept it and move forward a little more each day."

"Does it get easier?"

Miah's mother didn't answer immediately. Then she said, "With the appropriate support and time, yes, I believe it does."

"I know you have your reasons for not telling Miah about your ... rape ... but it's hard for me that he doesn't know."

Mrs. Detrone stood. "I understand. And I'm sure I'll tell him some day, when the time is right." With that, she gave Bella a little hug, and left the kitchen.

A small smile tugged her lips as Bella eyed the keys in her hand. She closed her notebook. If she stayed put, her mind would only wander again. There could be no harm in taking a drive to the local coffee shop. A good strong cup of joe was exactly what the doctor ordered. She jumped up, grabbed her purse, and ran out the door.

Settling into the driver's seat of the VW, Bella inhaled deeply, then coughed. The car smelled like stale mothballs. The last time she'd driven the car was just before it had been vandalized. All those awful words.

And now … She'd been called more than *slut* or *whore* over the last few days. Miah had been sweet and walked her to class almost every day when she'd been at school. They'd both believed having someone with her would prevent the name calling. And it worked—when they were in the hall. In class, all bets were off. People talked about her as if she wasn't even there. As if she was simply invisible.

But she had her car and her keys. Time to focus on the task at hand.

Turning over the engine, she rolled all four windows down, then backed out of the driveway. Bella inhaled a deep breath, and fresh air filled her lungs. God, it felt good to be on the road. Nothing in her way. The wind in her hair—which she'd regret later. It had grown out, and she hadn't been to the salon in months. Maybe … No … Miah's mother trusted her. Just a short trip, then.

She halted at the stop sign. The moment of truth.

If she turned left on Highway 666, she'd head toward the coffee shop in Nautica Valley. If she turned right, she'd drive toward the diner on the edge of Desemper Ridge, where she used to meet Tommy to get the pills. Her world hadn't seemed all that great with those pills, but the urge to use them remained with her every day. She struggled at the crossroads. If she turned right and returned to that life, she'd lose more than just herself. The price was too great to pay.

Bella turned left.

It took less than ten minutes to get to the coffee shop. Once there, she hopped out of the Beetle, smiling. She could almost taste the coffee. It didn't compare to the coffee her mother made, but it would suffice. With her hand on the door, she paused. Scrawled on a white sheet of paper taped to the door were the words: *Now Hiring*.

Jamar rubbed his eyes and looked at the date stamp of the security video. Which one was he on? Pausing the video, he glanced at the clock on his office wall. 8:00 p.m. He'd been at it longer than he'd realized—but he felt that somewhere in this video could be the break they'd needed. He'd checked in with Christine an hour ago to tell her he'd be working late. "Better than bringing the case home with him," she'd said. Now, if he took a small break, he could sift through another hour's worth before he called it a night.

He stood, stretched, and walked out of his office and across the squad room. In the break room, he found Russell lifting a mug. Apparently, Jamar wasn't the only one who'd begun to go cross-eyed. "Any luck so far?"

"All I can say is I've discovered what 'bored to death' feels like."

"Yeah, but somebody has to do it." Jamar grinned and poured himself a cup of coffee.

"What about you, Sheriff? You find anything?"

"No, can't say I have."

"Too bad Simms won't just give it up." Russell took another sip. "Not that I want to believe Simms would tamper with evidence, but after finding out he was working for Gervasio, seems likely."

"I know. Sometimes it's the people we trust the most who betray us. Listen, go for another hour, and if you don't find anything, then call it a night. The guy's not going anywhere and neither are the tapes."

His people shouldn't spend more time at work than he did, Jamar thought— and returned to his office. He'd split the surveillance tapes with Russell. They were searching three weeks of video. If Simms had switched out the DNA samples, he obviously hadn't signed the log to help them narrow down their search.

Sighing, Jamar dropped in his chair and started the video again, at August 30, 2013, 11:58 p.m. A few days after the rape. They certainly would've collected DNA by then. Sure enough, less than a minute had passed before Simms stepped into the frame. He had a quick conversation with the desk sergeant, and then the guy disappeared into the evidence locker.

Jamar jotted down the date and time. Then, he clicked a few keys and switched the frame view. Thankfully, the department had invested in proper surveillance equipment and the entire locker was covered. He waited a moment, and Simms entered the bottom right frame. He clicked and enlarged the picture. The guy shifted around a couple of evidence boxes, glanced in both directions, and placed something in a box. He appeared to remove an item as well, but Jamar couldn't tell what.

Only one way to find out. Stopping the video, he ejected the USB from the drive, snatched an evidence bag from his drawer, scrawled down the pertinent information, and practically jogged out of his office. He skidded to a stop at Ali's desk and set the bag down. "Need you to analyze this with those magic fingers of yours."

"Sheriff, you find something?" Russell called over.

"If we can identify the evidence box and get a better image of what he swapped out, I just might have."

The phone on Russell's desk rang. "Detective Russell. Yes, sir, he's right here. Incident? What happened? I see. We'll be there shortly."

"Dare I ask?" Jamar arched an eyebrow at Russell.

"You know that moment when you think you've got something, and it all turns to shit? This is one of those."

Luis lifted his gaze to the double doors that had *Valley Coffee & Beans* etched into the glass. He wiped his clammy palms down the front of his jeans. He'd never been this nervous in his life. So much depended on this meeting going right. Plus, it would be nice to actually have a relationship with his sister.

He peered through the window and watched as Bella plucked a pastry from the case and served it to a customer. He'd found out she'd gotten the job when he ran her credit. Now, although he desperately wanted to meet her, he worried perhaps it was too soon. Unfortunately, since Cristobal had kind of left him here, either he continued to act like a creepy stalker or he entered and introduced himself.

Plan B it was. Inhaling deeply, Luis opened the door and walked into the thick aroma of coffee beans. Cautiously, he made his way toward the counter. How should he approach her? It wasn't like he could go up and introduce himself as her brother. She'd look at him as if he were a lunatic. What was he thinking? He couldn't do this. No way, no how.

Luis lifted his gaze, and a pair of hazel brown eyes matching his own stared back at him.

"Hi. Welcome to Valley Coffee and Beans. What can I get for you today?" A bright smile crossed his sister's face.

His entire body flushed as if he were standing under a heat lamp. Sweat trickled down his forehead, and he swallowed to wet his parched throat. He opened his mouth and croaked out the only thing he could think of. "Hi."

"Do you need a few minutes to decide?"

"I ... yes." Luis squeaked. He stepped to the side. Thankfully, there was a customer behind him. He took three, deep, slow breaths and decided to try again.

"Have you decided on something?"

"Um, yes. I'll have an iced mocha and a slice of that carrot cake."

She put the cake on a plate and rang him up. "Here's your carrot cake, and the mocha will be right up. Your total is $7.53."

"You're Bella, right?" Luis handed her a ten-dollar bill. He simply had to ease into conversation and hope she didn't get scared off.

"Yes. How'd you know?"

Holding his hand out, he accepted his change and pointed to the tag on her shirt. "It's on your name tag."

"Oh, yeah." Her cheeks tinged pink. She stepped away, poured his mocha, then placed it on the counter.

He lifted the cup and sipped some of the ice cold joe. It was refreshing and sweet. Now, he needed to direct the conversation toward his true purpose. "We have someone in common."

"Who's that?"

"Ileana Costa." The name tumbled out of his mouth before his brain could stop it. He meant to say David or even Heather. Instead he blurted out their mother's name. Christ, what was wrong with him?

Bella gasped. This man couldn't have uttered her biological mother's name. Almost no one knew who her real mother was—not even Miah. Surely, he said some other name. Any other name. "I'm sorry. Can you repeat that?"

"Ileana Costa."

"No ... I ... how? How do you even know that name?" She backed away from the counter, and studied the tall guy who stood on the other side. Short, spiked black hair, hazel brown eyes, chiseled face, and mocha-colored skin tone. Who the hell was he?

He swept a hand through his black hair. "We should talk. Do you think you can take a break?"

"Emily, can you cover me for a few?" Getting a nod from her co-worker, Bella stepped around the counter and gestured toward an empty table in the back.

The guy followed after her, taking a seat to her left. "I'm not exactly sure where to start."

"How about with your name?"

"Right. I go by Luis Hernandez, but I was given another name at birth." He reached into his pocket, pulled out a folded photograph, and placed it on the table between them.

Shakily, she reached for the picture and unfolded it. Four people looked back at her. Two of the faces she recognized immediately: her birth mother and father. Jamar had once shown her a mug shot of Juan Castell, her biological father, but she'd never seen a picture of her real parents together. Standing in front of Juan was a little boy, perhaps two years old. And in her arms, Ileana held a baby with a pink ribbon in her hair. Tears rolled down her cheeks, as Bella eyed the guy who sat in front of her. Could it be? "How do you know her?"

"Ileana's my mother and ... you're my sister."

"I don't understand. How is this possible?" All her life she'd wanted a sibling. She'd hated being an only child. After a while, she accepted it wasn't in the cards. Her parents were meant to have one child and only one. And now, she was staring at a guy whose features were similar to her own?

"We were separated after our mother died. Our father believed it would be safer for us that way."

Obviously, he was wrong, Bella thought. She shifted her eyes back to the photograph. Yes. The children in the picture could be the two of them. She looked at Luis again. "How did you get this?"

"That's not important."

"Bullshit. It matters a whole hell of a lot." How long ago had he discovered they were related? Bella scrutinized him a bit further. He seemed familiar, but she couldn't say why.

"I found the photo among some of my baby things a few months ago. It took me a while to realize that you lived here in this county, too. We grew up in the same place, but never knew."

He sounded sincere. Was he as shocked as she was when he found out? What would this mean to her understanding of who she was as a person. Bella didn't know exactly what to say.

He seemed to understand. "I don't want to take up too much of your time. If you want to talk, you can reach me at this number." He set a slip of paper on the table and stood. With a quick goodbye, he left.

As Bella glanced at the scribbled numbers, the feeling that he was familiar nagged at her. She felt like she'd seen him, but where? Was it before the coma? *Holy shit! I know how I know him.* The last time she'd spoken with Tommy. The day she purchased the pills.

He knew Tommy. Had he recognized her then? Was that why he had been adamant about talking with the dealer? Her lungs tightened. She couldn't breathe. Bella ran to the front and grabbed her purse. "Emily, I need to go."

Her phone rang for the third time. She should've returned to the Detrone's an hour ago—but it was the last place she could go. Too many revelations had been dropped in her lap. The guy who'd identified himself as her biological brother had known her drug dealer. Not that she knew how. Asking Tommy was out of the question. Having only begun to pick up the pieces she didn't need to confront her dealer to find out.

Bella stared out over the lake. The sun cast a beautiful orange glow on the water. Another gorgeous view wasted on her. She'd done nothing to deserve the show. Not long after Luis left, questions bubbled to the surface. She could've called him, but she needed time to think.

Which was why she was here at the Hilliard's summer house. To think. She trekked through the back yard—the grass had grown above her ankles; it probably hadn't been cut in the last month—then climbed the three stairs to the back door and let herself in.

Strangely, although the house had always felt warm and inviting any time she'd been here before, now it felt cold and distant, as if the home sensed she no longer belonged. Nonetheless, Bella continued down the hallway, pausing at the basement door. She'd hung out with Vick down there over the summer. Funny, she'd also been forced to stay in the basement with Miah, and it was there that they'd truly spoken for the first time after their break-up.

That had been the same day she'd purchased the last bottle of pills from Tommy. Vick had called and insisted she drive out there to get him. Turned out the whole thing was a ruse, a plan to set up Bella so she'd finally talk to Miah. And because of that, she hadn't followed through with her plan.

Bella rubbed her arms just thinking about how the pills dulled the world. Those pills, those exquisite little pain pills made the world disappear for a little while. Right then, it would've been nice if the world faded away for a bit.

Her mind was spinning about the connection between Luis and Tommy. The guy admitted he discovered their relationship a few months ago. What did that mean, "a few months"? When had he found out they were siblings? And exactly what kind of connection could he have had with Tommy? So many questions ... and they could only be answered if she contacted Luis.

But she knew nothing at all about him. Nothing other than what he'd said. No reason for her to believe him without at least some corroboration. She didn't want to ask Jeremiah's dad for help, because that would involve the police, the last thing she wanted. Obviously, though, Luis and Tommy knew one another. She could ask Tommy, but that would tilt her too close to temptation. Unable to find a solution, she realized that there was one person who could help.

As Bella went to grab her purse, she stepped in front of a mirror by the door. Catching her reflection, she halted and studied her features. High cheek bones, mocha-colored skin, and wide hazel brown eyes. Her birth mother had the same features, and Luis had the same eyes and skin tone. His hair was even midnight black like her own.

She wondered what he had seen when he looked at her. Reaching to the left side of her neck, she let her fingers trace the line of her scar. At the coffee shop, her hair had been swept up into a bun, as required for the job. It always made her feel self-conscious, though. She hated the idea that the scar could be seen, so she disguised it with make-up. It took several layers to cover the awful truth of what she'd endured. Now, though, she could see the make-up had faded and the scar was peeking through.

Suddenly, she decided: She'd make two stops on her way back into Nautica Valley. If she was lucky, one would remove the mark embedded in her skin. And the other would provide much needed answers. While she deserved both, she had no clue if she'd get either one.

Bella snatched her purse and fled, leaving behind both the lake house and her reflection.

Jeremiah folded his arms behind his head and laid back in the bed. He'd gone by the coffee house after school to surprise Bella, but she hadn't been there. When she hadn't been at home either, he freaked out. Despite the number of times he called, she never answered her cell phone. She finally arrived home about an hour ago, but refused to explain what happened. There would be no dodging him tonight, though. She would tell him where she'd been all day.

Now, while he waited for her to finish her shower, thoughts were pummeling his brain. Where had she been? What had she done? When had she left work? Why hadn't she come straight home? He sighed and pinched the bridge of his nose. Stressing wouldn't make the answers come any faster—which was something he'd tried to remind himself of for hours on end, earlier today.

When he heard the water turn off in the bathroom across the hall, his body perked up at the image of his freshly showered girlfriend walking through the door any moment. Jeremiah frowned and adjusted his pajama pants. Maybe it wasn't such a good idea to wait in the bed after all. He eyed the desk against the wall. That would probably be the best place for him to sit. But just as he sat up to move, the door opened.

"Miah, what're you doing in here?" Bell whispered, clinging to the knot in the towel that was wrapped around her body.

He swallowed, and let his gaze trail from the towel on the top of her head all the way down to her bare feet. Had it gotten hot in here? "I, uh, I ... I wanted to talk."

"Are you trying to get us caught?" She peeked around the corner of the door and eased it shut. Holding tight to the towel, she tiptoed over to the dresser.

Oh, boy! Jeremiah dragged his hand across his buzz cut and gripped the back of his neck. Hormones made his entire body flush with heat. He yearned to have every part of her.

Bell opened a couple of drawers and pulled a few items out. She peered over her shoulder at him. "If you're staying in here, then you need to face the door."

"Um, okay." A small grin slipping to his lips, Jeremiah stood and turned toward the door. Then, unable to help himself, he glanced at her out of the corner of his eye. The glimpse granted him a beautiful view of her tugging on a pair of night shorts and the single tattoo on her lower back. Before she caught him, Jeremiah snapped his eyes away from her bare back. He'd always known she was gorgeous, but the sight of her skin blew his mind.

"Why'd you sneak in here so early, anyway? And you can turn around now."

Oh. Right. He had planned to talk to her about something, hadn't he. He spun towards her. "Where were you this afternoon?"

Bell tugged the towel from her head and picked up a brush. "Is that why you came in here? To talk about today?"

"Yes. I'd like to know where you disappeared to and why you refused my calls." Jeremiah crossed his arms. He had a multitude of questions. And they deserved answers.

"I'm sorry I didn't answer. Today was just ... a learning experience." The look on her face said a lot. Her forehead was creased with worry, and her eyes were filled with sadness—but it looked like a shred of hope existed.

He walked over and took the brush in his hand. Lacing his fingers through hers, he guided her to the bed, where he sat and pulled her up so she nestled between his legs.

"What happened?"

"It kind of goes along with something I found out a few months back."

Gently, Jeremiah brushed her hair. He started at the ends and slowly pulled the brush through her midnight black locks. Hopefully, it soothed her. "What'd you find out?"

"I'm adopted."

"What?" This threw him for a loop, momentarily. Then he recalled the picture of the "friend of the family" he'd seen on the mantel in the Kynaston house. He always thought Bell looked a lot like that woman—more than she did either her mother or father.

"Funny, how you think you know all there is to know about your parents, and it turns out you don't know shit. When I found out the truth, I didn't think they ever planned to tell me. They said they would have, when the time was right. Now, I'm not so sure."

He parted her hair down the middle, and took the right-hand section in his hand and brushed it, then inched his hand up and brushed through it again. "Why do you say that?"

"Actually, your dad kind of forced the issue, made my parents confess."

"I don't get it. Why would he make them tell you?" And why hadn't his father told him?

"From what I know, my biological mom, Ileana, came from Brazil with Milena. They were best friends. You've seen Ileana's picture in our living room. That's my birth mom. As for my dad, he's ... complicated. Your dad told me my birth father ran the local gang here for a while."

Wait. Did Bell just say her biological father was a gang leader? And she called that "complicated"? That was the understatement of the century. Jeremiah completed the right section of her hair and switched to the left. The local gang was called Grim something, he remembered. "Wait, I thought the guy who shot me was the leader."

"Apparently, he took over after my father disappeared."

"Okay, so what happened today?"

Bella tucked her legs up against her chest. "Turns out, I'm not the only child my birth parents had. I have a brother. We met today. And we've met before."

"What? When?" Jeremiah tossed the brush aside and swept Bella's damp hair back.

"The day I bought the pills."

Those six words reminded him of the day he nearly lost her. Those words also confirmed what he and Vick had speculated about just a few days earlier, when they discussed Bella's attempt to take her own life. Jeremiah wrapped his arms around her and hugged her against his chest. "What did this brother have to say?"

"Not very much. He gave me a number to reach him at, but I wanted to see if I could find anything out about him, first. That's part of why I was gone so long."

"What'd you find out?" He pushed her hair aside and kissed her shoulder. If possible, he avoided the scar on her neck. Hopefully, one day the mark would no longer shame her. Until then, he respected her boundaries.

"Nothing. A whole lot of nothing."

"I'm sorry, Bell. I wish there was something I could do."

She snuggled up to him. "You have. Just by listening."

He opened his mouth to respond, but something she'd said … "What was the other reason you were gone so long?"

"I went to the tattoo parlor."

"I don't understand. You didn't get any new work, did you?" Surely, he would've noticed. The image of her naked backside popped into his brain. Not what he needed to think about right at the moment.

"No. I asked, but the artist said he couldn't cover the scar. If he could have, I figured it would have been one less piece of me the bastard gets to keep. But I'm stuck with it."

Jeremiah kissed her forehead. "I think that scar shows you're a fighter. Some jackass tried to take you down, and not only did you survive, but you came out stronger."

Why was it that the elevator always took forever in the precinct? Sheriff Detrone knew she hated coming to the station, yet he still had requested her presence. Whatever he wanted to discuss had to be related to her case. Otherwise they could've discussed it at the house.

Bella glanced at her phone and pushed send. Hopefully, her brother—what a weird term to use!—would agree to meet with her.

Ding! The doors finally opened. She stepped in and pressed the button for the third floor. Maybe they'd found Gervasio. Nah, Miah's father would've told her that at the house. How nice that would be, though. She could call her mom, tell her to come home, and they could figure things out. She'd have to tell Milena about Luis. But maybe the woman knew about him already. Bella tugged on the hem of her shirt. God, the elevator took forever to climb three floors. Next time, she'd take the stairs.

Ding! The elevator doors parted too slowly for her. She squeezed through the moment there was enough room, then power-walked across the squad toward Sheriff Detrone's office.

"Hey, Bella. What are you doing here?" Detective Russell asked, before she could jet by his desk.

She crossed her arms and sighed. "Sheriff Detrone asked me to meet him here."

"Okay. Well, let me just poke my head in and let him know you're here." Detective Russell collected a file and disappeared before she could object.

Leaning against the detective's desk, she frowned. She never enjoyed dealing with any of the detectives. Who would? Probably no one; victims and suspects alike.

"He's ready for you."

Bella thanked Detective Russell and walked into Miah's father's office. Good Lord! The man had piles of files and notebooks stacked all over—a couple of boxes even cluttered the floor by the filing cabinet. He looked like he was in organization hell. "I hope you didn't call me in here because you need some help with filing."

Sheriff Detrone didn't crack a smile. "No. I have some news on your case. Why don't you have a seat." He crossed the room and closed the door.

His tone made his suggestion feel like a warning. Whatever news he had must be bad, she thought. "Mr. Detrone, what's going on? You're freaking me out a little."

"You recall we arrested Detective Simms for interfering with the investigation. Correct?" Sheriff Detrone said, settling into the chair beside her.

She remembered. He was the guy who'd shown her the first photo array, which hadn't included a picture of Gervasio. From what she heard, it had been left out on purpose. What did that have to do with her? "Yes. Did something happen?"

"A couple days ago we found proof he tampered with evidence. It seems Simms exchanged the sample in the evidence box with the one that was tested."

"That's good, right? I mean, the one that was tested belonged to Petar. Means he wasn't one of my attackers, right?" Yeah, Petar tried to kiss her once, but she never really believed he'd been capable of the rape. Even though the DNA tests proved he'd fathered the baby she'd lost, she never thought that made any sense. The guy was too sweet to be involved.

"Yes and no. We haven't located the original sample, yet."

What? She didn't understand. If they had Simms by the balls, why hadn't he told them where the sample was? Bella looked at Miah's dad, confused. "If you can't find it, why don't you just ask him?"

"I'd love to. Unfortunately, Simms was found dead the same day we discovered he'd made the switch. But we're doing everything we can to locate the sample."

"Was he killed?" She stared the sheriff in the eye. The guy always told her what he thought she needed to know when he felt she had to know it. This she needed to know. If the one person who had proof Gervasio raped her had been killed, it could only mean one thing.

"Yes."

Bella could barely keep herself from screaming. *He's going to get away with it. All of it. Gervasio attacks me, kills my father, and now this Simms guy. And he won't answer for any of it? I know he won't. This is bullshit! I'll be damned if he doesn't answer for it!*

Yeah, God had taken the weight of her pain. But this new shit didn't cause more pain. Instead, it brought anger and hatred. Bella ground her jaw and balled her fists. She wouldn't take this sitting down any longer. Her biological parents were who they were. It was time she lived up to the name *Castell*. Without a word, she stood and strode out of Sheriff Detrone's office.

seven

"Tell me we've got something to go on." Jamar eyed the warden. Two inmates killed in the jail yard less than two days apart. No witnesses to the first murder. Maybe this time they'd get lucky.

"I'm having my guys pour through the video feed right now."

The fact that two of the three witnesses in the case against Gervasio were dead created a huge problem. It was time to take control of the situation. "Tell your men to stand down. This place is on official lockdown. I want every inmate and guard interviewed by my detectives. I intend to find out how the hell this happened a second time."

"Yes, sir." Wisely, the warden walked away without an argument, leaving Jamar with Russell, Deegert, and the medical examiner.

Jamar would have his own tech go through the feed, too, he decided, to make sure nothing was missed. He made the call. "Ali, I need you down at the jail. Bring Reynolds and Alvarez with you, too."

Hanging up, he knelt beside the body of Rodney Harrison. The guy had family. Best if he delivered the news himself. Jamar glanced at the medical examiner. "What do we have, Joe?"

"Asphyxiation. There are ligature marks, some kind of cord was used. I'll know more once I get him on the table. I'll let you know as soon as I have anything." The medical examiner nodded to a couple of guys waiting nearby. They covered the body and loaded it on a gurney.

Sighing, Jamar approached Russell. "You and Deegert go pick up Gabriella Caprise. I want her somewhere safe. The two of you are on protective duty. I will not lose another witness."

"Not that she's talked to us," Russell said, crossing his arms.

"Harrison didn't say anything either, and you see what happened."

Russell pinched the bridge of his nose. "Point made. We'll take care of her, Sheriff."

"Let me know once you're set up. I'm going to wait for the others."

Jamar headed for the security office. Not that he didn't trust the warden, but he didn't trust the warden's men. Hopefully, the murder was recorded—but it was not bloody likely. Every prison had corners cameras couldn't reach. Rescate County Prison was no different.

With the video feed, and his having to make sure every inmate was accounted for, this would be a very long night. Jamar dug his phone back out and texted his wife.

B home late. Don't wait up.

Everything OK?

New problem. Same shit.

OK. B safe. I love u.

I love u 2.

Tucking his phone away, Jamar stepped into the security office. Good, the warden was still there. "How far along are we in getting this place locked down?"

"All inmates have returned to their cells."

"Excellent. Now let's get a head count. Every cell needs to be inspected."

"That may take all night."

Jamar folded his arms across his chest. "No worries. I'm not going anywhere.

The door to the warehouse opened. Bronco had returned. Hopefully, the fool'd completed his second task. If only Bronco had snagged the bitch like he'd been told, then none of these problems would've arisen. Gervasio rolled up the list of properties his New York contact had provided. In a matter of minutes, he'd leave this waste behind and move to a better location.

He stood and asked his executioner if the job was done. "*¿Se hace?*"

"*Sí.*"

"*Excelente.*" Only three tasks remained, but those he would handle himself. Gervasio rested a hand on Bronco's shoulder. Gervasio felt his executioner relax under the touch.

"*Gracias.*"

"*De nada.*" He grinned, and felt the jagged scar that ran down the right side of his face tug at his mouth. It was fitting that the coiled wire he pulled from his pocket was the same as that which Bronco used on his victims.

Swiftly, Gervasio wound the wire around his knuckles, jumped forward, and wrapped the wire around Bronco's neck, crisscrossing his wrists to tighten his hold. "You not fail me again."

Bronco grabbed for the wire digging into his neck. He flailed and attempted to free himself, gasping as his lungs struggled for the tiniest bit of air. After a moment, the fight in Bronco's body faded and he went limp.

Gervasio increased the pressure, the sound of tiny snaps of the breaking hyoid filling his ears, his mind buzzing with the thrill of another kill.

After all of Bronco's movements ceased, Gervasio held the wire tight another minute, then released the body, which dropped to the floor with a thud. He crouched down and observed his handiwork. Good to know he hadn't lost his touch. Lightly, he slapped Bronco on the cheek, then Gervasio stood and walked out the door whistling.

Bella slipped into the school library. She had to leave shortly to meet up with her brother at the coffee shop, and she wanted to see what she could find out about their parents beforehand. She eased into a chair at one of the computers and logged in, then typed in her father's name. Skimming the few items the search retrieved, she determined only one was relevant. The headline read, *Massacre in Mexico.* Though it populated because she'd searched his name, Juan Castell was only mentioned once in the article, which was about a large battle between two rival gangs. Several people had died, including a couple of bystanders.

She cleared out her first search and typed in her mother's name. The search returned several items, most referencing Ileana's modeling career—but only one link interested Bella.

Tragedy Strikes New York Model September 11, 1997

Fashion model Ileana Costa was found dead in her New York home yesterday morning. In a statement, local police indicated the 24-year-old model's death was being treated as a suspected suicide. Costa was last seen alive at the house she shared with her husband and children Wednesday evening at about 6 p.m., as reported by the detective on site.

According to sources, the model had been battling severe depression following the loss of her mother. Due to medical reasons, the Brazilian native had been unable to attend the funeral. Sources also report Costa has been in and out of rehab over the last few years. Though it has been rumored Costa recently saw a psychiatrist known to treat addiction, it's believed her suicide is drug related. The New York City Police Department neither confirmed nor denied this information. Toxicology reports will not be available for several weeks.

Costa is survived by her father, husband, and two children.

Had her adoptive parents searched for information regarding her mother's death? The article stated "two children," clear as day. If they had, they would've known about the existence of her brother. Neither uttered a word about Bella having a sibling, though. Not that they'd talked much about her birth parents, only that one time, when Milena told her Ileana had committed suicide—but didn't disclose how.

Returning to the search results, Bella reviewed the other links, but none of the later pieces mentioned her mother's death. Why?

Her phone buzzed. It was the alarm. If she wanted to be on time for Luis, she had to leave. Maybe he would know something more.

She logged off and left the library. The bell wouldn't ring for another ten minutes. She'd planned her exit for a time when the hallway wouldn't be crowded with students. Just then, she caught a glimpse of Miah at his locker. If she hurried, maybe he wouldn't see her.

As if he heard her thinking, he turned. "Bell? Where'd you come from?"

Shit! She plastered the sweetest smile she could muster across her face. "I had some research to do in the library before I go to work."

"Oh. I didn't think you had to be there for another hour." Jeremiah raised an eyebrow.

What had she told him? Had she mentioned any particular hours? Not that she recalled. "They asked me to come right after school. So, I've got to go or I'm going to be late."

"Okay. I have to make sure Mandy has a ride home, but I'll swing by after." He slung his backpack over his shoulder and shut his locker.

Not good. Her brother had only just come into her life. There was so much she needed to know before she introduced the two of them. Plus, who knew what she'd find out. "You know I'd love for you to, but you'll be a distraction. I don't want to get into trouble at work."

"Not trying to keep me away, are you?" Miah grabbed Bella by the waist and pulled her close. Caressing her cheek, he pressed his lips to hers, kissing her like he hadn't seen her in months.

The kiss stole her breath away. She hated lying to him. Part of her wanted to drop the bullshit and tell him the truth right then and there. If only she had a better idea of what exactly she was getting into. Keeping him safe required she proceed with caution. Hopefully, she wouldn't irrevocably damage their relationship in the process.

Their lips parted.

"I would never do that. Now, I really do have to go."

"Okay. Go on. I'll see you later." Miah released his hold of her.

Biting her bottom lip, Bella nodded, more to herself than to him. With a little hesitation, she walked out of the school.

"You might want to let me speak with her first," Jamar told the two US Marshals, a dark-haired female agent with her hair pinned back and a bald male agent. "She's been holed up for three days and was pretty steamed last time I came by." Although WITSEC had every right to his witness, the girl was a tad psychotic.

Given the nod by the marshals, Jamar opened the door—and a glass came flying at his head. Jamar ducked as it shattered against the wall.

Standing in the corner, Russell looked aghast. "I tried to stop her, sir."

"You better have my witness protection with you, or so help me God, I will throw every glass within reach at your head!" Gabriella screamed.

Jamar held up his hands. "They're outside. Calm down, and I'll let them in."

"Show me."

"All right." He opened the door and waved in the marshals— "Let me see your badges," Gabriella demanded.

The female agent swept her jacket to the side and displayed her credentials. Her partner followed suit. She gestured to herself, then to her partner. "I'm US Marshal Fox, and this is US Marshal Taylor."

"Oh, thank God! You've got to get me out of here."

"We leave at nightfall. In the meantime, Sheriff Detrone has some questions." Marshal Fox crossed the motel room, slid the curtain aside just an inch, and peered out the window.

"Why not now?"

Jamar pulled out a chair. "Better for cover. So, have a seat. We have a lot to discuss."

"Fine. What would you like to know?" Gabriella dropped into the chair.

The Latina who sat in front of him had knowledge of the inner workings of Gervasio's set-up. "Everything. Start with your role and go from there."

Gabriella smirked and folded her arms across her chest. "My role was simple. I kept the girls in line. Made sure they did what they were supposed to and that Papi got his money."

"Why do you call him 'Papi'?"

"We all have nicknames. Makes it easier to keep identities secret, along with fake IDs. Every person in the organization takes on the same last name."

"Smith? Like you used?"

"*Sí*. I'm also known as *Mamá Gallina* because I'm over the girls. I prefer that to Smith, but it was chosen because it is so common."

Jamar dug into his pocket and removed a stack of photographs. Some of the faces were reconstructions of those on the mangled bodies they'd found on the farm. He spread the photos on the table. "Do you recognize any of these people?"

"This one ..." Gabriella tapped a picture. "He uses the name Luis Smith, but Papi calls him Swifty. He was the messenger."

"Why was he called Swifty? And what do you mean he *was*?" The kid's body hadn't been found. But based on the information Russell collected, he might be Bella's brother.

"He could get in and out of anywhere. No fingerprints. Made him unidentifiable. I say he *used* to be the messenger because he disappeared. Papi thought he bailed. So, he got put on the list with the others. Papi's cleaning house. If he finds Swifty, he will kill him."

No fingerprints? Jamar dragged a hand down his face. That would make the guy impossible to identify without a blood or DNA sample. He'd have to get the DNA for the male bones tested against Bella or Juan Castell. If it wasn't Luis Smith, they would track the kid.

"Okay, anyone else?"

She pointed to another photo. "This is Enrique. The *verdugo*, the executioner. He was called Bronco. If he's not dead yet, he will be soon. He tried to kill the girl against Papi's wishes."

Yeah, Bella had survived. But with Gervasio roaming the streets, maybe he should put a protective detail on her. Better safe than sorry—even though she was living in his house.

Gabriella held another photograph up, a mug shot of the one body that had been identified. "This is *Bàrbaro*. Why is he included?"

"Because he was found dead."

Gabriella snapped upright. "What? No! That's not possible! That isn't how it works."

"What are you talking about? That's not how what works?"

The woman scattered the photos across the table and scanned them with wide eyes. "*¡Dios míos!* Are they all dead? You must tell me!"

"With the exception of the first two you identified, yes. These two men and these women have all been found dead, buried in the backyard of a house apparently owned by your Papi. Now, what do you mean, 'That's not how it works'?"

"*Bàrbaro*, he ..." Gabriella paused and wiped tears from beneath her eyes. "He was a soldier. These girls ... were my girls. Papi ... Gervasio, he breaks them before they come work for him. The first time, he drugs and rapes them. The second time, he takes a soldier with him, and they both rape her. He will only kill a soldier if they fail to perform. I know ... I know ... *Bàrbaro*. He would not have failed."

Jamar stared at Gabriella. She'd been broken by Gervasio Rodriguez. That was how she knew the man's methods. That was how she became *Mamá Gallina*. And the sorrow she felt for the tragic loss of those young girls and that young man *Bàrbaro* was real. He could see it in her eyes. For that, she deserved a moment of his sympathy.

Gently, he asked, "Who was the girl *Bàrbaro* was to rape?"

"The girl Papi is obsessed over. Bella." Gabriella traced the features on the mug shot, then looked to Jamar. "You have wrong man. Papi ... he set him up. I will tell you everything, but you must protect me."

Tears rolled down her cheeks as Bella eyed the driver's license she'd laid on the nightstand. All she'd wanted from her brother was for him to tell her what he knew about their parents. And to clarify his relationship to her dealer. Nothing more. Why'd couldn't he have kept the rest to himself?

"Here, I think you should have this." Luis placed a small box on the table in front of her.

Cautiously, Bella eyed the box. The last time she opened what seemed a harmless box, she'd found it full of red roses and rats. "What is it?"

"You don't have to open it right now. But it isn't anything bad. And it'll help with your case. I found this in the box." He held out her old driver's license.

The last time she'd seen it had been at the Fourth of July party she'd attended with Alex. Bella frowned. Her gaze shifted from the ID to her brother, who wouldn't meet her eyes.

"How did you get this?"

Luis didn't answer her, but from what she'd gathered, Gervasio had been at the party—and had drugged her. According to Alex, Bella danced with the guy, and the next morning her clothes had been disheveled. She could no longer ignore the truth.

Gervasio may have raped her for the first time last August, but he had assaulted her in July.

"Bell, what's wrong?" Miah climbed into bed.

She rolled over, buried her face in his chest and cried. A few days ago, the ache she'd released had been replaced with rage. Now, the pain seeped from her soul as if it had never left. There would be no reprieve, tonight. Tonight, she would have to face it again.

Miah wrapped his arms around her and held her tight. His hand made slow, comforting circles against her back. "Hey. Shh, whatever it is, you can tell me."

No, not yet she couldn't. She couldn't reveal the awful truth to Miah, yet. Finding out she had a brother was supposed to be a good thing. Except, it only worsened the pain she'd just been freed of. Brothers protected their sisters. Hers ... he might as well have raped her himself. More tears trickled down her cheeks.

"Did you know?"

"Not until afterward. I checked on you, but you kept going like nothing happened. I figured it was better that I stay out of the way." Luis slumped in his chair as if he was ashamed of his actions—or lack thereof.

Bella swiped at her tears. "Did you know he'd do it again? That he'd brutalize me?"

"I knew he'd planned something. I tried to stop him. You have to believe me. I did everything I could ... without putting other people at risk."

"What people?" As far as she could tell, the only person who'd been put at risk was her. If her life had nearly been sacrificed to protect others, she deserved to know who they were.

Luis swallowed. "I, um, it ... uh ..."

"Dammit! Tell me who!" Bella slammed her fist on the table.

That was one cat she wished could be shoved back in the bag. If the table hadn't been between them, Bella would've punched him the second he uttered that bitch's name. Her blood had boiled when she learned how far David's twin had gone. Not that Heather's involvement should've surprised her one bit.

Then the shit really hit the fan.

"Do you know why? Why he's targeted me?"

"I didn't. Not until I found that. Then I understood." Luis glanced from Bella to the box in front of her.

She leaned back in her chair. She refused to open the godforsaken box. He had to spell it out. Her brother owed her at least that much. "Enlighten me."

And he did.

Three days earlier, she'd decided to live up to the Castell name, imagining herself killing a man. Now, she despised that name and the person who'd bestowed it ... Juan Castell. He may have given her life, but she loathed him with every fiber of her being.

Bella sniffled. Her tears subsided and her breathing normalized. Miah had helped ease the storm that raged inside of her. Hopefully, the calm would remain—at least for a while. She had some explaining to do.

"I met with my brother today."

Jeremiah leaned against the wall. Bell'd shared one mess of a story. He had no idea how to process it all. Not only had she lied to his face, saying she'd done it to protect him, she'd also met with a guy who'd worked for her rapist. What was he supposed to do with that information?

Yeah, of course she had learned stuff from the guy—more about her parents, how Heather had been involved, and that her rapist had attacked her more than once. Of everything, that was what bothered him most ... for a few reasons. First, his father had to have suspected that had happened, based on Bell's memories. And no way was Alex dumb enough to assume Bella simply had too much to drink at that Fourth of July party.

He felt his shoulders tense. That brother of Bell's, the more she'd talked about him, the less Jeremiah liked the guy. If they ever met, he'd punch the living daylights out of him. The selfish asshole deserved that, if not more.

"Please say something." Bell tucked her feet underneath herself.

He glanced at her, arms crossed. "What exactly would you like me to say?"

"That you believe me. You understand why I went alone. You accept my apology. Most importantly, that you forgive me."

"One, I do believe you. Two, I don't understand. Three, I'm not sure on the last two." Jeremiah ticked each item off on his fingers. She was pretty good at lying, and this wasn't the first time she'd avoided disclosing pertinent information to him. He wasn't sure, anymore, if he could really trust her.

Bell dropped her gaze to her hands and fidgeted with the hem of her night shirt. "I'm sorry. I wish I could push rewind and take it all back."

"I'm sure you do." What would've happened if she'd told him, when they met at his locker, about her brother? Easy. He would've insisted he tag along to make certain she stayed safe. And, yes, he had to admit his presence would've made the situation awkward and possibly kept her brother from sharing anything. And, if he was being really fair, not that he wanted to be at the moment, he'd also admit they met at her job, a public place where people knew her. Not like it was a dark alley.

Dammit. Jeremiah walked over and sat beside Bell. "I'd do anything in my power to keep you safe. I can't help it, but I do get it."

"You do?"

"Yes. Just do me a favor." Jeremiah looked Bella straight in the eyes. "Tell somebody. If you aren't going to tell me, then make sure somebody here knows where you are."

"I can do that. I can absolutely do that."

"Good. Because I can't take a chance on losing you. I love you too much." Jeremiah caressed Bell's cheek.

She leaned into his touch and placed her hand on top of his. "I love you, too."

eight

By the end of the school day, Bella's anger had returned full force. She parked her car in the roundabout near the fountain, stomped to the front door, and started pounding on it. She wasn't sure if she hoped Heather would open the door or if it would be better if the butler did, so she'd have a brief opportunity to cool down.

It was Heather. "What the hell do you want?" the girl said, crossing her arms.

Bella answered by stepping through the door and punching Heather right in the nose. *Damn!* She shook her hand out. It seriously hurt to hit someone.

Heather stumbled back, and her hand flew to her nose. "Christ, Bella! What the hell was that for?"

"Payback. I don't know what I ever did to you, but I sure as hell didn't deserve any of the shit you pulled." She glanced at Heather's face. There was no blood seeping from the girl's nose, but Bella could see where it was starting to swell.

"I don't know what you're prattling on about."

What a total crock! For a split second, she thought of the ramifications for outing her brother, but if she were to trust him, she had to check out what he'd told her. "Bullshit! Luis told me everything."

"Oh? So, he told you he came to me? And explained about his obsession with you?"

Okay, so maybe *everything* was an overstatement. What her brother had said was that he'd used Heather to keep an eye on her. But he made it sound as if she'd then volunteered information to his ... boss. "What matters is that you helped my enemy. The guy who attacked me. You helped him keep tabs on me. You told him where I was going and how your brother felt about me. You even sold him on your computer skills."

Heather had walked over to a mirror to check out her nose. Now, seemingly shocked, she blinked wide eyes at Bella. "Luis told you that?"

"Yes."

"That son of a bitch."

Taking a step forward, Bella got in Heather's face, again. Whether it hurt her hand or not, she was totally prepared to punch the shit out of the girl. "Watch it. That's my brother you're talking about."

"Your *brother*? Are you kidding me?"

"Do I look like I'm joking?"

Heather stared at Bella. Once you knew she and Luis were related, Bella imagined it was easy to see the features they shared.

"Wow," Heather said. "I had no idea." She paused and glanced down. Then she raised her eyes to Bella's. "Look, you're right. I screwed you over, but Luis's boss was scary. Once I was in, I was in. I either did what I was asked, or someone I care for got hurt. Simple as that. I wouldn't wish what happened to you on anyone. Not even you. Okay? Are we done here?"

"No, Heather, we aren't done here. I believe you owe me—and I need your help." The idea came to her last night after she'd made up with Miah. She hadn't mentioned a word about the box Luis had given her to her boyfriend. And she hadn't looked inside of it, either, but she had hidden it in Miah's bedroom. She suspected the box held evidence against Gervasio ... but she was no longer interested in seeing him in jail.

"Excuse me?"

"You heard me." Bella smiled.

"And what makes you think I'll help you?"

"Two reasons. One, Luis gave me evidence that proves you helped Gervasio, which I'll be happy to turn over to the police."

Heather ground her jaw and narrowed her eyes. "You wouldn't dare."

"Try me." The meeting with her brother had taught her a few things. Her blood family, the Castells, lied to get what they wanted. They manipulated people and used them. And they only looked out for each other.

"What's the other reason?"

"You helping me will piss off my brother. And you can't tell me you wouldn't like to do that right now."

Vick pulled alongside the curb outside her house, and Amanda saw her brother's car in the driveway—but Bella's car was gone. She glanced at Vick. "Are you sure about this?"

"Yes. We agreed."

"I know, but Bella's not even here."

"Babe, come on. Why are you stalling?"

Amanda reached across the console and grabbed his hand. He meant well, but was it really necessary? Her brother and his girlfriend had acquired so much baggage, she was afraid the two of them would drag her and Vick down. "I just like the drama-free time we've had together."

"I know. Me, too. But we need to be supportive of them, especially Bella. She's had it tough. It's time we forgive her and move past all this. You catch Jeremiah now, and I'll try to reach Bella on her phone."

"You really are a good guy." Amanda leaned over and pressed her lips to his. The kiss deepened, and their tongues touched. Her body blazed at the instant connection, and she yearned for more. A soft moan escaped her mouth, and she released the kiss. If they started, they'd never stop, and she wouldn't get out of the car. Tempted, she bit on her bottom lip and eyed her boyfriend hungrily.

Vick groaned. "Yep, you need to go. And I need a cold shower."

"Sorry. I'll go. See you tomorrow?"

"Same time, same place."

Amanda got out, but then stopped. What if this was their last chance to be away from the disaster? "We should go to the lake house this weekend. You up for it?"

"Yeah. Sounds like a plan."

"All right. I'll text you later. Let you know how it went." Amanda waved goodbye and trekked up the driveway. She absolutely would prefer not to do this, but Vick had a point. They'd agreed to rebuild bridges.

Taking a deep breath, she stepped into the house. Her brother tended to do his homework in the kitchen. Taking a deep breath, she walked down the hall. There he was, in the nook.

"Hey," she said. "Can we talk?"

"I'm sorry. You want to what?" Heather dropped into the chair at her desk. No way she heard the geek right.

"Find Gervasio."

"Are you insane?"

Frowning, Bella propped herself against the wall by the closed door. "No. I'm entirely in my right mind, thank you."

"Okay. Then tell me what you plan to do if we find him."

"Turn him over to the police, of course." Heather noticed the girl didn't meet her eye as she said this. *Yeah, right!* If that wasn't a boldfaced lie, then she was Queen of Egypt. "Let's say I believe you. Aside from pissing Luis off, what's in it for me?"

"Satisfaction you got a bad guy off the street. No? Okay. How about I make that proof of your involvement with him disappear. You help me, you stay out of jail."

"Fine, but here's how this little arrangement works. You don't show up here whenever you damn well please. You only come when I call. I'll search the electronic trail, and you chase the lead down. If we find him, I take part of the credit. We don't talk in school. We don't even acknowledge one another. We go on ignoring each other like normal. Got it?"

"No. We'll check in daily, and if the lead is good, we'll follow it together. We don't have to be friends, but we can act like business partners. Agreed?" Bella shoved off the wall and held out her hand to confirm the pact.

Heather's jaw tensed. Had they both gone mad? Chasing some lunatic who nearly had his own brother killed. Damn that freak who'd shown up on her doorstep. He'd called the situation what it was and knew exactly what the geek would do. What an imposition. She stood, met the geek halfway, and shook her hand. What choice did she have? "Fine. Agreed. Worried you just made a deal with the devil?"

"No. Are you?"

Heather snorted, then stomped across her bedroom and pulled a painting off the wall. If someone told her yesterday she'd be working with one of the few people she disliked as much as her mother, she'd have called them a liar. Good thing the old man prepared for the unexpected. She unlocked the safe and removed two burner phones.

"What ...?"

Heather held out a phone to Bella. "A way for us to stay in contact. Our regular cell phones can be traced. If we're chasing a lead, your cell phone gets turned off, and you use this one. This is also how we check in with each other."

"Okay. Any particular reason you have burner phones?"

"You have your secrets, and I have mine. We're done for now. You can leave." Heather returned to her desk and booted up her system.

"I thought we were going to get started."

Rookie. The geek knew nothing about tracing electronic signatures and gathering leads. "I am. You don't have anything to do until I find something. And I can't do that if you hover. Besides, David should be home soon, and I prefer he didn't find out."

"I can't argue with that." Bella spun on her heel and headed across the room, but she stopped at the door. "Can I ask you a favor?"

"Depends."

"You know I'm adopted. I'd like you to find any information you can on my mother's death."

Not what Heather expected. The plea in Bella's eyes tugged at her strings. Despite what people often believed, Heather had a heart. In some small way, she even sympathized with Bella. Although she hated her mother, if the woman died, she'd want to know what happened. "Yeah, just, uh, text me what you know, and I'll look into it."

"Thanks." Without a further word, Bella left.

Heather turned back to her computer. She'd never attempted to get into police files, but maybe she could hack the county records.

His sister wanted to speak to him? Well, color him shocked. The last few weeks, she'd done nothing but ignore Jeremiah. Now, it was his turn. Acting as if he hadn't heard her request, he returned his attention to his math homework.

"I'd really like to speak to you," Amanda repeated, sliding into the nook next to him.

His sister could talk until she was blue in the face. He'd still pretend he couldn't hear her. Determinedly, he tried to understand the math problem in front of him—but it looked like gibberish. No way he'd make sense of it with his sister sitting there. Whatever. He wouldn't give her the time of day.

"Fine," she said, hefting her backpack onto the table. "Two can play that game. I'll just start my homework."

Jeremiah tossed his pencil down. "What the hell do you want, Amanda?"

She cringed at his tone. "I'm sorry. I know I kind of bailed with everyone else. I just ... I had to have some time to figure things out."

"Good for you." He slammed his book shut and headed down to the basement. He understood that all Bella's friends had a problem with what Bella had written them. But why had that affected his relationship with his sister?

Amanda clomped down the stairs behind him. "I'm not giving up. We really need to talk."

"Okay. Fine. Let's talk. Maybe you can explain why you stopped speaking to me."

"I'm trying to apologize. You don't have to be a dick about it." She turned to walk away.

Jeremiah jumped up and grabbed her arm. "You have a lot of nerve. You ignore me for weeks, and now you won't even explain why. Screw your apology."

"You want to know why? Fine! I'll tell you. Better yet, why don't I just show you," she said. "Come on." And she turned and stomped back up the stairs.

Jeremiah followed. "What? What are you showing me?"

Amanda didn't respond. She just stepped into her bedroom, walked over to the dresser, and pulled out a piece of paper from her chemistry book, which she handed to him. Then, in a serious tone, she said, "Until you read Bella's letter, you can't understand the pressure she put me under."

Fear coursed through his veins. What if what he read hurt him or pissed him off? Should he take the chance? Jeremiah rubbed the top of his head. His short hair prickled his fingers. Inhaling deeply, he unfolded the letter and sat on the corner of his sister's bed.

Mandy,

I want you to know that I believe you've been a good friend to me. I don't know many people who would punch Heather in my defense. Maybe Alex, but she'd do it for sheer pleasure. Anyway, I really appreciate it. It's one of the reasons why I feel I can come to you in my time of need.

I'm sure some of what I'm about to say may come as a surprise, but there's no one I trust more. You keep your word, no matter the consequence. I have faith you'll do as I ask. You're probably a bit confused, so I'll explain as best I can.

Every day that passes is worse than the one before. I can no longer deal with the pain. I just don't have the energy to fight anymore. Some people will likely take this harder than others, and I need you to look out for them.

Three in particular.

First, there's David. He's always cared for me more than I have him. Though, due to recent events, he may very well hate me. I hurt him in the most unimaginable way. You may want to give him time to cool off before you check on him.

Second, there's your brother. I used to think he loved me. Even if he doesn't, I'll always love him. The last thing I want is to hurt him, but I feel I've no other choice.

This is the only way I can be free. After I'm gone and enough time has passed, please make sure he moves on. I want him to love again when he's ready.

Lastly, there's Vick. He's family to me, so I want you to protect his heart. I know you're dating, and I know why you haven't told anyone. He loves hard and will fully give himself to you if you let him. If you can't give him your heart, then let him be. He deserves to be happy. You all do.

Bella

"Wow. She made you responsible for all of us." Jeremiah folded up the letter and handed it back to his sister, then rubbed tears from his eyes. All Bella ever wanted was for them to be happy. Even when she was barely coping, Bella thought about the people she loved most. He hadn't really considered that when he'd read his own letter. He'd been too upset to see it that way.

Amanda tucked the letter back in her book. "I'm sorry I cut you off, but it got to be a tad too much. I figured I had to limit my focus. With Bella okay, I thought you two would naturally just ... look out for each other."

"I guess we have." Of course, they hadn't exactly acted like a couple, recently. They only slept in the same bed for Bella's comfort. The last time he'd taken her out on a date had been the night of the Fall Harvest Dance. Maybe it was time.

"This isn't the only reason I wanted to talk. Vick and I think what you tried to do by pulling everyone together was a great idea. I kind of had a thought on it."

It was a relief. His sister was being kind. He glanced up at Amanda. "I'm all ears."

"There may be a way for Bella to deal with how her letters made us all feel ... safely. I know she still has regular therapy sessions. What if she took us all to one of her sessions so we could talk about it?"

"That's a good idea. I'll bring it up to her later. In the meantime, if you really want to make these past couple months up to me, then you can help me plan a date with Bell."

"A date?" Amanda raised an eyebrow.

"Yeah. Try and bring some sanity back to our relationship. A night out on the town like normal teenagers."

A smile tugged at the Amanda's lips. "I can do that. It might be just what I need to reestablish my own friendship with her."

After taking a sip of coffee, Luis stretched and rubbed his eyes. Their father had become even more determined to find Gervasio, since Luis had told him of his meeting with Bella. Now, between searching for Gervasio and reviewing his and Bella's adoption papers, Luis was exhausted—and worried about his sister. He'd texted her earlier, but she insisted she was okay.

He took another sip of coffee. The strong, bitter brew should keep him awake for a bit, he thought, then sighed and returned to reading the adoption documents. And then he saw it.

"What the hell?" *In the event of death.* What?

Quickly, he reread the paragraph that opened with that clause. What was this trust, the Rio De Angel Trust? And why was there a clause that willed all the funds in his sister's account to that trust if she died? Luis grabbed his own adoption documents and flipped frantically through the pages. Did his papers have the same clause? Sure enough. A few pages from the end, he found the exact same clause.

"Sabio!" Juan snapped his fingers to get his son's attention.

Luis looked up, startled. He hadn't heard his father enter. But it didn't matter. He shoved the documents in the man's face. "Do you know anything about this?" he asked, pointing to the relevant text.

"What is this?"

"Gigi's and my adoption papers. Just tell me. Have you seen this clause before?"

Juan took the papers and eased into a chair. After a moment, he said, "Your mother had the adoption documents prepared ahead of time. I have no knowledge of this trust."

"You do understand what it says, correct?"

"Yes, but I do not understand why. I cannot believe your mother would've established a blanket authorization for funds to be transferred to a trust in the event of either your or your sister's death. This makes no sense to me."

"What about the lawyer? Could he have included this clause without my mother's knowledge?"

Juan folded his hands in his lap. "I do not believe he would have drafted the adoption papers in a way that favored some mysterious trust. I have known him for years, and I trust him with my life."

"I'll dig into it a little more." Luis said. He wasn't convinced of the lawyer's trustworthiness, based solely on his father's testimony. His parents may have trusted the man, but sometimes the people we most trust betray us the most badly. He'd also inform his sister. This could mean her life was in more danger than he and his father had thought.

"A date?" Bell's hazel brown eyes lit up like the stars in the night sky.

He'd do anything to keep the sparkle on her face. Jeremiah caressed her cheek and tucked a few loose strands of hair behind her ear. She looked absolutely exquisite in the soft light of the lamp. "Yes. How's tomorrow night sound?"

"That sounds perfect, but we don't have to do anything special."

"Of course. we do. We have a lot to celebrate." He played with the ends of her midnight black locks. They were smooth like silk. Running his fingers through her hair was a bit like heaven. The night she'd allowed him to brush her hair had been wonderful. One of the most honest and intimate moments they'd shared. A moment he'd like to have again. But those moments were fleeting, more rare since they got back together. And they were also moments he couldn't plan for. They simply ... happened.

"What are we celebrating?"

"You finding your brother, for one thing. Although, I guess he technically found you. And there's your new job. Your upcoming one month of sobriety. But, most importantly, us."

"You want to celebrate us?"

"Yeah. I know it sounds weird, but I feel like we're starting to find each other again. Like every day, you let me in a little more. Does that make sense?" There was probably a better way to say it, but words weren't exactly his forte.

Still, Bella understood. "I get it. We're kind of like children stumbling through out first steps, learning to trust one another."

Jeremiah pressed a tender kiss to her lips. Yes, she got it.

"So, what are we doing on our date?"

"I'm not saying. It's a surprise."

"Then how will I know what to wear?"

Sweeping her hair from her shoulder, Jeremiah stared into her beautiful brown eyes. No matter what she wore, she'd look perfect. But she was right. She had to wear something suitable for what he planned. "Mandy will help with that."

"Does this mean she's speaking to me?"

"Yeah. We kind of cleared the air earlier."

"Explains the call I got from Vick today. We agreed to meet at school in the morning and discuss things. I assume he wants to talk about his letter. And why he stopped talking to me."

Jeremiah ran his hand over his brush cut. Should he tell Bella he read the letter she wrote to his sister? Or should he keep that to himself? He'd recently chastised her over being secretive. It would be a bit hypocritical if he didn't tell her. He rolled over onto his back. He should tell her. Avoiding the truth never ended well. Plus, it would weigh on his conscious. "I have to tell you something."

"Okay?" Bell propped up on her elbow.

He glanced at her nervously. He felt like he'd invaded his girlfriend's private thoughts. While he didn't demand the letter, he'd sort of pushed his sister's buttons until she didn't have a choice. Had that been his plan all along? No, it hadn't ... yes, it had.

Jeremiah sighed. "It's difficult."

"You know you can tell me anything."

Remembering the letter Bella'd written to his sister, Jeremiah felt again how much she loved him, how much she cared about her friends, and how much she wanted to make sure they were looked after. This caring was why he'd fallen in love with her to begin with. Would she understand that? Or would she just be upset that he read something she'd written to someone else. He took a deep breath. He guessed he'd find out.

"Well ... I didn't give Mandy an easy time. She tried to talk to me, but I didn't listen. Finally, she felt the only way for me to understand why she'd been ignoring me was to show me."

Bell sat up. The covers shifted and slid down to her waist. "Show you how?"

"She, uh ..." His eyes trailed from the gentle curve of his girlfriend's neckline down to her collarbone and continued to the swell of her breasts. A tank top and shorts were all she normally wore to bed. They'd been sleeping together for a few weeks. He should be accustomed to how she looked in bed, but it still awakened his blood and stirred his body in ways he couldn't control. *Man, she's one gorgeous woman.*

Snap! Clicking her fingers in his face, Bell yanked Jeremiah back to the conversation at hand. "What did Mandy show you?"

"Your letter to her."

Bella paused for a moment. "That's why she stopped talking to us?"

"Yeah. I think she was overwhelmed by all you asked. And since you were okay, she felt like she could focus elsewhere. Not on us. She figured we'd be okay." He kept his gaze glued to Bella's face. What was she thinking?

Bella shook her head. "I guess I understand," she said, slowly.

"You're not mad?"

"Well, no. I mean, I figured Mandy at least discussed her letter with Vick. As for you reading it … it just explains a lot."

"Do you feel that way about all the letters? That it would be okay if other people read them?" He hoped not. He felt like now he'd relinquished his right to say no if one of the others wanted to see it.

"What? God, no. Mandy's letter, that was mostly instructional. Everyone else's was really personal, just between me and them. I wouldn't want anyone else to read those."

Jeremiah sat up and cupped Bell's cheek. "Meant for one pair of eyes only."

"Exactly." She covered his hand with her own and bit on her bottom lip.

He had to brush his thumb along her bottom lip to prevent himself from kissing her. If he kissed her now, they'd never get to the end of this conversation. Jeremiah stared into her eyes. "What if we each wanted to talk to you about our letter, would you do it?"

"I don't know. I mean, I've talked to you about yours, and I think Vick will bring his up, and, yeah, Mandy's has been referenced. I know eventually I'll probably have to, in order to make amends, but right now, I don't know … Does that sound bad?"

"No, not at all." Jeremiah kissed her forehead and hugged her tightly. *One day at a time* had been the anthem, and it had worked wonders. He'd rather keep her tucked safely in her comfort zone than put her under some sort of pressure that might send her running back to drugs to help her cope. For now, his sister and Vick would have to accept that. Surely, they understood how important it was for him to protect Bell—no matter the cost.

nine

As the elevator doors closed, Jamar began to read over the medical examiner's notes on the body that had been proven to belong to Hector Rodriguez, father of Cristobal and Gervasio Rodriguez.

Eight bodies had been discovered in the back yard of the cabin. Thus far, six had been identified, and all eight had been brutally beaten, prior to death. Then, Hector and the female victims had been strangled, while the other male victim, Rolando, had been stabbed.

While Jamar believed they'd all been murdered by Gervasio, he had next to no evidence to support his theory. Jamar pinched the bridge of his nose. Everything related to this case gave him a migraine. Something had to give. They had to get a break.

With a *ding*, the elevator doors parted, and the sheriff headed toward his office, but was stopped at Russell's desk by an argument between his two best detectives.

"I tell you we missed something." Ali stabbed her finger at a sheet of paper on the desk.

Russell groaned. "And for the fifth time, it's his parents' estate, and it was checked out. There's nothing there."

"What's going on here?" Jamar asked.

"I keep trying to tell this jackass about unexplained transactions on an account for the estate of Simms's parents. It warrants further investigation, sir. But Russell says there's no need—it's been done. My gut says we need to look at it again."

Hmm. He saw no harm in letting Ali follow her gut. "If you think something's there, then check it out. Go with your instinct, Ali."

"Thanks, Sheriff." Ali spun on her heel and stalked across the squad room.

Russell rolled his eyes, but had the good grace to say nothing more.

Jamar let the eye roll pass and asked, "You get records on Hector Rodriguez?"

"Yeah. And you won't believe what I found."

"Walk and talk." Jamar headed toward his office, noting that Russell sounded optimistic about whatever he'd found. Gervasio's father's body had been so decomposed, it had been difficult to glean much about his attacker—just that the person was right-handed and had a great deal of strength. Hector Rodriguez had been no small man. It would've taken extraordinary force to knock him down, beat him, and strangle him to death.

Russell glanced at a file as he followed the Sheriff. "There was nothing in our database on Hector Rodriguez, so I researched the addresses listed in his credit history. Surprisingly, our guy lived in New York around the same time as Juan Castell. I made a call to the NYPD, and sure enough, he was on their radar. They think he held two positions in the Grim Reapers, Enforcer and Lieutenant."

Enforcer. That seemed logical. The guy had been built for it: six feet tall, around two-hundred fifty pounds. But the other position? To be made second in command in any organization required skill. If Hector Rodriguez had been the Grim Reapers' Lieutenant, that might have been the motivation for his murder. Especially since Gervasio, the man's oldest son, had taken over leadership at about the time Hector had been killed. "Any idea how he ended up in our neck of the woods?"

"None. We know the family lived here, but the only name on the house in Desemper Ridge is the wife's. As far as we can tell, Hector Rodriguez never lived in Rescate County."

"Then how the hell did he end up buried at that cabin?" From NYC to Rescate County, that was a hell of a long way to go just to dispose of a body.

Ali poked her head in the doorway. "I might be able to help with that." The detective walked in and stood beside Russell. "Hector didn't live with his family. He had a small apartment in a building that was abandoned five years ago in Desemper Ridge."

Frowning, Russell crossed his arms. "How'd you find that out? The guy had nothing in his name."

"The house has a landline. When we first started searching for Gervasio, I pulled the phone logs. The number belonged to Hector Smith. I also happened to find an address in the same name." Ali handed a note to the sheriff.

In exchange, he held out the folder with the medical examiner's notes to Ali. "See what scenarios you can configure that would lead to this outcome."

"Will do, but that isn't why I came in here. It's about Simms. He was named executor of his parents' estate, which included their house in Amorte Cliffstone. The house was willed to him, but that isn't what's interesting. What is interesting are the electrical bills. The electrical usage for the house never changes. Almost as if the temperature is climate-controlled." Smiling broadly, she held out another note.

"Warrant?"

"In the works. You should have it by the time you get there."

Jamar nodded. "Good work, Ali." Then he handed the address she'd just given him to Russell. "Take Reynolds. You may find a lead to Gervasio. I'll head to the Simms residence."

"You sure you don't want me to go with you?"

Bella squeezed her boyfriend's hand. His concern was sweet, but unnecessary. Vick was her best friend—or had been. She lifted her gaze to Jeremiah's emerald green eyes. "I'll be fine."

Jeremiah kissed her tenderly on the lips. "Okay. I'll see you after first period?"

"Yep." Bella gave him one more quick kiss and walked toward the door. She and Vick had agreed to meet on the bleachers. Just to schedule their first conversation in weeks, they'd argued over every possible thing: date, time, location. What a way to rekindle their friendship. She sighed. If he could manage not to annoy her, then she could manage not to strangle him.

She trekked across the courtyard and climbed halfway up the bleachers. Where was he? Vick was usually more punctual than she was. Of course, he was also more secretive. Maybe 'private' was a better term. Either way, the likelihood he'd done as she'd requested in her letter was slim.

"Couldn't have chosen a more convenient spot?" Vick said, interrupting her thoughts.

Bella shrugged. "This seemed good enough."

Vick dropped his backpack on the bleacher and sat beside her. "Fine."

"Would you like me to apologize?" While she sort of intended the question to be rhetorical, in another way, she meant it literally. And she knew that he knew she wasn't asking about their meeting place. They'd learned as children how to read one another. Well, more like how to read each other's mind.

"Yeah. Not that it'll do a lot of good. You really put me in a tight spot. How could you even consider asking me to tell Amanda?"

So, she was right. He hadn't told Mandy the real reason he'd left his old school. Bella glared at him. "Tight spot? I told you to be honest with her. She deserves to know the truth."

"Seriously? Tell her about Taryn? You can forget it."

"You know what, never mind." Bella stood and shrugged her backpack over her shoulder. They were supposed to be mending fences, but she refused to sit there and argue with him.

"Wait." Vick gave her a wry smile. "Look, I'm sorry. I didn't come here to fight about the letter."

"Then why did you want to meet?"

"Because, for the life of me, I can't figure out how we got here. We used to tell each other everything. I understand the rape changed you, but I don't get why you didn't think you could come to me with whatever you were facing." Lacing his fingers together, he leaned on his knees and looked up at her. Sorrow and pain filled his brown eyes.

Biting the inside of her cheek, she sat back down. How to begin to explain? Slowly, over the course of many sessions with her psychiatrist, her ability to give words to her emotions had gotten easier. So maybe she could give Vick a reason he could comprehend. "Honestly, at the time, I didn't feel like anyone would understand."

"And now?"

"I'm trying, but I'd be lying if I didn't tell you every day is a struggle. Believing you're not alone is difficult when your faith has been lost." Her whole life had changed. With all she'd been through, her peace of mind had been tainted. For a long time, she stopped believing that God would always be there. Recent events had altered that perception, though, and going forward, she'd no longer be the victim.

"And we didn't help. I'm sorry. We could've done more, listened more or something."

The knowledge she'd gained over the last weeks had taught her something, that her biological history made her susceptible to drug use. Who knew what else it caused? Clearly, it made her mentally unstable. And now, was it her DNA that made her want to chase a killer? Bella smirked at the thought. "I don't think it would've changed anything, Vick. Not really. And, hey, look, we can't go back now. We can only move forward."

"'Forward.' I like the sound of that."

"Yeah, me too." Had they made up? She hadn't told him everything … not about her family or her recent discovery. Still. Bella gave him a tentative smile, as she stood up again.

Vick returned the smile, standing as well and slinging his backpack over his shoulders. "I guess it is about that time."

"Vick?"

"Yeah?"

"Don't worry. I won't tell anyone your secret. But Amanda does deserve to know."

Bella'd chosen a silk, ivory razorback blouse and a pair of black skinny jeans for their date. Now, she twisted her hips in the outfit and slid her body to the right, the way Miah'd shown her. Or so she hoped. If the dance step wasn't up to par, at least she could blame her two left feet. She peeked up at him as she kicked one foot out, then the other. The smile on his face and the hand over his mouth said it all. "You're laughing at me."

"No, I'm ... Okay, maybe a little. But I can't help it. You look so cute trying to do the Cupid Shuffle."

"I told you I wasn't any good at dancing."

Miah placed his hands on her bare shoulders. "Doesn't mean you can't learn.

Come on, I'll walk you through it step by step, and then we'll do it together."

"One more time, but if you laugh, I'm not doing it again." Her skin tingled where his hands lingered.

A new song came on, as upbeat and up tempo as the rest of the songs he'd played. Miah stepped to her left and showed her the Cupid Shuffle for the third time … or the fourth. She'd lost count. Not that it mattered. The entire point of the night was for them to have a good time. Mission accomplished.

She attempted to mimic his movements—again. She twisted three steps to the right, then to the left, then kicked each foot out with a heel tap, the heel of each ankle boot clicking against the hardwood floor. It definitely wasn't as awful as her first few tries.

Miah scooped her up in his arms and swung her around. He set her down and brushed his hand over his hair. "That was great!"

"Yeah, it was pretty awesome, if I do say so myself."

"Modest, aren't we?"

"I have no idea what you're talking about, sir." Beaming brightly, she folded her hands across her chest and batted her eyelashes, in the most demure gesture she could think of.

Jeremiah laughed. Then, a slow song began, and he offered her his hand. "You may not be modest, but if you give me this dance I think I can overlook it."

"So easy to please." Bella giggled and settled her hand in his.

He spun her out and back in, then held their clasped hands against his chest and dropped his other hand to her waist. "In the right circumstances, I can be."

"Are these the right circumstances?"

"Well, perhaps. I've got one hot girl in my arms, and thus far we've had a great time."

"All quite true. It helps that the guy who's holding her is rather handsome himself." Handsome didn't come close to describing how Miah looked tonight. He'd worn black jeans also, and they hung perfectly on his hips. A sky-blue shirt complemented the pants and his skin tone beautifully. The close cut of his hair capped his natural sexiness. Yup. It was true. Her boyfriend was drop-dead gorgeous. She was lucky to have him.

"But what if he was ugly?" Miah whispered in her ear.

"To her, that's simply not possible. I mean, beauty is in the eye of the beholder."

Miah leaned down and tenderly kissed her lips. "I can't argue with that logic."

Bella rested her head against his chest, and they swayed together. The singer's voice was sultry and seductive. Her eyes shifted to Miah's face. At first, she'd hardly noticed the way his hands set fire to her skin. Or how she felt every passionate kiss down to her toes. But somehow, this one part of her world had begun to right itself. And she longed for him to know exactly where she stood.

Keeping her gaze steady, she slowly ran her hands up his arms and paused at his broad shoulders. Softly, she dragged her right hand over his chest.

His breath quickened, and his eyes widened at her touch. Then, Miah laced his fingers through one of her hands and trailed his other hand along the curve of her spine, all the way to the top of her jeans, his fingers warming the skin of her lower back. He turned her and pressed his chest to her back, and then let his hands drop to her waist, so together their hips swung from side to side.

Her heart raced and goosebumps crawled up her back. With his hips grinding her ass, she rolled her head back, exposing her throat to him. Miah kissed along her neck and jaw, and hovered over her lips, until, hungrily, his lips crashed down on hers.

Their tongues touched, and her blood boiled. She hooked her hand around the back of his neck, pulling him closer and deepening the kiss. As following the singer's instructions, he slipped his hand to her belly and caressed the sensitive skin there. Arching her back, she thrust her ass into his groin, and her grip on his neck tightened.

A new song filled the speakers, one that turned up the sensuality even further. Miah shifted her body so she faced him. Without breaking their kiss, he dropped his hands to her hips. Using the gentle beat of the song as a guide he swung her hips along with his own, generating so much friction between their bodies, Bella could barely breathe.

She dug her nails into his shoulders and thrust her breasts into his chest. Miah moaned in her mouth. He shoved her back against the wall and grabbed her ass. Longing for more, Bella dragged her nails teasingly down his back. With his hands dug into her ass, he lifted her off the ground, and she wrapped her legs around his waist.

As his groin pressed into hers, heat coursed through her body, and that secret place between her thighs pounded with the flow of blood. She tightened her grip on Miah and crossed her ankles behind his back.

Then a snatch of a different song came from the front pocket of her jeans. *What the hell?*

Panting, Miah leaned his forehead against hers. "Don't answer it."

"I have to. It's my brother's ringtone." Whatever he wanted better be damn important. Not only had he called on a Saturday night, he'd interrupted ... well, something quite pleasurable.

"Dammit."

Bella untangled herself from Miah and dug the phone out of her pocket. Still breathless, she answered. "Hey, Luis."

"You all right? You sound winded."

"Yeah. I'm out with Miah, and we were dancing." It wasn't entirely a lie. They were at a dance studio and they had been dancing. Sort of.

"I need to see you. There's something I have to show you."

She eyed Miah and bit her bottom lip. "Now?"

"Yes, now."

At that moment, she truly hated having a brother. "As long as you don't mind me bringing Miah, I guess I can come." *Damn him to hell.*

"Fine. I'll text you the address."

She opened her mouth to reply, but the line dropped. Had he really hung up on her? She stared at her phone. The bastard actually hung up on her. Oh, he'd certainly get it now.

Miah raised an eyebrow. "What's up?"

"Apparently, my brother needs to see me."

"Well, all right, then. We should probably freshen up before we leave."

Bella giggled. "Yeah. We'd better."

Jeremiah frowned. The drive to the address her brother provided had been quiet. Besides the directions from Bell's cell phone, he'd mostly heard only their breathing. Was it his fault? Did Bell blame him? He had to admit things had gotten out of hand back at the dance studio.

He turned onto yet another dirt road. Where in the world was this place?

Egypt? Was there a reason the guy lived in the middle of nowhere? Jeremiah glanced at Bella. "You really trust this guy?"

"I know we're going far out, but I swear he's trustworthy."

"Okay. But just so you know, if I die tonight, I'll haunt you for the rest of your life." It was a horrible joke, but she cracked a smile—and at least it lightened the mood between them.

Should they discuss what happened? One minute they were slow dancing to John Legend and the next they were grinding to Kevin Lyttle. Then J. Holiday's "Suffocate" came on and ... Had he really pinned Bell against the wall? Had she actually wrapped her legs around his waist?

Jeremiah gave Bell a sideways glance. She definitely hadn't stopped him when they began grinding. In fact, he was pretty certain her body had come to life under his hands, like it was responding to his touch. A part of him felt guilty, but what if she wanted him, too?

Bell lowered her phone. "Is everything okay?"

"Yeah. Why?"

"Because you slowed down so much."

Twisting in the seat, Jeremiah grinned at her. "Sorry. I, uh, I keep thinking about the dance studio and what happened."

"You mean because my brother interrupted?"

"Um ..." Jeremiah frowned. "No. I think ... I mean, it's been a while since we talked about sex and ... not that it would've happened there, but something was happening." He let the car come to a complete halt and put it in park. Not like anyone was going to come flying down this track through the middle of nowhere.

Bell unbuckled her seatbelt and climbed across the console and into his lap, straddling him, then tenderly kissed his lips. "Being in your parents' house has been hard for me, but having you there's made it easier. I don't know why, but our relationship has started to fall back into place. As for what happened at the dance studio, I want you. It's as simple as that."

"I want you, too. I just don't want to push you into something." He leaned his forehead against hers, inhaling her lovely lavender scent and kissing her tenderly on the temple.

She bit her bottom lip and lightly brushed her fingers over his neck. "You won't. To tell you the truth, I should've ignored the phone."

"I'm not going to lie; I wish you had. But I don't think our first time should be in a dance studio ... or a car, for that matter." Jeremiah grinned at his seductive little minx, then wrapped his arms around her and kissed her like he meant to ignite a fire.

Thrusting her breasts into his chest, Bell nipped his tongue and eased from the deeply passionate kiss. "So cruel. Come on, we should get moving before my brother calls again."

"You first."

"So cruel." With a lopsided grin, she crawled out of his lap and returned to her seat, buckled in, and brushed her fingers through her hair.

Jeremiah put the car back in drive. "How much farther is it, anyway?"

"Looks like we take the next right, and the cabin is just up the way."

"Do you have any idea why he's all the way out here?" Suddenly, despite Bell's refusal to do so, he wished they'd told his father where they were going—and had the guy checked out.

"He hasn't said ... but I think it's, like, a safe haven."

Following her final directions, Jeremiah turned at the next dirt road. He couldn't fault the guy for trying to stay alive. There might come a time when he needed the guy's help to protect Bella. In his book, that made the trip worthwhile. As they approached a cabin, he slowed.

"That's him," Bell said, gesturing toward the door.

All right then. Jeremiah shut the car off, and they both got out. He offered his hand to her, and she laced her fingers through his.

The guy standing on the porch was wearing jeans, and had his arms folded across his chest. Jeremiah could see that his eyes, his features, even his skin tone, all looked like Bell's. It wasn't hard to tell they were related.

Smiling, Jeremiah extended his hand. "You must be Luis. I'm Jeremiah."

"Ah, so you're the guy dating my sister."

The crushing grip of the guy's handshake amused Jeremiah. He'd just appeared in Bell's life, and he had the audacity to express seniority? Jeremiah grinned wide. "Yep. Might as well get used to it. I don't plan on going anywhere for a while."

Bella interrupted. "You know, if you guys want to see who has the bigger cock, I can leave." Bell glared briefly at Jeremiah, but focused most of her annoyance on her brother.

Jeremiah snorted, and they both released their grip on the other's hand.

"No?" Bell said. "Good. Then why don't we get on with it."

"If they want the money that bad, they can have it." Bell crossed her arms and stared at her brother.

Shifting his gaze from his girlfriend to her brother, Jeremiah wondered how he was he supposed to trust her when she continued to keep things from him? "You're serious?" the guy said. "Never mind. The money isn't the point. It's the fact that the clause exists at all. That's the problem."

Bella turned her attention to the documents Luis held. "I think you're missing the bigger picture. This all leads back to him."

"I understand that, but it also means your life could be in danger."

"Like it isn't already?"

As much as Jeremiah hated to admit it, Bell had a point. She'd been beaten within an inch of her life and force-fed pills and booze. And the person responsible for her attacks was still at large. Jeremiah opened his mouth and quickly snapped it shut. He stepped over and eyed the two-monitor computer setup. Several sequences of numbers raced across both screens. What was that about?

Luis gripped the back of his neck. "Dad told me not to tell you about it, but I thought you deserved to know."

"Excuse me? Are you in contact with that bastard?" Bella glared at her brother and dropped her hands to her hips.

"He is our father."

Jeremiah glanced over. He knew those had been the absolute wrong words for Luis to say. Steam was practically pouring out of Bella's ears, and her eyes were narrowed directly at her brother. She might have even snarled. Jeremiah backed up. Sometimes, like now, his girlfriend frightened him a touch.

"Bullshit!" she said, exploding. "He was nothing but a sperm donor! And if you have half a brain, you won't try to defend that man to me."

Luis sighed. "You're not even giving him a chance, Gigi."

Whistling low, Jeremiah shook his head. Yep, she'd definitely snarled. This guy was putting his foot in his mouth. Hell, Bella might shove that foot right down her brother's throat, if he didn't stop talking about their father.

But while she didn't resort to violence—not yet—she did make her views known. "Juan Castell had every chance to be a father to me, to us. And not once has he taken any of those chances. I had one father, and he was killed. As for Juan Castell, he can stay gone for all I care." Bella stormed out, slamming the cabin door.

Left alone with Luis, Jeremiah eyed the floor. She might not have thrown any physical punches, but she'd certainly knocked her brother on his ass. Lifting his gaze to Luis, he hooked a thumb over his shoulder. "I should go after her."

"Will you talk to her for me? I don't think it's too much to ask for her to give him a chance to explain."

"I'll see what I can do, but she has a right to be angry."

"I know. I'm not asking her to forgive him, just give him a chance to make things right."

Brushing his hand over his head, Jeremiah nodded. All he could do was try. He walked out the door.

Bell was standing by the car. "If you don't mind, I'd like to go home."

"Okay. We'll leave." Wrapping his arms around her shoulders, he hugged her close.

Inhaling deeply, she snuggled into his chest. "Thank you."

They got into the car, and he started back down the maze of dirt roads that had led them to the cabin. Jeremiah gave Bell a sidelong glance. The way she reacted to what her brother said bothered him. So much anger in someone who used to be so sweet and innocent. Where had the girl he'd fallen in love with gone? Tonight, it was as if someone else had taken her place.

Or was he overreacting?

After all, the information about the money pointed to yet another reason someone would want her dead. Plus, there was her biological father. Jeremiah had to admit, if he'd been misled his entire life, and his real father not only ignored him, but turned out to be psychotic, he'd be ticked off, too. He meant it when he'd said she had every right to be angry.

He turned onto the main road. He hoped any dirt in the tire treads cleared out on their way back to the house. Otherwise, he'd have some explaining to do to his father. Jeremiah eyed the clock. It was already after eleven. There might be questions, regardless.

"I'm sorry I didn't tell you about the money," Bell said quietly.

"I understand, but I would like you to involve me in whatever you decide. You're finding out a lot about your family, and I want to be a part of it."

Bell reached over and rested a hand on his leg. "Thank you for being there tonight."

"I'll be wherever you need me." He laced his fingers through hers and gave her hand a gentle squeeze. His stolen glance was rewarded with a heartwarming smile.

"Did he say anything after I walked out?"

Jeremiah considered lying, but knew it would compromise the trust they were rebuilding. "Yes. Your brother asked me to talk to you about giving your birth father a chance. Just know," he said, before she could respond, "I'll support whatever decision you make. If you don't ever want to see him, then you don't have to. And if you decide to hear him out, I'll be by your side."

"Thank you. I really appreciate it."

"But Bell? How come he called you Gigi?"

She looked out the passenger side window. "I was born Giovanna. He couldn't say my name as a child, so he called me Gigi. He was born Sabio and renamed Luis. Then we were both renamed as part of our adoptions."

Bella paced from one side of her therapist's office to the other. She had no right asking Heather to research her family. But it would be stupid of her not to investigate, especially since Heather was such a computer whiz. And most especially since the newspapers seemed to have no conclusive information about how her mother died. Suicide? Maybe. Maybe not. So, yes, she had every right. Right?

"Would you like to tell me what has you so anxious?"

"I'm confused." She knew next to nothing about her family. Several weeks ago, she'd shared that little tidbit with her therapist. Was it too much to ask to learn something about the people who gave her life?

"What are you confused about?"

Everything. Had her mother truly taken her own life? If so, why? And would that make Bella herself susceptible to suicide, too? And what about her father? What kind of role could he have in her life?

Whoa. Bella stopped mid-step. For sure, he was the most confusing element of her life, right now. DeWei, the man she'd grown up calling "father," had been killed trying to protect her. Then this man, this Juan Castell, comes out of nowhere—and she knew almost nothing about him. All the knowledge she'd gained about him, she'd learned from the police. And she didn't even have a way to contact him. Hell, she wasn't certain she wanted to. What had he done to deserve the chance her brother asked her to give him? "Mostly, I'm confused about my father."

"I'm assuming you're referring to your biological father."

"Yes." Bella lifted her eyes to her therapist. She scratched at her arms and slowly eased onto the couch across from the dark-skinned woman.

"What do you find confusing about your birth father?"

Her therapist looked at Bella closely. She could see the woman was scrutinizing her arms. Yeah, so they itched. That meant nothing. Right? Okay, so maybe being slightly numb to all the words tumbling around her brain would be nice right about now. But no. She had to talk things through. That's what her doctor was there for.

Bella sighed. "My father's resurfaced, and my brother wants me to meet him."

"And you're unsure if you'd like to agree to that?"

"Yeah. I mean, I had a father. A man who loved me like his own, and he died protecting me. And this man, who I know nothing about, appears and suddenly he wants to play daddy."

"Are you sure that's true?"

Bella bowed her head. She wasn't sure what Juan Castell's motivations were. But what if her father did want to be a part of her life? As far as she knew, he wasn't a wanted man. But she didn't know everything about him. Hell, she knew hardly anything about him. What if she let him in, and then he got ripped out of her life as quickly as he'd entered it? Bella dropped back against the couch cushion. *Holy shit.* Had she discovered her real problem? "No, but if it is true, and I let him, and he has to leave again …"

"What if he did?"

"I'm not sure I could deal with that. I get him just to lose him? It wouldn't be fair." Although she knew practically nothing about Juan Castell, he was her birth father. They shared DNA. His blood pumped through her veins. She could try to deny it, but she had to admit it, at least to herself: she had an inherent love for a man she couldn't remember. But she'd already lost one father. She didn't know what would happen if she lost another.

The last couple of days had been a complete nightmare. Simms had screwed the entire precinct. The sheriff walked into the bullpen where his troops were gathered. If he was honest, this wasn't just bad news he was about to deliver, it was a shit storm, and he'd stepped right into it. Dirty cops gave all cops a bad name. Now, it was up to the good ones to fix the problem.

"As you know, two days ago we located a built-in evidence locker in a residence that once belonged to Simms's parents. Final count indicates twenty cases were affected. As of now, I'm splitting those cases between you, to add to your caseloads. Reinvestigate them from start to finish. Look for anything new, anything Simms hasn't previously touched, verified, or checked. I want every guilty person he set free in jail where they belong."

There was a collective groan from the group. Reynolds was the first to speak up. "Sheriff, you can't be serious. We can't backburner our current cases so we have the time to spend reviewing old ones."

"I know, which is why, effective immediately, all overtime will be approved. Every case gets reinvestigated. No stone is to be left unturned. We clear?"

Whatever gripes the individual detectives might have, not a single person uttered another disapproving word. Instead, they responded as a unit that was determined to get their good name back—however many extra hours it took.

As the group dispersed, Jamar headed to his office. "Russell and Ali, with me."

"Yes, sir." The two jumped to their feet and followed him.

He stepped around his desk and removed his suit jacket. "Give me a status update on Hector Rodriguez's apartment."

"The building's been abandoned for years. The apartment is in shambles. Only thing I found was a bunch of squatters. Two talked to me, but they couldn't tell me much about the place."

"Find the last owner. I want to know why it was abandoned, exactly when Hector left, any information they have on him as a tenant, and what has gone on with the building since. From now on, you two partner up on everything."

"Sir?" Russell looked from Jamar, to the woman next to him, and back to Jamar.

Ali raised an eyebrow. "No offense sir, but we don't exactly work well together."

"After what I saw the other day, I think you two will do great together. You're both competitive enough to push each other. Use it. Now, go do some digging on that building. I want answers like yesterday's news."

After the two left, Jamar rubbed his temples. Another migraine had begun. Jamar picked up the phone and dialed the lab. It was a long shot, but he wanted to ensure the DNA sample they located for Bella's case got tested as a priority. It couldn't be used in the case, but it could give the girl some peace of mind. When he got no response, he sighed. Nothing about the aftermath of Simms's double-dealing was going to be easy, it seemed.

The place reeked of feces, but structurally it suited Gervasio's purposes. Rats tended to take up residence in abandoned buildings, along with the homeless. Typically, he'd only had to get rid of one of the two species. And most people hardly noticed when the homeless disappeared. But today, the bums were lucky. None of them were occupying the building, at present. Good thing, too, since his body farm had been compromised, and there'd been no time to find someplace new. Truly, though, there was no need for him to stay and find a new spot. Roots could be laid elsewhere. He was tired of the heat. Perhaps he could return to New York. It was quite beautiful this time of year.

Gervasio carried in the final bag of fertilizer and dropped it on top of the others. Several cans of diesel fuel sat on the floor beside them. He still required a few more items, as he'd been purchasing what he needed from different shops, so as not to raise any alarms.

He glanced at his watch. It was time. He walked out to the truck the New Yorker had obtained on his behalf. The F150 had originally been blue, but the color had been changed at a chop shop outside of town. Gervasio tugged a hoodie over his head and leaned against the truck, waiting.

Bella stepped out of the coffee shop, phone to her ear. Gervasio scanned the parking lot. Aside from his whore, there was no one around. Dare he risk getting closer? It would be nice to hear what she was discussing. The information could prove useful, but if he were exposed, that would halt his plans. And he wanted to grab her without witnesses. Plus, he had to make sure she had no one left to look for her.

Her conversation didn't last long. She returned to the coffee shop, then came back out a few minutes later, a bag slung over her shoulder, and went to her car. Interesting. No way her shift ended so early.

He ignited the engine of the F150 and followed the black VW at a safe distance. This time of day, most of the traffic was heading into downtown. As for his whore, she was driving away from town. This meant that the further out of town they drove, the more space he had to put between them. He wasn't ready to be sighted. Soon, she would see him again, but not yet.

Following her onto the highway, he wondered where she was going. Over the last few days, the whore's travels had been limited to school, work, and home. This trip was out of the ordinary. Then he caught a glimpse of the sign as they exited. Oh, this was too perfect.

Approaching the traffic light, Bella slowed. "Left, or right?"

"Umm, hold on."

"Heather, come on. You're a horrible navigator." Bella groaned into her phone. If she wasn't paying attention, she could've missed the exit. How was it possible someone as tech savvy as Heather couldn't get directions faster?

"Shut up. Go left."

Bella smirked. "Okay. How far am I going?"

"It should be about eight miles on your right."

"Are you sure? It seems like the middle of nowhere." It had been the first tip they'd gotten in days. Hopefully, it would pan out, especially since she left work to check out this restaurant.

"Yes. According to the tip line, one of the waitresses reported him eating lunch there the other day."

"Servers," she corrected Heather. "It isn't exactly a gender-based profession."

"Do you have to be so damn literal?"

"Do you have to be so damn disrespectful?" Bella snapped in return.

"Remind me again why we're working together."

"Because you want to stay out of jail." The corners of Bella's lips tugged into a smile at the way she'd convinced Heather she had evidence proving the girl had helped Gervasio—non-existent proof—which could land Heather in a whole heap of trouble. Bella was unlikely to ever tell the girl there was no such evidence. Especially since the threat had convinced David's twin sister to help her get Gervasio.

"Right. You're still a pain in my ass."

"Tell me something I don't know." If nothing else, the banter distracted her from thinking too much about what she was doing. Every fiber in her being longed to see Gervasio Rodriguez dead. Could she be the one to kill him—if she managed to find him?

"You're a bitch."

Bella rolled her eyes. "I said, tell me something I don't know."

"Hold on. I have a call coming in."

"What? Are you—" With a click, Heather actually put her on hold. There had better be a good reason for it. Bella leaned a little closer to the steering wheel and peered ahead. In the distance, on the right, stood a building. Wow. Heather managed to get her there.

Heather still hadn't clicked back. And, Bella realized, holding the burner phone to her ear waiting for the girl, she'd never explained why she had burner phones locked in a safe in the first place. Oh, well. Whatever else she had going on, Heather came through.

She hoped. But Bella could be chasing her tail for all she knew. Her partnership with Heather required more trust than she believed she'd been capable of. Therapy apparently had accomplished something.

Maybe more than she'd imagined. Saturday night, there had been magic between her and Miah. They hadn't just taken their relationship to a new level, they'd also had an honest conversation about it. Feelings and concerns had been expressed and addressed. At least Miah's had. She, though, hadn't uttered a word regarding her recent discussion with her therapist.

Bella slowed down and pulled into the parking lot of the mom and pop restaurant. She stared at the sign that simply read *Diner*. Was she really going to ruin all she'd begun to rebuild with her boyfriend? No. This wouldn't hurt their relationship. By not telling him, she was keeping him safe. Plus, if things went according to plan, she could get closure and truly move forward with her life. Having convinced herself, Bella walked into the small diner.

Three patrons occupied the place, and a stocky brunette approached her. "You need some help, darling?"

"No, yes. I, um, have you seen this man in here before?" Bella presented a mug shot of Gervasio. She'd borrowed it from the case file Jamar had on the guy.

"Yeah, but I don't think he's been here for a couple of weeks. Hey, Sharon, you 'member that guy with the scar? You 'member last time you seen him?"

"Not since Earl brought in that rattler he killed."

The brunette nodded and handed the photograph back to Bella. "Yeah, been two weeks."

"Thank you." Offering the woman a brief smile, she left the diner. Had to have been a stale tip—or a false one. Those two women didn't seem to have any reason to lie about when they'd seen Gervasio. Heather'd warned her about the possibility of bad leads. And she still hadn't been prepared for the disappointment.

Just then, the burner rang. It was Heather. "Sorry about that. I have some good news."

"At least one of us does."

"It didn't pan out?"

"He was here a couple weeks ago, but not since. So, share your good news with me."

"I have information on your mother's so-called suicide."

Juan lifted the binoculars and eyed the diner. He knew the Warren girl would assist Giovanna in her search for Gervasio. Now, he had taken cover in a small copse of trees opposite the small restaurant and, locating his best vantage point, had climbed one of the trees. From there, he had seen his daughter return to her car after being inside for just a few minutes.

She hadn't started her car yet. She was talking on her phone. He surveyed the road to his right, then his left. A truck ambled back toward the highway. Was that the same truck that had driven by the diner not five minutes ago? He zoomed in and got a close look at the driver. *Son of a bitch.*

He shifted in the tree and angled his rifle toward the truck. But moving targets were difficult. If he shot now, he might miss. And he'd give his position away. Lowering his weapon, he dug out his phone.

"Hey, Dad. What's going on? That lead pan out?"

"It has, though not as we believed. I have an eye on the target." As the vehicle drove past him again, Juan peered through the binoculars. "Black Ford F150, New Mexico Plates, Golf, Romeo, Mike, Romeo, Three, Papa, Romeo, Sierra."

"Got it," his son replied. "Let me see what I come up with."

"Work fast."

He turned his attention back to the parking lot. Giovanna still hadn't departed, but the truck was heading on toward the highway. For now, it seemed Gervasio had gotten what he wanted—whatever that might be. Juan had learned something himself, as well: that Gervasio was moving faster than he'd believed. That the situation was now officially critical.

ten

The gate had been open, so she'd gone ahead and driven up the long driveway. Now, three stories of white glory stared Bella in the face. The last time she'd been inside the place had been before David entered the picture. So much had happened since then.

Today, her plan was simple. Since she was too young to receive instruction from any gun ranges in the area on safety, she'd considered asking the few people she knew that handled guns on a regular basis to teach her—but most of them would question her motives. It was possible the father of Sarresh's baby would do the same. But she had to try.

What if Mike refused? And what if he agreed? Her heart raced at both possibilities. Books and YouTube videos could educate her on the use of guns, but that wouldn't compare to the feel of a piece of steel in her hands. Then, what if she couldn't handle the shock of actually shooting a gun? Even target practice certainly wouldn't be the same as turning a weapon on a person and pulling the trigger.

Though she had attempted to take her own life, taking someone else's was an entirely different thing. On the other hand, how many times had she imagined killing Gervasio? Too many to count. Bella nodded to herself. Yes. This was the right thing to do. She absolutely had to be prepared in case she actually found him. Otherwise she'd be the one who ended up in the morgue. A result that would only suit one person.

Sitting in her car, staring at the gorgeous mansion, Bella scratched at her arms. God, what she wouldn't give to not feel so antsy right now. She took a deep breath. It was a bad moment, but it would pass. It always passed. She always managed to get through the longing for a pill to help kill any hint of emotion. Now, she silently repeated the mantra her therapist drilled into her head: *Embrace your feelings. It's okay to cry. It's okay to scream. It's okay to get angry.*

The front door opened. Sarresh leaned against the door frame, arms crossed. "Are you going to sit out there all day?"

"Shit." Bella muttered. She climbed out of the VW, tucking her keys into her pocket.

"Did you forget about the camera at the gate?"

To Bella, Mike's super-secure house had always been the perfect fort for hiding. How could she have forgotten one of the features that made her feel so safe? "I guess so."

"Well, I'm assuming you're here for a reason." Sarresh looked tense.

"Yeah. You probably know I'm in therapy. Part of my ... healing process, I guess you could say, is to make amends with the people I've hurt." None of that was a lie. Jeremiah had suggested talking to people about the letters. Her therapist thought it was a great idea. Since it wasn't like she could admit her true purpose for the visit, the letter would be a good excuse.

Sarresh moved aside. "Come on in. Mike just took Takina upstairs for some playtime. We can talk in the living room."

"Sure." Bella stepped inside and headed directly for the den. Inwardly, she was shaking her head. Who was she kidding? Her drinking had been a problem for Mike. The likelihood he'd think it was a great idea to show her how to properly handle a gun was practically nonexistent. She'd simply have to figure it out on her own and pray she didn't kill herself in the process.

"I'm not upset about the letter, you know."

Caught off guard, Bella stopped. She thought everyone was angry about their letter. She eyed her best friend. "Then why'd you stop talking to me?"

"Because I felt like I failed you."

"What?" Of all the reasons she'd imagined, that certainly wasn't one of them. Bella would've believed that Sarresh would be annoyed that, in the letter, she'd asked her friend to give Mike a chance. It seemed so simple, but Sarresh was stubborn. Even more stubborn than Bella. Part of what made them such good friends.

"Before you started dating David, you spent a lot of time here. Several of those nights you got drunk, and I took advantage of your inebriated state to keep an eye on you. When you stopped, I thought maybe things were getting better."

Bella bit the inside of her cheek. Once again, she'd nearly forgotten her friends had their own battles—but still tried to help her with hers. Would chasing her real-life demon damage all she was trying to rebuild? No. She refused to accept it would do anything save make it all better. "You couldn't have known. I kept everything well hidden. I mean, I spent a lot of time with David, and he didn't even realize it. You can't blame yourself."

"I just feel like I could've done more. Maybe pushed Jeremiah harder to make things right. Told Aunt Christine sooner—not that I meant to do that to begin with. You dealt with so much by yourself. Kind of makes me feel like a shitty friend."

"I chose to deal with it alone." Or not at all. Was she doing the same thing by going after Gervasio? No. This time she had help. Coerced help, but still help. Although Heather didn't fit what Miah had in mind when he requested she let someone know where she was at all times, at least someone knew where she was and what she was up to.

"But you didn't have to."

Funny, Amanda uttered those same words to her five days ago. That conversation hadn't gone the same route, but Mandy and Sarresh both asked why she'd believed she had to face everything alone. And if she was honest with herself, she'd have to admit things hadn't changed. She still dealt with it all by herself. At least the new stuff. God and her psychiatrist helped her process the old stuff. "Maybe. But I didn't think any of you could understand."

"What about now?"

"Everything's different …" How could she explain? Bella played with the hem of her skull t-shirt.

"How?"

Funny. That's exactly what Amanda asked, too. But she would never reveal the entire truth to her friends. She'd give the same answer to Sarresh she'd given Vick and Amanda. Best to stay consistent in case they eventually compared notes.

"Because I'm not the same. There's so much more I have to deal with than I did before. I have to deal with the drug addiction, and I have to learn to accept who my parents are. You guys can't do that for me."

"Your birth parents don't change who you are. It doesn't matter if your biological father was some kind of drug king or something. You're still the same girl I met at camp all those years ago. You know that, right?" Sarresh cocked her head.

"Yeah, of course. Listen, I, uh, I have to go to work." This was a topic of conversation she refused to debate. Of course, her birth parents impacted who she was. They created her, gave her life. She shared their features and personality traits. Everything about them influenced her.

"Right. Well, I'm glad we talked."

"Me, too." With that, Bella left, having never even seen Mike, never mind having asked for his help in learning how to shoot a gun.

"Don't you think it's time for a break, Mother?" Heather scooped up her bottle of water and gulped it down as if her life depended on it. Her parents had been back for almost three weeks, every day of which she'd been tortured with a ridiculously health-conscious diet and a minimum of two hours in the gym. Her body had grown tired of the regimen and her mind weary. At this point, she dreamed about wrapping her hands around a thick, juicy burger with the works. She might even throw in a slice of greasy, fattening pizza for shits and giggles.

"The scale can be the judge of that."

Heather swallowed a groan. The scale had become her worst enemy—but it could also be her savior. Without griping any more, Heather stepped on the scale and closed one eye. No part of her wanted to look, but she had to face her enemy. Standing as still as she could manage, she saw the digital reading stop on three beautiful numbers: 122. But she couldn't jump off the scale and celebrate. Like a trained dog, she wasn't allowed to move until her mother released her.

"Well, we can break for now. But we need to get those last twelve pounds off."

Heather followed her mother. "You mean, seven pounds."

"Oh, no, dear. One hundred-ten is now in. Think of it this way—you'll fly that much higher when the cheerleaders toss you up into the air." A bright smile crossed the woman's wrinkle-free face.

The doorbell rang. Heather refrained from slapping the smile off her mother's plastic face. Her mother had been saved by the bell. "I'll get it."

"Excellent. I'm off to shower. Tell Chef I'll be down in an hour to discuss this evening's menu."

"Of course, Mother." She'd never wanted so badly for her parents to leave again. Heather walked to the door and opened it. Luis. He was the last thing she needed right now.

Her former boyfriend pushed past her and into the house. "We have to talk."

"Sure, come on in." She loaded up her response with all the sarcasm she could manage and, seeing as he obviously didn't intend to go anywhere, reluctantly shut the door.

Luis turned and glared at her. "Stop helping my sister."

She scanned the open-floor foyer. Thankfully, her mother had gone up to shower. However, her father had last been seen in his office. Heather grabbed Luis's arm and dragged him up the stairs to her bedroom. If he intended to hash things out, they required privacy.

"What the hell?" she hissed, once the door was closed behind them. "Have you lost your mind showing up here unannounced?"

"You're the one who's trying to help my sister find a freaking psycho."

"I didn't have much choice, did I?" Heather spat out. Luis was the one who'd given Bella proof of her role in the whole situation. All Bella had to do was turn the evidence against Heather over to the police, and it would be the cops knocking on her door, next.

"And why's that?"

"Like you don't know."

Luis raised an eyebrow and propped himself against her bedroom door. "I have no clue, so enlighten me. Because last I checked, you hated my sister."

"I do, but I'd rather my brother and I didn't go to jail." Heather dropped into her desk chair to emphasize her point.

"What're you talking about? There's no proof you were involved."

"Excuse me?"

A smiled tugged the corners of Luis's lips, like everything suddenly made complete sense. "Let me guess. Bella made you believe she could prove your involvement."

What? The geek had pulled one over on her? Heather had underestimated the girl. But Bella's threat wasn't the only reason she was helping the girl. Only a few people actually scared Heather. And one of them was the man who had contacted her a day or two before Bella showed up on her doorstep. That man had knowledge of things Heather had never told anyone. Not even her twin brother. And when he instructed her to "fight with Bella" a bit on the matter, but to ultimately accept whatever the geek proposed—or else—Heather hadn't argued. The cold stare in his brown eyes had convinced her he meant business.

No way Heather was going to tell Luis about this guy, though. Instead, she quickly formulated a lie. "That was only part of the reason," she said. "The other part was that I knew that my helping your sister would piss you off."

"There's more to it than that. What're you hiding? You get this little twinkle in your eyes when you're lying." Luis pushed off the wall and closed the distance between them.

Son of a bitch. Heather narrowed her eyes, folded her arms across her chest, and glowered at her ex-boyfriend. She had one fallback tactic. "What? Like you're not doing the exact same thing? Is it a guy thing? What? You think because you have a dick you can do something better than us girls?"

"I see."

"What the hell is that supposed to mean?" How had he not fallen for her pissy attitude? If lying failed, starting an unnecessary argument always worked. No guy wanted to fight with her; she fought dirty and had a tendency to hit below the belt.

Shaking his head, Luis shoved his hands in his jeans pockets. "Do me a favor. If you find the guy, don't let her go after him. She'll get herself killed."

"I make no promises. I mean, it isn't like I can tie her up and stop her." Heather smirked.

Luis gave her a long stare, then crossed the room and opened the bedroom door. "Try your best. I'm sure you can figure something out. After all, you're quite resourceful."

After Heather heard the front door close behind Luis, she took a deep breath. Bella sure as hell had some explaining to do. Not that it would stop her from helping the geek—not after that threatening visit from the mystery man—but once Gervasio was found, she was done. If she survived the shitstorm, she'd jump ship and escape this dreadful city. Screw her parents. Only one problem existed ... her brother. Maybe she could talk him into leaving, too.

"You have a lot of nerve lying to me."

"I didn't ... okay ... I might have exaggerated a bit." To Bella, the lie had been small—and justified. She hadn't expected Heather to help, but she needed the girl. She had mad tech skills. Maybe she disliked Heather, but even she had to recognize the talent the Heather hid from the world.

"A bit? You flat out let me believe you had proof of my involvement."

Bella fidgeted with the ends of her braid. "I'm sorry, but I needed help. And you didn't jump in when I said it was a chance to get back at my brother."

"Right. Because that wouldn't have made me agree to your crazy scheme. But, anyway, he is certainly pissed."

"What? How do you know that? What does he know?" She sank to the bottom step of the staircase. Luis knowing what she was doing could mess everything up. He'd given her the evidence. His plan had been for her to deliver it to the police. Instead, she'd scanned the material he'd provided her and hidden the package.

"He knows I'm helping you. I don't know how. Mostly, he told me to stop."

"Are you going to?"

Heather sat on the stair beside Bella. She leaned her elbows into her knees. "No."

"I don't get it. We aren't friends. Now that you know I don't have anything on you, why would you keep helping me?" Bella studied Heather. What could the girl possibly get out of helping her find the monster who ruined her life?

Heather stared her straight in the eye. "My reasons are my own. All you need to know is I'm not backing down until we find that bastard. Got it?"

That statement was likely the most honest thing she'd ever heard from Heather. She couldn't fault the girl for keeping her reasons to herself. There had been a lot she'd kept secret, too. "Thank you."

"Yeah. Don't mention it. And I mean that. Same rules apply."

"Agreed."

Heather stood and offered a hand to help Bella to her feet. Then, their brief moment of cooperation having passed, the girl gestured to the door. "You should go before David gets home."

"At some point, I need to talk to him." So far, they'd arranged to meet when he would be away from the house. Bella also avoided him at school. But it couldn't last forever.

Just as she thought this, the front door opened, and David walked in. "Bella."

"She was just leaving." Heather tried to shove her past David, but Bella swatted at her. This was an opportunity. She had no way to tell if the timing was right or not, but she would take her chances.

"No, I wasn't leaving." She looked at David.

"It's okay, Heather," he said. "I have questions that need answering."

"Fine. Whatever." Heather threw her hands in the air and stalked out of the foyer. The squeak of her sneakers against the marble floor could be heard the entire way to the kitchen.

David stared. Why couldn't Bella have looked ugly in her uniform? No. His ex-girlfriend had to look as beautiful as ever. He gripped the back of his neck. It was true what he just said. He had lots of questions. But right then, every single one of them escaped him.

It was Bella who broke the silence. "You said you have questions?"

"I do. I, umm …" He'd thought about this moment a lot. Now it had happened, and his brain up and decided to take a timeout.

"Okay, well, I'm assuming whatever you want to know has to do with the letter."

Yeah, the letter. David propped his hands on his hips and truly looked at her. Her face and body were quite nice, but those hazel brown eyes of hers told a story. One of love, loss, and devastation. But she had taken actions that hurt a lot of people. He needed to know about them. "Did you really do it? Try to kill yourself."

"Yes."

"When?" He knew her answer might cause him more heartache, but nothing could hurt him worse than her betrayal. The images of the kiss she had with her ex had broken his heart. Still, he'd been willing to forgive her transgression. Then she'd gone and spent time with the guy before their official split. She'd stabbed him and destroyed all they could've shared. He hadn't fully recovered from the knife in his heart.

"David, you don't really want to know the answer to that."

Her response should've clued him in, but he was stubborn and tired. Too much had been hidden from him. "Answer the question, or you can leave."

"You have to understand. I was in a bad place. Nothing was right in my world."

"Dammit! Answer me. When?" The demand came out harsher than he intended, but her incessant need to explain everything away wore him out.

She took a breath before answering. "The day you found out about the kiss. Our fight was the last straw. I couldn't deal anymore."

David swallowed. Wow. That wasn't what he wanted to hear. But he knew it couldn't have occurred any time except those last days of their relationship. The things she'd written in his letter matched what she said the day they broke up. "Did you try again after that night?"

"No."

"What stopped you?" Perhaps the more appropriate question would've been, *Who stopped you?* Which he thought he knew. But he needed her to say it.

"Miah."

His own heart plummeted, as he realized that no part of *her* heart had ever really belonged to him—no matter how hard he'd tried to claim to it. They'd been doomed from the beginning. David brushed tears from his eyes. Their false relationship hardly deserved any emotional display of his pain. "I don't get it. Why'd you even agree to go out with me?"

Bella's face softened, as she answered him. "A lot of reasons, but, mostly, you made me feel almost normal. With you, my past didn't exist. I could forget about the past because we were in the present."

He fastened her with his gaze. "Did you always intend to end the relationship?" That was the million-dollar question. Had they ever had a shot? Could they have worked out?

She didn't flinch. "I don't know. I spent so much time avoiding the pain of what happened to me, I never really focused on the possibility of a future. My heart was in so many pieces, I never felt like I had anything to give."

David was stunned. Bella'd never been this honest throughout their entire relationship. But that honesty shattered what little of his heart remained intact. If only he hadn't asked, then he could keep pretending they'd had a chance. The truth warped his momentary hope into a reality he wished he'd never seen.

"I'm sorry. I probably shouldn't have told you that, but I just ... I couldn't lie to you anymore."

"No. I'm glad you did. I mean, maybe it'll give me some closure." He wasn't sure he meant it, but, eventually, he probably would feel that way.

"I never wanted to hurt you." Were there tears in her hazel eyes? If there were, he was going to ignore them.

"I think it was inevitable." He shrugged, not sure there was anything left to say. She'd claimed his heart three years ago. In the end his heart was bound to be broken.

Suddenly, a movement caught David's eye. He looked up. They weren't alone anymore.

Bella followed David's gaze and saw an older man stepping into the foyer. He and David shared similar features. They had the same blue eyes. The only difference in their blue-black hair was the gray that dusted the older man's head. And he scowled, where David often smiled.

Folding his hands behind his back, the man scrutinized Bella. "Who's this?"

"Dad. This is, um, a friend of mine, and she was just leaving."

"It seems my son has forgotten his manners. What is your name young lady?"

His voice demanded, not commanded, respect. She was polite in her reply, but something about him told her he didn't necessarily deserve it.

"Bella Kynaston, sir." She tucked her hands in her khakis' pockets and stole a quick glance at David. Her ex-boyfriend shifted from one foot to the other. His twitchiness suggested that this wasn't going to end well.

The man circled her, as if she were prey to be watched, then stopped in front of her again. "Are you seeing my son?"

"She doesn't feel that way about me, Dad," David said.

"I believe I was speaking with Miss Kynaston. Do not interrupt again," the older man snapped.

Bella saw David ball up one hand into a fist at his side. "Yes, sir."

"Now. Miss Kynaston, are you dating my son?" Another glance from her shoes to the top of her head ... with what looked like a sneer at her uniform.

"No, sir."

"Have you ever dated my son?"

Bella had had it. Enough people had bullied her in her life. Whether this man felt she owed him some deference or not, she refused to be studied like human trash. She stared him straight in the face. "Yes, sir. We dated for a couple of months. Our relationship ended, but the details are strictly between David and me."

The man smiled—a smile that didn't make it to his eyes. "Feistiness in a young woman is like fight in a mare. It requires a man with a strong hand to break it. If you're smart, Miss Kynaston, you'll not sass me again. I'll ask only once. What caused the relationship you shared with my son to end?" David's father narrowed his eyes, glaring as if she had no choice but to answer him.

No way. Not going to happen. She stood her ground. If she refused to discuss the specifics of her relationship with Miah, what in the hell made this man think she'd tell him. The sweetest smile she could muster spread on her lips. "I mean no offense Mr. Warren, but that's none of your business. There's nothing you can do that'll make me tell you otherwise."

"We shall see about that Miss Kynaston." Another smug smile settled on his face—and he swung at her.

David jumped in front of her, just in time. With one hand, he blocked his father's wrist and used his other arm to move Bella behind him, in a half-arc of protection. "Leave her alone."

"You have one opportunity to step out of the way," his father growled.

"No. I won't stand by and watch you beat someone else I care about." He grabbed Bella's hand and squeezed.

Bella was shaking—with fury or fear, she couldn't tell. But what was clear was that David's father had shown him how to treat women. This was obviously where his temper stemmed from. Whatever happened before, this moment changed how she understood David. She'd ask Amanda to forgive him. And she'd ensure he knew he had her support. Bella squeezed his hand in return, offering him all the reassurance she could manage.

"Then you leave me no choice." The man's feet and arm shifted, but he didn't get far.

David threw a right hook and knocked his father off point.

The guy stumbled backwards and stared at his son with wide eyes.

David shoved a finger in his father's face. "Go after her again, and I swear to God, I'll call the cops and have you arrested."

"You'd have your own father arrested?"

"Try me. I'm sure the newspapers would love a story about an abusive, high-powered CEO who gets hauled away in cuffs."

Carefully, David's father studied him. Then, slowly, the man wiped the blood from the corner of his mouth and walked away.

David held onto Bella while his father ascended the staircase and disappeared from their view. Then he turned and asked, "Are you okay?"

"Yeah. I'm okay. What about you?"

He nodded. "I'm good. But you need to go. I don't know what's going to happen, but you don't need to be here to see it."

Of course, he was more concerned about her than his own safety. "Only if you promise to go to a hotel or something." The situation had become ugly fast, and she wanted to make certain he'd make it through the night, alive.

"That isn't necessary. I'm fine here, but I need you to go." David ushered her toward the front door.

"But won't he come after you?"

"No. He won't." Her ex-boyfriend sounded sure, but she wasn't as certain.

Bella reached for his hand and squeezed again. She couldn't leave him here with things like this. "But David—"

"No buts. There was a time when you didn't want to talk about things that happened to you. Now, I'm asking the same. Let me handle my business."

She hated how he turned her own actions against her. It wasn't fair play. Then again, when had he ever played fair? "Okay, but can you do one thing for me?"

"I make no promises."

Bella placed her hands on either side of his face and forced him to look in her eyes. She had to make him understand. Maybe she'd never loved him, but that didn't mean he wasn't important to her. "Check in with me. I want to make sure you're okay. I may not have shown it so well when we were together, but I do care about you."

"I'll try."

"I suppose that's all I can ask." Given the circumstances of their breakup, she was unlikely to get a better promise. Bella squeezed his hand one last time and slipped out the front door.

Aurora gathered what she needed for her first class. In a little over two months, she'd graduate under her assumed name. Provided she could remain hidden. Maybe it wasn't the wisest decision to stay in one place so long, but she'd kind of become attached. The town had its quirks, as did everywhere she'd ever stayed. But they were part of what made the place special.

Besides, she still hadn't found her uncle. And she desperately needed his help. At some point, she'd have to stop running. Not as if her refusal to leave had anything to do with a certain dark-haired guy she'd kept at arm's length. Why couldn't she get David out of her head? Even though she avoided him like crazy, which had become increasingly difficult, she thought about him more than she should.

Her locker, worse luck, was right next to his. She'd actually learned his schedule so she could hit her locker, the gym, and even the cafeteria when he wasn't around. And at least they didn't have any classes together.

Behind her, she heard a low whistle, followed up by, "Hey, sweet thing. You look like the kind of girl who'd like to go on a date with me this weekend."

Oh, dear Lord. Maybe if she ignored whoever it was, he'd go away. Aurora fished around in her locker and pretended to search for something she had to have to get through the morning.

"In fact, I bet you're the kind of girl who likes a strong man."

Right. Because that line is so much better than the first. Instead of hoping he'd just disappear, she decided to take advantage of the opportunity. How many chances does a girl get to teach a douche-bag a lesson? She glanced back at the guy. Blonde hair, blue eyes … and a soccer jersey. Dammit. Of course, he had to play on the team with her dark-haired guy.

He grinned at her. "It's your lucky day, because I'm that kind of man."

Really? No girl, unless she was absolutely desperate, would fall for such cheesy lines. This guy definitely deserved a lesson. A smile crept onto her face. She shut her locker and turned to face him. "Would you really like to know what kind of girl I am?"

"In every way."

"Tell me your name, and I'll show you." Seductively, she licked her top lip. The move worked like a charm.

"I'm Keith, but you can call me anything you want, babe."

And the cheesiness continued. Somebody really had to teach him how to pick up girls. But it wouldn't be her. Maintaining her bright smile, Aurora stepped closer to the moron, and traced her fingers down his chest, lingering near his belt buckle. The hitch in his breathing pleased her. She continued to his crotch, where, suddenly, she squeezed. Hard.

"Keith, I'm the kind of girl who'll cut off your balls if you don't get the hell out of my face."

"Got it! Just let go!" he squeaked out, his face flushing bright red.

Good thing he got the picture. Otherwise, she would've tightened her vice-grip, and they would've had to pry her fingers from his nut-sack. And that would've drawn way too much attention. Aurora looked past Keith, and saw—of all people—David, standing among the small crowd of students who'd gathered to watch the scene unfold.

Shit! She pushed through the gaggle of her classmates and sped down the hall. If she was lucky, the dimwit would be too embarrassed to tell the principal what happened. While Keith might not be able to identify her by name, he knew where her locker was, and that would be all the principal needed. She really had to stay under the radar. What was she thinking? Teaching that idiot a lesson wasn't worth getting caught.

"Hey! Wait!"

She glanced back. David had chased after her. Really? Was he going to scold her because mere moments ago she had her hand clamped around his friend's balls? Aurora turned her attention back to the slowly emptying hallway. "Tell him to put some ice on it. and he'll be fine."

"Look, if Keith was hitting on you, then he got what he deserved. That's not why I came after you."

"Then why?" The words shot of out her mouth before she had a chance to stop them. *Dammit!* What the hell was wrong with her? She shouldn't encourage him to explain anything. Talking to her was dangerous as hell.

David quickened his pace until he fell in step with her. "I don't know exactly."

"Then maybe there is no reason. Maybe we're not meant to cross paths."

"I don't believe that for one second." He grabbed hold of her arm.

The sensation of his hand on her body halted Aurora in her tracks. Her entire mind went blank, and chills crawled down her spine. Her skin burned beneath his fingers. His touch on her arm, innocuous as it seemed, set her body on fire. Aurora faced him and lifted her eyes to his blue orbs. They were exquisite, and they fueled the sensations racing through her body. "Why?"

"Because for some reason I feel like I'm supposed to protect you. I don't know why, but I do."

"You need to forget that feeling. The last thing I need is a hero. Please, for your own safety, stop chasing me." Despite how good his touch felt, she had to let him go. It was the only way. With all the power she could muster, she pulled her arm from his grip, pivoted on her heel, and walked away.

eleven

Cautiously, Gervasio scanned the alley. He'd already confirmed a lack of police presence in front of the residence. Obviously, they assumed he wouldn't return to the house he'd spent half his life in. Wrong. Unfortunately, since *Mamá Gallina* had disappeared without a word, he had to see if his secrets remained hidden.

He'd been told she'd gotten arrested with his brother. But while Cristobal had knowledge of one of Gervasio's secrets, his young brother had no knowledge of the lock box. No one did. It was the only piece of insurance he had when it came to his New York contact's involvement, the evidence he'd collected—which served one purpose and one purpose only. If he was arrested for the death of Ileana Costa, suffice it to say he wouldn't be the only one going down for her murder.

Satisfied the alley was empty, he slipped over to the wall and checked the window. Unlocked, as always. After one more glance down the alley, he climbed inside his brother's bedroom, then headed down the hallway, where he opened the basement door and went downstairs. It was possible his brother had located the materials hidden in the wall. There'd been no indication of how long Cristobal had been inside the house before *Mamá Gallina* discovered his presence.

And *Mamá Gallina* still would've spoken to Cristobal, despite his orders. She'd been a good leader for the ladies, and a semi-decent fuck, but she hadn't been good at much else. Though his soldiers all adored her, especially the last addition. Now, that had been a kill he'd enjoyed. Come to think of it, *Mamá Gallina* probably cried when she learned of his death—which gave him at least some satisfaction. Though he would've preferred her dead, her pain over the loss would have to suffice.

Slowly, Gervasio wiggled the brick back and forth and eased it out. Once it was free, he reached into the hole. The box should be right there, but there was nothing. Damn it. His brother must have remembered where he'd stowed his books. It was all encoded, but Luis had the brain to decipher the records, even if Cristobal didn't.

The lockbox must have remained undiscovered, though. Heart beating faster, he mounted the stairs two at a time and headed for the bedroom that used to be his. Moving directly to the dresser, he yanked out the bottom drawer and lifted the thin board beneath it. Also empty. "Shit."

Though the lock box had more protections than the box hidden in the basement wall, it wasn't impossible to crack. If he was right that Luis was part of all this, there was a good chance both Gervasio's books and the lockbox might be at the guy's residence.

His schedule had just changed, but the plans had not. He simply had to execute a quick scare tactic, let that bitch know he was coming for her. He'd get a rise, even if his time had been cut short. Then he'd search Luis's house. Even if he found nothing, the bitch's brother should get the message. Then, just one final component for the warehouse, and the thing would be wired exactly as he intended.

Bella dragged a damp cloth across another table. Only a few customers were still scattered around the dining room, but her shift wasn't over, so she was using the down time to clean up. Made the rushes go smoother. Though nothing could make them go by faster. Pausing mid-swipe, she dug the disposable cell phone out of her pocket. Still nothing from Heather. Seemed finding this guy was easier said than done. Aside from the one lead, Heather hadn't found anything worth following up on. Bella typed out the beginning of a text message, then quickly deleted it. Trying to rush Heather would get her nowhere.

Tucking the phone back in her pocket, she scanned the occupied tables to see if any of the customers needed anything. Her eyes stopped on a man in the corner booth. Hadn't that table been empty just a few minutes ago? He could've come in through the back door, she supposed, while her back was turned. Weird. It was warm inside, but he had on a black sweatshirt, hood up. Between the shadows and the hood, she could hardly make out his face.

Had he already placed an order? She glanced at the counter where orders were assembled, but nothing was being prepared. Shifting her gaze toward the black-clad man again, she studied his features as best she could. The beat of her heart quickened. One thing stood out—a scar. A scar she'd recognize anywhere. A scar that was embedded in her memory as if it were a part of her. Her grip on the wash rag tightened.

Gervasio Rodriguez obviously wasn't done with her—and now he was playing cat and mouse. It had to be the reason he'd shown up at her job. None of her co-workers had any knowledge of her rape, but for a moment, she almost wished they knew. At least then, if she ran at her rapist, the man responsible for so much death, including her father's, they wouldn't be surprised. Maybe they'd let her lose control. Not that she had any control.

That wasn't the case, though. So what the hell was she supposed to do? If she called Sheriff Detrone, Gervasio would be long gone by the time the police got there. Same if she called her brother or Heather. She had to think of something, and fast. What would Giovanna Castell—the girl she'd have become if she'd grown up with her biological parents—do in the situation? Surely, the daughter of a drug lord would've learned a thing or two about self-preservation. Only one reaction made sense—do nothing. Bella squeezed the cloth again and continued wiping tables as if she didn't notice Gervasio.

And while she did so, a plan formulated in her mind. Bella inhaled deeply and quietly exhaled. First, she had to calm down. Then she'd ease her way to the kitchen. Once she disappeared from view, Gervasio probably wouldn't stay long, so she'd have to move fast. There might not be time for her to grab a knife, but hopefully she could snatch her purse and clock out without anyone stopping her. If she was lucky, she'd be able to follow him and discover his hideout. Then she'd find a way to repay him for all her suffering—and he would see, then, who was the cat and who was the mouse.

His eyes narrowed as he studied Bella's sudden change in posture and focus. Her gaze had stayed on him for a moment, before shifting away—but he was certain recognition had flashed in those pretty hazel eyes of hers. Readjusting his hood so his face remained shadowed, Gervasio lowered his head. Had his girl figured out how to play the game? Impossible. It took most people years to perfect their moves. But he had definitely seen two versions of his girl in less than five minutes.

One version was the frightened girl he'd taken back in August. The girl whose adoptive father had been killed by his men. The girl whose family he planned to rip apart piece by piece. The girl whose hazel eyes had faded from drug abuse. The girl who'd nearly died twice. The girl who carried his child for a few short months. Who would carry his children in the future.

But the other version … intrigued him. The young woman who quickly gained control of her emotions. The one whose eyes flicked to the kitchen door as she appeared to formulate a plan. A plan of what though?

Gervasio slid a hand to the butt of the gun tucked in the back of his pants. He despised guns. Not because they weren't an efficient means of killing, but because he preferred the feeling of life slipping away from his target. Close up. Still, he had no intention of going anywhere unprotected, not even to his girl's job. He had to be careful. Wary. He'd been smart thus far. A few more days, and everything would finally come to an end. Then he could leave the desert behind. New York would still be cold this time of year. Perhaps he should head down to Florida instead. Miami would not only be warm, but also overflowing with opportunity. His girl would fit in perfectly there.

Knowing his point here had been made, Gervasio got out of the corner booth and slipped back out through the back door.

Biting on her bottom lip, Bella eyed the clock on her car stereo. 5:27 p.m. It had been nearly thirty minutes since she texted Tommy. He should've been at their meet spot by now.

Her plan to chase Gervasio had gone all of nowhere. Despite the fact that she'd run out of the coffee shop only a minute or so after he slipped out the back, she hadn't seen any cars leave the lot. Where had the guy disappeared to? How had he managed to escape unseen?

She shook her head. None of that mattered now. All that mattered was that next time he appeared she'd be prepared. Yeah, she'd chickened out on asking Mike to show her how to handle a gun. But she could learn on her own. How hard could it be? Aim and pull the trigger. Simple, right?

Bella wiped her sweaty palms on her pants. Where the hell was Tommy? She gazed at the clock again. 5:32. Shit. She reminded herself that she was doing the right thing. No one else could keep her safe. She only had herself to depend on. Giovanna Castell would buy a gun. Hell, Giovanna probably would've gotten one a long time ago. It was the smart thing to do.

And Bella had no other choice.

An old black sedan pulled into the alleyway beside the diner. About damn time. Bella climbed out of her car and strode across the parking lot. She had the cash. All she needed was the weapon. A quick exchange, and she'd be on her way home. With a gun tucked away in her ... God, where would she hide it? Her purse would be the logical choice, but Miah's dad might find it. Her car? It wouldn't do her any good there.

Uncertainty crept in. This was dumb. If she was smart, she'd turn right back around, get in her VW, and race out of there. No. No. She had to do this. She had to protect herself. It was the right thing to do. Okay. She'd stow it in her car, then transfer it to her purse while she was at work or ... wherever. Good. Problem solved. Chewing on the inside of her cheek, she slipped into the alleyway.

Tommy got out of the sedan and popped the trunk. "Got to say, I was surprised to hear from you."

"Yeah, well, things change." Who else could she have called? Shifting her gaze from the trunk full of guns, Bella raised an eyebrow at Tommy.

"That they do," he said. "Listen, I know you're here for one of my fine handheld items, but I got you a little something extra. You know, between old friends?" Tommy lifted her hand and placed a pill bottle in her palm. It had maybe twenty pills in it, more than enough for a good fix. Enough to get her hooked.

"What's that?"

"It's new. Not on the market, yet. It's better than the last stuff you bought from me."

She swallowed and stared at the bottle. Four weeks and four days. She'd stayed clean for nearly five weeks. Now, in her hand sat a small break from the never-ending battle she faced. No. She couldn't. But … what if she found Gervasio? What if she needed a small pick-me-up to help encourage her with her plan? No. She could kill the bastard without pills. But maybe it wouldn't hurt to accept them. In case it was harder than she imagined. Bella curled her fingers around the bottle and shoved it in the front pocket of her pants.

"Good. Now, about the guns. I'm thinking you'll want one of the 9MMs I have here. The baby Glock would suit you well."

"Dammit! This isn't working." Luis dragged his hand down his face and pinched the bridge of his nose. He'd attempted to get into the lockbox for days, now, and he still couldn't crack the code. Screw the fingerprint. If he couldn't figure out the code, the print would serve no purpose. The lockbox wouldn't open without both.

"I understand this is frustrating, son, but you must not give up. This item was hidden for a reason. We simply—"

His father's words were interrupted by a car door slamming. It was too soon for Cristobal to be back with food. Luis crossed the small room. Lifting the curtain, he peeked out the window, then glanced at his father. Shit. "Hide. Now."

"Who is outside?"

"Luis? Are you here?" Bella's voice, coming from the porch, answered their father's question.

With a half-nod, Juan disappeared into the bedroom and eased the door shut behind him. Luis waited for a split second before he opened the front door. "Gigi, what're you doing here?"

"I need to talk to you. I need some insight. I'm freaking out a little. I don't know if I did something smart. Or stupid. Or … I just, I need my brother right now." Bella's words came out in a rush, as she pushed past him into the computer-filled room and started pacing.

Luis placed himself directly in front of his sister, put his hands on her shoulders, and escorted her to the nearest chair. "Okay. Let's sit down and talk. Tell me what's going on."

"Gervasio showed up at my job today."

"What?!" He jumped up and stumbled to his computer. Hadn't he scheduled a search for updates on the guy earlier that morning? He scanned the screen. Everything was working fine. But nothing turned up. What the hell? If Gervasio made an appearance at the coffee shop, why hadn't it shown up in any police reports? Unless ... Luis eyed his sister and frowned.

Bella rolled her eyes, then stood and began pacing again. "No. I didn't say anything ... to anyone. I thought about all the possible scenarios and only one made sense. My boss wouldn't have been able to do anything. And even if I called the police, Gervasio would've been gone by the time they got there."

"You went after him, yourself, didn't you?" His sister could be so stupid sometimes. It was bad enough she'd been looking for the guy. And that she had help from Heather, but for Gigi to actually go after him? It was too much. She'd been raped and left for dead how many times? And still she chased the one responsible for all of it. Luis dropped his gaze to the floor. He had no clue how anyone was supposed to keep her safe when she was determined to put herself in harm's way.

Coming to a halt and staring at him defiantly, she said, "Of course, I did. Well. I tried, but he just disappeared. I don't know how, but he did."

"Because he's smart. He's been doing this a long time. And if you keep going after him, all you're going to do is get yourself killed!"

"No, I'm not! He's the one that'll die."

The fact Gervasio deserved to die was unspoken between them. Evidently he was going to have to find the bastard first. He was confused, though. Every action the guy ever took was purposeful. His appearance at the coffee shop would've been no exception. So why had he shown up there? He shook his head. Bella's safety was his first concern. "I need you to be reasonable. Even if you do find him, he out-skills you in so many ways. You'd never be able to outmaneuver him."

"Why? Because I'm a girl? I managed to find out what happened to Mom, when you didn't."

"Don't change the subject, here. Your gender and what happened to Mom have nothing to do with this. Gervasio is simply better trained than you. He's killed multiple times. You have no idea what you're getting yourself into." His sister needed a frigging reality check. Maybe if he showed her the pictures of the decayed bodies it would snap some sense into her. Let her know what she was truly up against.

Grinding her jaw, she glared at him. Then she threw her hands in the air and stomped over to the chair. "Screw you! I know exactly what I'm doing."

Shaking his head, Luis turned to the computers. No. She had no idea. But he was about to show her exactly what she was walking into. As he bent over the keyboard, out of his peripheral vision, he saw his sister snatch her purse off the chair. *Thud.* He turned to see what had landed on the wooden floor—and blinked. No way he was staring at a gun. No flipping way.

Bella lunged for the weapon, but Luis pushed her back and grabbed the gun first. A baby Glock. He studied the 9MM. The serial number had been filed off. A street gun. Perfect. He removed the magazine and checked the chamber. Safely unloaded, he placed the gun in a desk drawer and closed it. He could ask how she obtained the gun, but only one person he knew of would've sold it to her.

Damn Tommy. The guy never learned. He'd be dealt with soon enough. One thing at a time. First, smack some sense into his sister. Then Tommy. And, lastly, Gervasio. Gigi mentioned knowing something about their mother's death, but it wasn't necessary to discuss that right now. Keeping his sister alive needed to be his focus.

Saying nothing about the gun, Luis finished what he'd started, pulling up the photographs from the police files. "Come here."

"Why?" Quietly, she sniffled and swiped beneath her eyes.

And now she was crying. Great. Sighing, he wrapped his arms around Bella and hugged her tight. Upsetting her wasn't on his agenda, but what she was doing was dangerous. Even self-destructive. Was she so hell bent on extracting revenge, she'd put herself in the line of fire? "I want to keep you safe. Is that too much to ask?"

"You don't trust me." Bella said, shoving at him and trying to escape his hold.

He tightened his grip on her. Oh. She was crying because he'd grabbed the gun. "I'm sorry. It's not that I don't trust you. It's just ... do you even know how to use that thing?"

"No, but I can learn."

"If you think I'm teaching you, you can forget it. It's a weapon, and it's dangerous. One wrong move, and it's no longer in your possession. Instead, it's being used to kill you. I'm not ready to take that chance. Are you?" He'd found his sister such a short time ago. No way he was prepared to bury her.

"I can't sit by and do nothing. I have to protect myself."

Luis stepped back and stared at his sister. "Then take a self-defense class. Leave Gervasio to me. Gigi, I promise you, I'll take care of him. I'm not going to let him take you away from me. Got it?"

Jeremiah surveyed the finished product. He'd spent the better part of the afternoon transforming his bedroom into something a bit more to Bell's taste. To accomplish this, he and his younger brothers had gone by to collect a few items from the Kynaston house. When they'd gotten there, the place looked so abandoned. All the more reason for him to make his room a tad more like home for his girlfriend.

A few of the things they'd snagged were Bell's favorite mirror, the one with the oak frame, which he'd now hung over the dresser. Then, he'd taken down his own posters and replaced them with some of hers. There was the Maya Angelou poster that said, *The more you know of your history, the more liberated you are*, and the Evanescence poster. Last, he'd put up her poster with the big treble and other musical notes streaming from it. He'd also remade the bed, using her purple sheets and her comforter patterned with book covers, which he was fairly sure had been a gift from one of her grandmothers. He'd also switched out his books for hers, and placed some of Bell's family photos around the room—including one that was pretty old, of Bell's birth mother and her adoptive mother together.

Jeremiah glanced to the keyboard he'd set up in the corner. Above it he'd hung a collage of pictures of Bell and him together that he'd found hidden in the back of her closet. It had been only partially complete, so he finished it.

He peeked at the clock on the nightstand. She should be home from work soon. Folding his arms across his chest, he stood back and admired his handiwork. The room was perfect. Well, except for one minor detail. Jeremiah maneuvered around the bed and peeled the back off a red bow, which he stuck to the top of the keyboard. At least this way, she'd have a place to play besides church or the chapel at the rehabilitation center.

Just as he ducked into the hallway, Bella stepped through the front door.

Talk about timing. Jeremiah closed the distance between them. "Hey."

"Hi." Bella wrapped her arms around his waist and buried her face in his chest.

Holding her tight, Jeremiah rested his chin on her head, trying to act casual, but thinking that she hadn't ever hugged him the moment she walked into the house before. What could it mean? "Everything okay?"

"Just a long day." She held on another second, then released her grip. Stepping back, she grinned through semi-gritted teeth.

Jeremiah narrowed his eyes. Her half-ass smile. The one Bell used as reassurance. Something had happened, but she had no intention of talking about it. Like usual. For now, he wouldn't challenge her. Maybe his surprise would help open the line of communication between them—which, admittedly, had been eased a bit. But it could be loosened a little more, for sure. He laced his fingers through hers. "Come on. I have something to show you."

Without further explanation, he tugged her down the hall to the bedroom door. So much was riding on this. He'd worked hard to make the room feel like home for her. To show her he'd truly listened.

Bell looked up at him, eyebrows raised. "Okay. We're at the bedroom. Why?"

Placing his hand on the doorknob, he grinned at her, feeling like a kid on Christmas morning. The look on her face would be worth the hours of busting his behind. "Close your eyes and don't open them until I tell you."

She shook her head at him, but obediently lowered her lids.

He opened the door and slowly ushered Bell inside, escorted her around the bed, and stopped. This spot gave her a view of the entire room—almost. Her back was to the keyboard. He'd save that for last. "Open them."

Bella gasped. What had he done? Those were her books on the shelves of the bookcase. That was her comforter, the one her father's mother made for her last birthday covering the bed. The purple pillowcases—hers. Her posters. Her mirror. And the pictures ... they were all hers.

Bella threw her arms around Miah's neck and held on tight. Everything about the room was perfect. Her new room. Her room. *Their* room! He hadn't taken himself entirely out of the room. Instead, he'd combined it so they truly shared the room. "I love it!"

"Really? You're not just saying that."

"Yes! I love it!"

"Woohoo!" Holding on to her, he lifted her off the ground and swung her around.

His enthusiasm was contagious. She laughed. For a second, the awful truth of her day slipped her mind. She forgot about Gervasio making an appearance at her job. She forgot about illegally purchasing a gun. She forgot about the visit with her brother. For a second, her world was all right, as her boyfriend spun her in circles.

Setting her back on the ground, a wide grin spread across his face, and Miah brushed a soft kiss across her lips. "I have one more thing to show you."

"One more? No. This is enough. My books, my posters, my mirror ... the pictures. I couldn't ask for more."

"Then it's a good thing you didn't." Slowly, he turned her around toward the right corner of the room.

Even with all the spinning, she'd missed the keyboard on the stand. Red bow and everything. Bella blinked and swiped at the tears that threatened to spill over. Then her gaze lifted to the wall behind the keyboard. Her collage. The one she intended as a Christmas gift for Miah. And it had been finished.

He had done so much in one day to make her world right. And all she had given him in return were lies, omissions, and grief. Bella glanced at the warm, loving smile on Miah's face. Could she tell him everything that was going on? Lord knew, she wanted to open up to him. Let him in on the ugly parts of her world. Hadn't he already been through the worst with her? "Miah, I—"

"Knock, knock. Hope I'm not interrupting anything." Miah's father stepped into the room.

Bella turned her attention to the man, welcoming the distraction. Her mouth had opened, but she wasn't certain how much of the truth she was ready to reveal.

"No. What's up?" Miah said to his dad.

"Detective Russell is here to speak with Bella. Think you can join us in the kitchen?"

"Um, yeah, sure." Bella paused and glanced at her boyfriend. "Come with me?" Bella turned to Miah's father. "That's okay, right?"

"It's your call," his father said.

Jeremiah eyed his girlfriend. He swore she was about to say something when his father showed up. He would rather he and Bell finished their conversation, but they could take it up later.

Hand in hand, the two of them followed his dad.

His father glanced at Detective Russell as they approached the dining room table. "Bella's requested Jeremiah be present."

"Of course." The detective gestured to two chairs across from him.

As they sat, Bella asked, "Is something going on with my case?"

"I do have news, as well as a few questions."

"Okay."

"Petar Jacobs is being released—"

"What? Why?" Jeremiah was stunned. The guy'd raped his girlfriend, and he was being let out of jail? How the hell had that happened? One of her rapists was still on the loose, and the other one was getting off scot free? The freaking justice system at work.

He turned to see Detective Russell pulled a manila folder out and slid it across the table toward Bell.

"I know the sheriff told you about Detective Simms's involvement," the detective said. "That he switched the samples. We finally located the original DNA sample from your rape kit. We had it tested, and Petar Jacobs wasn't a match. Since we've been able to prove chain of custody, the charges against him are being dismissed."

"Did you find a match?" Bell asked.

Jeremiah was confused. She acted as if none of this was news to her. It sure as hell was news to him. Had she planned on telling him any of this? Or was Bell keen on keeping even more secrets. Internally he sighed. Great. Just when he thought things were improving.

"Yes. It matched Gervasio Rodriguez."

At that, Bell dropped her gaze and sudden tears spilled down her cheeks.

Damn it. He was being a selfish jackass. There she was, hearing someone she once considered a friend wasn't one of her rapists, and that they had DNA confirmation for someone else, and all he could think about was what she was keeping from him.

Jeremiah wrapped Bell in a hug and held her for a moment. "Do you need a break? Or do you want to pick this up at another time?"

"No. I'm okay. Really. I'm just ... I'm relieved. I never wanted to believe Petar could hurt me like that." Bell swiped beneath her eyes.

His father handed Bella a tissue. Jeremiah watched as she wiped away the rest of her tears. Not that they appeared to be tears of relief, despite what she'd just said. Her shoulders slumped a little, as she spoke. It was such a tiny gesture, if he hadn't been so close, he might not have noticed it. There was something she wasn't saying. But what?

Collecting herself, Bella looked back to Detective Russell. "What about my other attacker? Have you ... you been able to identify him?"

"I believe so. I've got a photo array for you to look at, if you're up for it."

"Yeah." Bella nodded.

The detective pulled out a stack of photos and laid them in front of Bell, one by one.

Jeremiah studied Bell's features as she focused on each picture. It was hard to tell at this angle, but something seemed off with her. Now that he thought about it, she'd seemed out of it when she walked in the door. What was going on? It definitely—

"Him. It's him," Bella said, pointing at the photo in front of her.

"Are you sure?"

"Yes. It's the eyes. I know them. He's my other attacker."

"His name was Rolando Gomez," Detective Russell said.

"What do you mean 'was'?" Jeremiah raised an eyebrow.

"He was among several bodies we found in a mass grave behind a cabin under a name we've linked to Gervasio Rodriguez," Jeremiah's father said.

Jeremiah blinked. Bodies? How many people had this Gervasio killed? "Tell me you're going to catch this guy."

"We're doing everything we can, son." His father rested a hand on his shoulder and squeezed.

"That's what I wanted to talk to you about, Bella," Detective Russell said. "It isn't a coincidence that Petar was framed. He's connected to Gervasio through his younger brother, Cristobal. Do you ever remember running into him at the detention center?"

Jeremiah leaned back in his chair and draped an arm behind Bell's shoulders. Now, she looked tense. Seemed logical, though. This couldn't be an easy conversation for her.

"Once. The guards usually tried to get me through when the halls were empty. But I remember one day, Cristobal was leaving my dad's office, and we bumped into one another. Bad timing, I guess."

"Did you talk to him at all?"

"Not really. Just apologized and then my dad stepped out of his office. I went in, and my dad sent Cristobal on his way."

Crossing his arms, Jeremiah looked back and forth between Detective Russell and Bell. Petar was connected to Gervasio through Gervasio's brother, Cristobal. Bell's brother, Luis, was connected to Gervasio because he once worked for the guy. Would make sense that Luis knew this Cristobal guy. Jeremiah had agreed to keep the information about Luis between Bell and himself, but it seemed important to the case. Why wasn't she saying anything?

Detective Russell stood. "All right. I appreciate your time."

"I'll show you out." His father and the detective left the dining room.

Bella slid her chair back. "Thank you—"

"You aren't going to say two words to them about your brother?"

"There's nothing to tell." Bell stood. "And you agreed to keep that to yourself."

"Yeah, but what if he can help? He may know this Cristobal kid, which could help the police find your rapist."

"Let it go. Luis can't help." She turned around and disappeared down the hallway.

Something was definitely going on with her. But what? He wasn't going to get any answers like this. And she wasn't going to offer any, either. Jeremiah frowned. How in the world was he going to get her to open up to him?

t w e l v e

The computer *beeped*, snapping Luis out of snooze land. He rubbed his eyes and eyed the monitor. It had been a long night watching the system running a decoder. The lockbox had an eight-digit combination, and the options were numerous. Now, though ... Was he seeing this right? Blinking, he leaned over, knocking a file off the desk in the process, scattering the pages within it. Bending over, he grabbed the file and the loose pages—and stopped. What the hell?

It was the folder Bella had shoved into his hands last night. He'd forgotten all about it. But ... what were these pictures of their mother? What were all these reports? He gathered the papers and sat back in the chair. He scanned the photographs first. Bruises on his mother's face, neck, arms, and thighs. Cigarette burns. Then there was the picture of the rope. And her clothes. These were crime scene photos. He'd seen enough of them to know.

Luis turned his attention to the other pages. Two police reports. Two medical examiner reports. But hadn't his mother committed suicide? So why would there be these reports claiming the manner of death as murder?

The cabin door opened, and his father stepped inside. "Have you accessed the code?" the man asked—a reasonable question, but not one Luis could answer at the moment.

Instead, the question "How did my mother die?" propelled from his mouth. He needed answers. The information in his hands contradicted everything his father had ever told him.

"I told you before, your mother was very sick, and it forced her to take her own life. Why—"

"Then why the hell am I looking at a report that says she was killed?!" Luis glared at his father. The man was lying. Something he was good at.

"What are you speaking of?"

Luis jumped to his feet and shoved the police report in his father's face. "This! This is what I'm talking about."

His father took the report and glanced at it, then shifted his gaze to Luis. "Where did you get this?"

"That's not important."

"*¡Mierda! ¿De dónde has sacado esto?*"

"*¡De mi hermana!*" Luis spit the words out before he could stop them. He hadn't meant to tell the man where the documents had come from. Not that he knew how Gigi ... he sighed. Who was he kidding? Only one person could've found this. Heather.

"Get rid of it. Forget you ever saw any of this. Do you understand?" his father demanded.

Luis crossed his arms. "No. I want answers. I deserve to know what in God's name happened to my mother. Now, you either tell me the truth, or I go to the police with everything I know. *¿Comprende?*"

His father leaned back against the wall and crossed his arms. "Your mother was murdered. I used my influence with the police and the medical examiner to have new reports generated deeming it a suicide. I thought it was safer for you and your sister."

"Why?"

"Because I could not take the chance of our enemies discovering the truth."

The guy was still dodging questions. A master manipulator, his father was, but that wouldn't stop Luis from getting what he wanted. He closed the file and stared at his father. "Which is what?"

"That there was a traitor in our family."

What? No way his father meant someone in the gang killed his mother. No way. It simply wasn't true. The gang didn't—the computer *beeped* again. Luis glanced over his shoulder. No. That was not the code to access the lockbox. He looked from the monitor to the lockbox, then back again. It had to be wrong. It absolutely could not be 09101997.

Luis keyed in the eight digits, praying they would not work. But the lockbox clicked. One half of the puzzle. "Dad, why is the access code to Gervasio's lock box the date of my mother's death?"

Gervasio yanked open the drawer and tossed out all the clothes. Fuck! Nothing. He searched the entire dresser and found nothing. He kicked the piles of crap all over the floor. Where could his lockbox be? Maybe there was a hidden panel under Luis's bed. He knelt down and checked the bed frame. Gervasio felt along the crevices and scanned the bolts. Nothing out of the ordinary. No special spring action panels.

He stood and eyed the piles of clothes and books scattered everywhere. He'd covered every part of the room, from the desk to the closet to the dresser to the bed. He'd smashed the computer monitors. Nothing in them. There was nothing left to touch.

Scanning the room one last time, his eyes stopped on the clock on the wall. Shit. Was it really almost three o'clock? His girl would be out of school soon.

He had to go.

Leaving the room as it was, Gervasio strode toward the front of the house, halting at the window. He pulled the blind aside, just a sliver. Nobody on the sidewalk. No cars coming. He was good to go. Moving around in broad daylight on his old side of town wasn't the wisest decision, but it was necessary. Gervasio slipped out the door, tugged his hood up, and made his way across the street, keeping his head down as headed to his truck.

He drove toward the high school. His girl had been back in school full time for a few weeks, now. Visiting her at the coffee house yesterday was the beginning of a fresh start for them. This time, he'd get her all to himself—as long as he planned everything right.

She would serve as the perfect bait. He'd get all the incriminating documents back and destroy the warehouse, Luis, and his girl's boyfriend all at once—then he'd leave with his girl.

If he was lucky, Juan would arrive in time to enjoy the show, then die, too. No way was he leaving that bastard alive this time around.

About six car lengths in front of him, a black Volkswagen pulled out from the school parking lot. It was his girl, but she was going the wrong way. The coffee house was the other direction. So, where the hell was she heading?

He preferred to tail someone with at least two cars between him and the mark. Unfortunately, traffic was light and there weren't any cars between him and his girl.

Gervasio slowed as Bella turned into a business driveway. He passed her, so as to be inconspicuous, then turned around at a gas station down the road and headed back to the driveway where she'd pulled in and spotted her car parked three spots down. Seemed she'd already gone inside. Parking himself, he shut off the ignition, pulled his hood back up, and got out of the truck. Keeping his head down, he stopped at a bench by the building's entrance, lifted a foot, and pretended to tie his shoe. He glanced up. *Luna Hills Recovery* was scrawled across the doors.

So. His girl had gone into rehab. At least Tommy had done one thing right. Gervasio shoved his hands in his hoodie pockets and headed back to his truck. This would prove useful. It might even be the opportunity he'd been seeking. She drove herself to this place, regularly, he guessed, along a rather long and empty stretch of road. With no cameras. The perfect place for a snatch, but it would require some planning.

Her car couldn't stall out too soon or too late. It had to be just right. She had to be left alone. Gervasio smiled. And the only person she would have is him.

"Bella, would you like to address the group?" The group leader asked.

No. Not really. Bella leaned forward, digging her elbows into her thighs. She wasn't ready to talk about it like the others did. Their stories were almost all the same—they knew their attackers—although the circumstances differed. One girl had been assaulted by an ex-boyfriend. Another had been raped repeatedly by an uncle. Only one other girl had been attacked by a stranger. Her attacker had never been caught, either. The girl still had no justice. Their situations were almost the same. Almost.

But there was something else they all shared. As if wasn't enough that they'd all been attacked, they'd all been ridiculed too. People whispered behind their backs, called them names to their faces. It was horrible. Like Bella, these girls all had some days at school that were harder than others because of what people said about them. Like they were at fault.

"Okay, maybe tom—"

"You know what I hate the most?" Bella interrupted the group leader. "What people say about me. Like I deserved it. Like, somehow, it's all my fault, like I did something ... something to provoke ..." Bella paused. That word. That word. She still struggled with it. Why was it so hard to say? Because it made her a victim. And she was not a victim.

"It's okay. Go on." The leader nodded, with a kind look on her face.

Bella lifted her gaze to the girls in the group and eyed them, one by one. That's when she realized why they talked about their attacks. It was a way for them to take their power back. So, they were no longer victims. Maybe she didn't like the word, but ... the attack, the ... rape ... It did make her a victim. But she didn't have to stay that way.

Bella sat up straight. "They talk about me like I provoked my rapists. I always knew people could be naive, but it just seems downright cruel to blame me for the rape. It wasn't my fault! It wasn't my fault. I didn't ... I didn't do anything wrong. I didn't even know him or that he knew me. How can I be responsible for someone I don't know?"

"I used to think the same thing," Margot, a quiet girl, sitting to Bella's left, said. "I didn't know my rapist. How could it be my fault? I asked some of the people who blamed me how it was my fault. No one ever had an answer. It took me a little while to realize they weren't really placing the blame on me. People just don't want to believe anyone could be that evil. It's easier for them to believe I somehow encouraged him or that I misinterpreted the events."

Bella looked around the group, at the faces of the girls who'd experienced such terrible things. "There are evil people in this world," she said. "Yesterday, I found out my rapist not only framed somebody else for raping me, for getting me pregnant, but that one of his ... associates tried to kill me and caused me to miscarry. How is that not evil?"

"I'm so sorry you had to go through all that," the group leader said. "I wish there was a better answer than the one Margot pointed out. Unfortunately, she's right. We desperately want to believe there is good in people. Thinking anyone could be that evil, it contradicts that, and some people don't know how to wrap their head around it. It's hard for them to understand that, while most people fall in the middle of the spectrum, some go to the extreme—on both ends."

Even as Bella was shaking her head, she could see the sense this made. "So, it's easier for them to blame me than to accept that someone would go that far to hurt another person." Yep. The world was an ugly place. Well, not all the time. Bella eyed the other girls. Each one of them had experienced something awful, but it brought them all together. And that was comforting.

The leader responded. "Yes, but that's why we talk about rape. That's why we share our stories. Not just so we can heal, but also so we can educate the world and let people know that rape is not okay."

Bella dropped her gaze to the floor. Yeah. That's what she was trying to do. Heal. But not just by talking. Gervasio was definitely evil. And she was chasing him. With everything she knew about him, she was deliberately hunting for him. If she did find him, and something happened, there would be no way to redirect that blame. It would be on her. Her fault.

Was she willing to put Miah through that? To make him face all that again? Or worse, to mourn her? All because she was so determined to do something she had no business doing. No. He deserved better. He deserved the truth.

Okay, then. She'd talk to Heather on her way home. And tell Miah the truth, tonight. Bella sighed. What fun.

"If we're going to discuss this, can we at least do it upstairs?" Heather started up the stairs toward her bedroom. What was it with Bella and Luis and surprise visits? Was it something in their blood?

Bella followed after her. "There's nothing to discuss. I'm done looking for Gervasio."

"Then I guess you don't want to know what I found out." Done, her ass. She'd spent the last two days digging into Petar's background. It sure as hell wasn't going to be for nothing. And if they gave up on looking for Gervasio. then that's exactly what it would be for—nothing.

"Why? What did you find out?"

Heather opened the door to her bedroom and headed to her desk. Her laptop, a Dell XPS 15 9530 got the job done, but what she really wanted was an Alienware. She'd kill for it. Dropping into her chair, she glanced over her shoulder. "Close the door behind you."

Shutting the door, Bella sighed. "What's with all the cloak and dagger? Couldn't you have just told me what you found downstairs?"

"I'm going to remember that the next time you ask me to do something illegal." Heather scanned the information on the screen.

Bella walked over. "What exactly are we looking at?"

"An arrest record for Petar. Do you see what I see?" Funny. She knew about the arrest in Rescate County, but she hadn't expected to find the one in New York. Heather glanced at Bella.

"Does that really say he was eight?"

Heather nodded. "Joyriding." What eight-year-old joyrides? Not the point. She scanned the rest of the report. "Holy shit."

"What—wait, does that say he was arrested with Cristobal Rodriguez?" Bella pointed to the screen as she asked.

"Guess they've known each other longer than we thought." Heather hadn't expected her search to actually lead somewhere. She'd been bluffing, just wanted to keep Bella from quitting. But the fact that Cristobal and Petar were arrested together ten years ago in New York City, that was huge, no doubt.

"They were both underage, so it would make sense this hasn't shown up on any records. Does it say what happened?" Bella was practically fogging the screen with her breath, she was bent so far over Heather's shoulder.

Heather's eyes flickered over the screen. Then she saw it. "No fucking way." She pointed. "They were released into the custody of a Jorge Wong." Could it be another alias? Oh, please let it be another alias. She had run out of steam on the other two aliases she had found for Gervasio.

Bella read what Heather highlighted with the cursor, then backed up and sat on the edge of the bed.

"Look, this could be the break we've been searching for," Heather told her. "It could be exactly what we need to find this guy." Heather spun the desk chair to face the geek. Thus far, it had been one dead end after another. But this could be the thing he didn't want anyone to find out about. It was another alias they had to explore.

"And it could lead us nowhere."

"I get it. You're frustrated. We haven't really done anything, but chase our tails. That has to give at some point, right?"

"I just don't know how much more of this I can take."

Boy, did she understand that feeling. Heather leaned back in her chair. She was good at hacking and finding things and people. No one had ever eluded her the way Gervasio had. The guy was better than most at staying hidden. He didn't have much of a paper trail. At least not that she'd been able to locate. And money was obviously no object. This, though … She just hadn't thought about using Petar as a starting point before.

"I know. But let me see if I can find anything under this name. See if it pans out. And if it doesn't, we'll stop looking."

"You don't get it. It isn't just the endless searches that don't lead us anywhere. It's the constant lies. Every time I have to tell Miah another lie, it hurts us. At this point, I'll be lucky if he forgives me, let alone stays with me."

"Is that what this is about?" Heather narrowed her eyes. The geek could've told her boyfriend the truth—although the fact that her boyfriend's father was a sheriff would have complicated things.

"Sacrificing my relationship with Miah? Yeah. That's enough to make me quit."

Heather sat up. That was complete and utter bullshit. When they began this whole thing, the geek had seen red. It was all about getting back at the person who'd hurt her the most. And now she was quitting? Whatever the reason, they needed to get some things straight. "Then you need to think about why you're really doing this. Because I thought you wanted to find Gervasio so he couldn't hurt another woman. So you could keep your boyfriend safe. Maybe even make Gervasio pay for killing your father. Or did I miss something?"

Bella sighed. "That is why, but I realized I was causing more damage than doing good. And that some things aren't worth the price."

"Then just tell your boyfriend the truth. Hell, while you're at it, tell the sheriff all the information you found on Gervasio. Including the fact that he's responsible for your mother's death." Heather reached over for the file she'd put together earlier and handed it to Bella. Turned out there had been a couple more reports tucked away on the Ileana Costa murder. It was a low blow, but it was all she had left.

Bella opened the file and scanned its contents. She looked up, a shocked expression on her face. "What?"

"Yeah. His thumbprint was found in the master bath." Heather paused. She had no clue how much of the information had been shared with Juan Castell. Or if any of it had. With what it took for her to find it, it had probably been overlooked. "People don't always think about wiping off the toilet handle."

Bella slapped the folder shut. "Fine. See what you can find on Jorge Wong."

Jeremiah stared at the basement ceiling. He'd turned the lights off at least a half hour ago. Maybe longer. This would be the second night he'd sleep without Bell in his arms. He hadn't joined her in bed last night. Nor would he tonight. Not after he suggested she tell his father about Luis. After that, she shut it down and walked off. So, this was on her.

Weren't things supposed to be getting better between them? Weren't they at a point in their relationship where they talked things out? He sighed. They should be and yet—

He heard the door at the top of the staircase creak open and someone start down the stairs. They weren't his father's footsteps. Much lighter.

Jeremiah rolled over to see Bell stopping at the last step.

"Hi," she said, quietly.

"Hi." Should he say something else? Like, *Hey, come join me in bed.* Ugh. The situation wasn't his fault, and he didn't want to be the one to initiate the conversation. Still. It was better than silence.

Jeremiah opened his mouth, just as Bell said, "I'm sorry about last night. I know you mean well, I just ... I don't think it's a good idea to get your dad involved. Or, rather, the police."

Jeremiah sat up. "Why not?"

"Because ..." Bella paused and sighed. "Luis is already looking for Gervasio."

"What? Wait, back up. How do you know this?" Jeremiah frowned. All right, the guy was Bell's brother, but how much time had she spent with him? He only knew about the time in the coffee shop and then the night of their date. Had she gone back to the cabin since then? And why hadn't she told him? Had she ever intended on telling him?

"I've seen it on his computers."

So. Apparently, she'd spent a lot of time there. And it had to be recent. Obviously, she lied to him about some of her comings and goings. Jeremiah reached over and flipped on the light. He needed to see Bell's face, to see if she was lying about anything else.

Bell looked ashamed. "I know I should've told you sooner, but I think deep down I kind of hope Luis finds him before the police."

That was insane. Bell had been thrilled to find out she had a brother. Why would she be so quick to sacrifice him? Jeremiah thought back to the night he'd met Luis, when Luis asked Bell to give their father a chance. A chance to do what? Why hadn't Jeremiah asked then?

Bella stepped closer and sat on the bed, looking at him closely.

Jeremiah stared back. "Does this have something to do with your birth father?" It made sense. Why else would her brother have brought the man up? Jeremiah ran a hand across the top of his head. Lord, this was some messed up shit.

"Yes," Bella said, taking his hand. "I think he's working with Luis."

"And if they find him? It isn't like they're going to turn Gervasio over to the police."

Bella glanced down. Should she say it? "No. They'll probably kill him." She regretted the statement as soon as it left her mouth.

"Please tell me you're joking."

Bella sighed. She didn't know much about her birth father. But there was that new information about her mother's death. Plus, there was the way her brother had become so adamant about finding Gervasio, himself, and keeping her safely away. "I'm not. I really believe they intend to kill him."

"You can't be okay with this?"

"Honestly, I don't know." It was true. Part of her wanted Gervasio in jail. Part of her, actually most of her, wanted Gervasio dead. She wasn't sure if she was okay with her brother and father planning to kill someone. Even if that person had ripped her apart. But maybe she was.

Miah dragged his hands down his face. "Okay, how do I not tell my dad about this? I need you to help me understand, because I don't really want to be in this position."

"What? Don't want to feel like you're stuck between a rock and a hard place? Welcome to my club." Bella flopped back on the bed. She'd been in that position so many times over the last couple of months. It sucked.

"Bell, come on. Please explain this to me. You want me to back you? Then I need to understand where you're coming from."

She turned to look at him. She owed him that much, she thought. Earlier she'd promised herself she'd tell him whatever he wanted to know. Now, Bella stared at the ceiling, hands folded across her stomach. "I keep thinking about what happens if the police find him. They have all the proof they could ever ask for that he raped me. But then what. Would they try to make a deal with him? Plead him out so I wouldn't have to testify? Or would we go to trial? What if a jury finds him not guilty? Or what if he goes to jail and escapes again?"

"I get it, but that's the justice system at work."

"But how is that justice? And who's getting justice? Me? My dad? What about all the other lives he's destroyed? Or the lives he could still destroy?" This wasn't something she'd pieced together overnight. It had taken her weeks to come up with all the ways things could go wrong.

"It's you getting justice. Your dad. All the people he's hurt. That's how it works. We don't exact our own justice—we let the jury decide. As for what happens afterward ... I don't know." Miah echoed her sigh with one of his own.

Her boyfriend was talking to the angel on her other shoulder. The one who knew that the whole eye-for-an-eye thing was outdated. That the person getting revenge wasn't any better for it. It just ended the fight. Or added to it, depending on the revenge extracted. Which was really the reason she'd wanted to get out of the search. But then Heather had thrown fuel on the fire in her heart that Bella had almost extinguished. Jorge Wong, indeed.

She still hadn't answered Miah, though. "That's why I gave serious thought to what I think Luis and my father are planning."

"But how can you even justify that?"

She tried to explain. "Because it would be over. There would be no court, no people to convince I'm telling the truth, no possibility of him escaping. I wouldn't have to look over my shoulder, anymore. I could move on. My mom could come home."

Miah dragged a hand across the top of his head. But before he could speak, Bella had one more thing to say.

"That's why I decided not to tell your dad or Detective Russell about my brother." Bella leaned up on her elbow and eyed Miah, closely. That was it. She'd laid everything out. Well. Sort of. She hadn't uttered a word about her own search. Or that Heather had been helping her. She bit the inside of her cheek.

Now would be the time to tell him. Except deep down she knew the new alias wouldn't lead anywhere. Nothing would come of it. So, why shake the foundation of their relationship over something that was going nowhere? Bella sat up and pressed a kiss to Miah's cheek.

He smiled at her and said, "I get it. I don't entirely agree with it, but I get it. If you don't want to tell them about Luis, then I've got your back."

"Thank you."

"You're welcome. Now, what do you say we head upstairs and go to bed?"

Bella smiled. "I'd like that."

thirteen

Thursday afternoon, and the last bell had rung. Bella had everything she needed for her homework tucked safely in her backpack. Tightening her hold on the strap, she looked at the lockers across the hall, where her best friend was standing talking to another girl. Alex was the last person Bella had to speak to about the letter.

When the other girl walked away, Bella strode across the hall, weaving around the gaggle of students trying to rush out the door. "Hey."

"Took you long enough."

"Huh?" Okay. She deserved that. A week had gone by since she dealt with Sarresh's letter. There had been other pressing matters. Not that she—

Alex gestured to the other side of the hall. "I saw you hanging around. I thought you were going to hover all day."

Oh. "Sorry about that. I didn't want you to think I was trying to pin you down or anything." Bella felt her face heating up. "God, that came out wrong. I just meant … we don't have to talk about it if you don't want to. The letter that is."

"B, it's okay. I know you were going through some shit. And I know you wrote it because you care." Alex smiled.

"So, we're good?"

"Yeah. We're good."

Bella blinked. Wow. Talk about easy. Wait, that was too easy. "I'm confused."

"About?"

"How's it possible you're all right with everything and everyone else had questions?" Bella shifted her backpack. She'd prepared all day for this conversation. And it wasn't even necessary?

"Mandy and I talked a few days ago. After you told her about the whole David situation. I guess I realized I wasn't mad. And the questions ... I kind of figured it out for myself. I know I always talk about a silver lining, but I don't think I could've found one, either, if I'd been in your shoes." Alex shut her locker, slung her backpack over her shoulder, and gestured for them to walk.

They walked side by side, like they used to do. Something so small and it mattered so much. "You're the first one to say that. I can't tell you what it means to me."

"I do have a favor to ask."

"Anything." Her best friend had handed her forgiveness on a platter. Given the secrets Bella'd kept from all of them, she probably didn't deserve it. But she'd take it, anyway.

"We may not understand everything you're feeling, but please, still talk to us. I promise we won't turn our backs on you if just talk."

Talk to her friends. That would be easy—and complicated, too. On future issues, she could absolutely do that. But past stuff? That wasn't included. Right? Right. "I can do that."

"Good. I'm glad to hear that. Think we can hug on it?"

"I thought you'd never ask." Bella and Alex hugged. Bella missed having her best friend around to hash things out with. It was nice to have that back.

"Thanks, Sergeant. I appreciate you letting me know." Jamar hung up the phone. Another juvenile file for Petar Jacobs and Cristobal Rodriguez to be unsealed. This time in New York. How long had these two known one another? He sighed. With Petar's release, he figured they had gotten all the information from him that was pertinent to the case. Guess the kid would have to be called in for another conversation. That could be handled by his detectives. Right now, he had adoption documents to review.

It had taken four long, overseas calls to convince Milena to send him her copy of Bella's adoption record. It had come in a couple days earlier, but the legalese was tough to get through. A lawyer could've probably read it over and found the answer faster, but he didn't trust anyone local to handle the job.

There was a knock at his door. "Come in," Jamar said, without looking away from the computer.

Ali poked her head in. "Hey, Sheriff. The ADA has been updated with everything we've gathered on Gervasio Rodriguez."

"Good. I take it he upped the charges?"

"Yeah. Said it's all been filed."

"Now, we just have to find him." Jamar muttered. Not that they weren't searching every part of town for this jackass. He had every available resource scouring warehouses, cabins, even abandoned buildings for this guy. Not to mention the digital stuff Ali had been digging through.

"Sheriff?"

Jamar looked up to see Ali still standing there with a manila envelope in her hand. He waved her in. "What's going on?"

Ali stepped in and closed the door behind her. "You know I've been going through all the evidence stored at the Simms's ranch, right?"

"Sure. You find something?"

"You could say that." Ali held out the envelope.

"Is it on Gervasio?" A lot of the evidence that had been stowed away was linked to Gervasio or his gang. Most of it kept gang members out of jail. Something he'd begun to rectify.

"No, sir."

"Anyone we know?" he asked, opening the envelope.

"Sir, it's about Russell."

He paused. "As in Detective Russell?"

"Yes, sir. I found it tucked away in a desk in Simms's parents' home."

"Of course, mother." Heather smirked as she stepped into her bedroom and shut the door. Another workout after dinner. Sure. She had nothing better to do on a Friday night. She flopped back on her bed, grabbed a pillow, and screamed into it. This was the longest her parents had been home in months. Why couldn't they leave already?

Sneaking out to eat a burger and the greasiest fries she could find sounded better and better every day. If she had to eat one more salad, she might stab herself. Then again, maybe she would die from dehydration with all the sweat she'd been pouring out at the gym lately. These last five pounds were going to kill her. No doubt about it.

Her laptop beeped and pulled her out of her pity party. Heather dropped into the chair at her desk and scanned the monitor. "Holy shit."

It had been a long shot, but her search paid off. She snagged a pen and scribbled down an address, then dug out the burner phone. She dialed and drummed her fingers against the desk. One ring. Two rings. Three rings. "Come on. Pick up."

"Hello?" the geek said.

"What took you so long?" Heather got up and headed over to her closet.

"I'm at work. I couldn't exactly rush to the phone just because you called."

Black jeans. Dark t-shirt, Heather thought. "Well you're going to have to leave. I found something, and we need to check it out tonight."

"What? No. I can't leave, and I've got Vick's birthday party tonight."

"You'll have to be late. Besides, nobody arrives at a party on time." Heather crouched down and scanned the closet for the perfect pair of shoes. Yes. Her black combat boots.

"Can't this wait?"

"No. Listen to me. There's a warehouse just outside the county limit that came up under my search for Jorge Wong. It's scheduled for demolition on Monday." This would be their best chance to sneak in unnoticed. Places like that always had people buzzing around a couple of days ahead of time.

"Shit."

"I'm going to text you the address of a diner not far from it. Meet me there in an hour. And make sure you wear black." Heather figured this would give her time to shower, change, and get past her mother. Plus, it would be dark enough for cover by then.

"Okay." The line went dead.

Heather disconnected her own phone. Now for the fun part.

Bella swept the flashlight beam from one side of the warehouse to the other. Her phone buzzed in her pocket. She dug it out and saw another text from Amanda. At this point, she was only a half hour late. Yeah, well, she was going to be a hell of a lot later. It would take at least forty-five minutes to get to Vick's house. She sighed. This better not be another bust.

Tucking her cell phone in her back pocket, Bella took another step into the warehouse. "It looks empty," she whispered to Heather.

"This place has been on the chopping block for a while. So, people have probably been working to clean things out."

"Great, so he may not have even been here recently." She was no more likely to find Gervasio than she was to cross paths with her birth father. How had she let Heather talk her into this? This was such a waste of time. Time she didn't have.

Heather shone her flashlight to the right. "Hey, what's that?" she asked, moving toward a desk the beam illuminated.

Bella followed Heather. The desk itself didn't look very interesting. What caught her attention was the map of Rescate County and outlying counties spread out across it. There were black dots all over the map. "What is this?"

"I think he's been here."

"You think?" Playing her flashlight across the map, Bella studied the dots. One looked like it could mark the diner she checked out a couple weeks back. Another appeared to be the warehouse where they were standing. She didn't recognize any of the other marked spots.

"Wait a minute," Heather said. "Isn't this where the Detrones live? Where you've been staying?" Heather pointed to a dot just outside Nautica Valley.

Bella looked closely, hoping Heather was mistaken. But she wasn't. "I think it is." If this map belonged to Gervasio, he'd known where to find her all along.

"We need to take this back to the diner so we can study it. Figure out what all these places are." Heather rolled the map up.

"I can't. I need to get to Vick's party."

"But this is what we've been looking for."

Yeah, and it had been easy to find. Too easy? Bella shook her head. "It could be a trap. You ever think about that? Gervasio is too smart to leave something like this by accident."

"All right. I see your point. So, take me back to the diner. I'll get my car and check these out at home," Heather said.

Bella's agreement with Heather was that she would only keep searching for Gervasio if this lead panned out. The map seemed like the perfect clue. Too perfect?

Her cell phone buzzed again. This time the text was from Miah. She had to get to the party. Putting her phone back up, she sighed. "Okay, that's fine."

"Good. Let's get going. This place is starting to creep me out."

"Really? Now it's creeping you out?" Bella asked, as they headed toward the back window they'd climbed in earlier.

With her backpack slung over one shoulder, Aurora handed a couple of dollars over to the vendor in exchange for a hot dog slathered in mustard, peppers, and onions. It wasn't like the dogs back home, but it sufficed. Another cheer erupted from the stands behind the vendor. She nodded toward the stadium. "What's going on there?"

"Soccer game."

Right. Just head straight to the parking lot. She'd been successful in avoiding David all week. Spying on him would not help keep the separation between them she believed was necessary. Aurora walked away, took a bite of her hot dog—then stopped and glanced back toward the stadium. Even if she did watch the game for a couple of minutes, it wasn't like David would notice. He'd be too busy on the field. Maybe she could—

No! Had she learned nothing since she left home? Aurora inhaled deeply and continued forward. She pulled her phone out and checked the location of her taxi. Crap. Still a good fifteen minutes away. She looked at the stadium. Five minutes couldn't hurt. Right? Right.

Aurora finished the last of her hot dog and tossed the trash as she headed toward the central divide in the stands, stopping at the bottom of the upper level. From there she had a perfect view of the field. She shoved her hands in her pockets and stared across the field, spotting David just as he scored a goal. Yes! The stands erupted in another cheer.

She scanned the bleachers behind her. Aside from the incident earlier in the week with that douchebag Keith, she had paid her fellow students no mind, and they barely even noticed her, which was exactly the way it should be. So, what was she doing standing here? She couldn't attract anyone's attention. She had to stay low-key. It was the only way to find the person she came for. Not to mention, stay out of trouble.

The crowd broke into a groan. Aurora shifted her gaze back to the game. The other team had scored. Damn it! Come on.

Soccer wasn't really her thing, but she knew enough to follow the game. She watched as the ball got kicked out of bounds, and David tossed it back into play from the sidelines. The way he moved amazed her. She'd seen him work out in the gym, but to see the results of it …

The crowd erupted into a full-blown cheer. Aurora looked down to see David high-fiving his teammates. They'd won. She smiled. Team spirit wasn't high on her agenda, but his happiness was a good thing.

As David turned toward the crowd, his eyes met Aurora's, and he waved.

Just then, her phone vibrated and snapped the connection. Shit. She turned and practically ran toward the parking lot.

What the hell? Where was she going? David jogged up the bleacher stairs two at a time, not stopping until he reached the top. His girl had just been there. Where'd she—? Then he spotted her about thirty feet in front of him. He pushed his way through the throng of students heading toward the parking lot. When he got to the front of the stadium, he scanned the lot and saw her climbing into a taxi.

He sighed. Why would she have watched the game? Watched him, only to jet the moment their eyes connected? It didn't make any sense. Maybe if he knew who she was, he could figure out why she affected him the way she did. She wasn't like any woman he'd ever met, including Bella. And that was saying something.

David cut through the bleachers and walked to the locker room. He stepped in just as one of his teammates popped Keith in the ass with a wet towel. Ouch.

Then he remembered. The guy had a run-in with the girl. Maybe Keith had gotten her name before she grabbed his gonads.

David swallowed a chuckle. It was funny, but only in principle. "Hey, Keith. Can I talk to you for a sec?"

"I had nothing to do with that ball going out of bounds."

"Oh, yeah. I know. It's not about that." David crossed his arms. Actually, Keith had been at fault, but he wanted information, and playing the blame game would get him nowhere.

Now that he had the guy in front of him, he had no clue how to approach the topic. Though avoiding any mention of the guy's nut-sack sounded like a good call. David eyed the floor for a second, then lifted his gaze. "You know that girl you hit on, Monday? The one who's locker is beside mine? You ever get her name?"

"You mean the redhead with the tits? Nah. She never mentioned it."

David inhaled through his nostrils and forced himself to stay in control. Popping the guy in the mouth for a chauvinistic asshole comment would end in a fight. And he definitely didn't need that. At least not with his parents still in town. "You know anyone who might?"

"James might. He has Spanish with her. Hey, James. You know that redhead in your Spanish class? You know her name?"

James joined Keith and David. "Um, I think it's Aubrey or Arlie or something like that. I'm pretty sure it starts with an 'a'."

"Thanks guys." David gripped the back of his neck and headed for the shower. At this rate, he'd never find out who she was or get her to talk to him. He looked back at his friends. At least they hadn't asked him why he was asking. There were just some things he wasn't ready to own up to. Not yet, anyway.

fourteen

Jeremiah parked just outside Valley Coffee and Beans, pulled out his phone, and shot his sister a quick text. He'd waited at Vick's party for over an hour, but there'd been no sign of Bella. And she hadn't answered any of his texts. As he climbed out of the Dodge, his cell beeped. Checking Mandy's response, Jeremiah sighed. Bella still hadn't arrived. He scanned the parking lot. His girlfriend's Beetle was nowhere in sight.

He stepped inside the coffee shop, surveyed the tables and the counter. No Bella, but he did know the cashier. Jeremiah smiled. "Hey, Jamie, is Bella around?"

"Nope," the cute, silver-haired cashier replied. "She left a couple of hours ago."

Jeremiah crossed his arms. That made no sense. If Bella had been gone for over two hours, where the hell was she? And why wasn't she answering his texts or calls? "I don't suppose she left her phone here by accident?"

"I doubt it," Jamie said, in a weird tone.

"Why do you say it like that? Like she isn't coming back any time soon." Jeremiah frowned and stepped closer to the counter. Something was going on, but what?

"Well, she may come back, but only as a customer."

"What are you talking about, Jamie? She works here."

The woman glanced over her shoulder, then leaned towards him. "Not as of a couple hours ago," she told him in a low voice. "She got a phone call and said she had to leave. Frank told her if she left this time, not to come back."

"Phone call? From who?" Jeremiah watched Jamie straighten up as the manager poked his head around the corner. Okay. He could play this game. Jeremiah pointed to a scone in the display case and dug out his wallet. Information on his girlfriend was worth a five-dollar scone.

Jamie boxed up the pastry and shrugged. "I don't know, but it's always the same. She gets a phone call, takes it outside, and five minutes later she walks out the door."

"Thanks." Jeremiah paid, collected the box and left. No way he was going back to the party, now. He needed answers. And that meant he'd have to do something he swore he'd never do. Trust was a two-way street. His girlfriend had broken his for the last time.

Bella eyed the clock and drummed her fingers against the steering wheel. *Come on, come on.* The party had started over two hours ago, and now the traffic light was taking forever to change. When it finally turned green, she gunned it through the intersection. Taking a right two blocks up, she clipped the curb—and inhaled deeply. Running late was no excuse for driving like an idiot. She narrowed her eyes at the almost-empty street. No way the party had broken up already.

Bella pulled into the Hilliard's driveway just as Amanda and Vick exited the house. Shutting off the ignition, she grabbed the bag off the passenger seat and got out of her Beetle. "Hey," she called. "Where is everybody?"

"Probably halfway to the bowling alley, by now," Amanda said.

"Wait. I thought the party was here."

Vick shook his head and crossed his arms. "It was ... two hours ago. I'd ask where you've been, except I don't care. No one was dying, and that is the only thing that would've been more important than you missing my birthday party."

Bella sighed. He was right. Her explanation would be complete bullshit. "I'm sorry, Vick. I meant to be here sooner. This wasn't what I planned. I know nothing I say will change the fact that I'm late, but I did get you something." She tried to hand him the birthday present she held. "Here, this is for you."

Vick wouldn't take the gift. "Intentions don't equal actions," he said. "And actions are what matters. I thought we'd gotten past all this. Guess I was wrong." Vick turned around and got into his truck.

"Mandy—"

Her friend's face was stony. "Save it. Nothing you could say right now will make this better. So, take your present and go home. At the moment, none of us want you around,"

Of all the reactions Bella had anticipated, she certainly hadn't expected to be shunned. Her friends were turning their backs again, except this time she deserved it. Today had been all about her, not the one person it should've been about. "Mandy, I know you think I'm a horrible human being, but will you at least take Vick's gift? It'll be something for him to open later, anyway."

"I don't think you're horrible. Selfish, but not horrible." Amanda sighed and accepted the gift bag.

"I really am sorry."

"I'm sure you are, but apologies won't fix this. You really screwed up. I hope it was worth it. I think you should go home, now, though." Amanda turned and climbed into the passenger side of the truck.

Bella stood watching as Vick backed the truck out of the driveway and drove off down the street. Why couldn't she have just told Heather no? Or suggested they go to the warehouse after the party? Except then she would've had to tell another lie to make it out there. Nothing about this situation was simple. Damn it. She kicked at the driveway.

Then the burner phone in her back pocket vibrated. She dug it out and said, "You find something?"

"Yeah, and it's not good."

"Great. Like my day hasn't been bad enough." Bella frowned. She'd been fired. Missed one of her best friend's birthday parties, then got into an argument with said friend. What else could go wrong?

"As much as I hate it to make it worse, I don't feel like I have much of a choice."

"Just spit it out already, Heather."

"Those dots on the map? They represent places connected to you. The sheriff's house, the school, your job, your friends' houses. Even the facility where you've been getting treatment at. They're all on this map."

Bella swallowed. *Worse* didn't begin to describe how bad her day had just gotten. He'd been watching her. She surveyed the dark, empty street. He could be watching her now. Shit. *Okay. Keep your cool,* she told herself. She had to stay calm. Inhaling deeply, she opened the door to her Beetle and climbed in.

"Heather, look carefully. Are there any of the places I go that aren't marked on there?"

There was silence for a moment. Then Heather said, slowly, "I think there's only one. Look, you know I'm the last person to suggest this, but I think it's time we got your boyfriend's dad involved."

Yeah. Telling Sheriff Detrone was a great idea. They could tell him all about their hacking and sneaking around. Not to mention the warehouse they'd broken into earlier. Sounded like a plan. Bella backed the car out of the driveway. "Just tell me what isn't on the map, Heather. Then we can talk to the sheriff in the morning … after I figure out what to tell him."

Jeremiah's gaze drifted from the dresser to the bookcase to the closet to the nightstand and stopped on the bed. It had only crossed his mind once in the last few weeks to search his girlfriend's bedroom for answers. Tonight was the second. But he had no clue where to start. Or even if he should. He rubbed the top of his head. Then he decided. He had to do this. Bell was hiding something. He was certain of it.

Jeremiah strode around the bed and opened the closet doors. He looked in shoeboxes, checked through Bell's backpack, shoved clothes around, but found nothing of interest. Getting down on his hands and knees, he lifted the bed skirt and looked under the bed.

What the hell?

He tugged out the box he'd found and plopped it on the bed. It was an ordinary, brown box, with flaps that were tucked into one another.

When Jeremiah opened it, although he could see several notebooks and a few photo albums packed into it, what caught his immediate attention was the opened letter resting on top of them. He scanned the letter not once but twice to ensure he'd read it correctly.

To the Rescate County Sheriff's Department,

Enclosed is everything you need to fully convict Gervasio Rodriguez for sexual assault and drug possession and distribution. Decoding information has been provided and attached.

Sincerely,
An anonymous friend

Who the hell was this "anonymous friend," and why did Bell have a letter from them tucked in a box under her bed? Lifting the letter to set it aside, Jeremiah's eyes stopped on a bottle of pills nestled tightly between the notebooks and the photo albums.

Just then, his phone rang. He checked caller I.D. Mandy. Jeremiah answered, "Hey, sis."

"Listen, I only have a couple of minutes, but I thought you should know Bella showed up as we were leaving."

"She tell you where she'd been?"

"No, but I didn't ask. Vick was upset, and honestly I just wanted to get him away from the situation," Mandy said.

"I take it she's not joining you at the bowling alley, then."

"No. I told her she should just go home."

"Good." Jeremiah picked up the pill bottle. If she did come home, she could answer some questions.

"Everything okay?" Mandy asked. "You sound weird."

Yeah. He probably did. It's not every day one finds a bottle of pills belonging to a recovering addict who got addicted in the first place due to a brutal rape. Never mind the fact that the pills were hidden away with evidence of said rape under the victim's bed. The reality he knew had just shifted on its axis and knocked him to the ground. "I'm fine. No worries, sis. Go back to your boyfriend."

"All right. Call me if you need me."

"Will do." Jeremiah disconnected the call and tossed his phone on the bed. He had no idea what kind of painkillers Bell had gotten addicted to, never mind what they looked like. But he was certain these pills had not been purchased from a local pharmacy, since the little bottle had no label.

"Miah? What're you doing?"

He turned around to face his girlfriend and held the bottle up for her to see, clear as the night sky after a heavy rain. "I'd like to ask you the same thing."

"Where did you ..." Then Bella spotted the box in her boyfriend's lap. Shaking her head, she walked around the bed and headed straight for the closet. This was the last thing she needed to deal with right now.

Jeremiah set the box aside and stood. "That's it? You're not even going to try to explain this to me?"

"There's nothing to explain. I haven't taken any of them." She'd forgotten Tommy had even given her the pills. They'd been tossed into the box of evidence she had yet to turn into the police. Hmm, that might be the answer she and Heather needed. Instead of telling the sheriff about her's and Heather's antics, she could just turn over the box of evidence. Something else she couldn't deal with right then.

"And I'm just supposed to believe that?"

Bella grabbed a small suitcase out of the closet and dropped it on the bed. Then she began pulling clothes out of dresser drawers. "Why would I lie about it?"

"Why would you lie about it? You mean like you've been lying about work?"

"What're you talking about?" Bella tossed a handful of clothes in the suitcase and stopped. She looked at her boyfriend. What did he know?

Miah narrowed his eyes and crossed his arms. "Oh, I don't know. Maybe about you getting fired because you just had to leave again like you've been doing for weeks. Where the hell have you been going? And who the hell have you been talking to?"

Shit. This should've been a quick in and out for clothes—she didn't have time for this conversation right now. Bella dragged a hand down her face. "Miah, please. It's not what you think. I'll explain everything, but I can't do it right now."

"I don't know what the hell I'm supposed to think, Bell. You've been lying to me for weeks, now. Not to mention this secret stash of evidence you've kept hidden away. And let's not forget the pills. Or that you've been unreachable for hours. You don't think any of that warrants some explanation? That's bullshit, and you know it!"

"Dammit! I didn't say I wouldn't explain. I just can't do it right now." God, why couldn't he just accept that? Bella frowned. She couldn't stop. She wasn't safe here. She yanked out another drawer and shoved more clothes in the suitcase.

Miah flipped the lid of the suitcase shut. "I don't think you get it. There is no other time besides now."

"You don't mean that." Bella stared into those bright green eyes of his. Her favorite part of him. She loathed the idea of walking out the door and leaving him so angry, but she didn't have a choice … even though this was definitely not how she'd anticipated her night going. Fighting with her friends, with her boyfriend, and all because she'd been determined to find her rapist and avenge her father.

"Yeah, I do."

Bella dropped her gaze to the suitcase. Seconds mattered when it came to safety. Not just hers, but the Detrone's as well. Miah's safety. As much as she wanted to explain everything to him, his life was more important than answers. She closed the suitcase, picked it up, and lifted her eyes one last time to Miah.

"I'm sorry," she said—and walked out the bedroom door.

fifteen

Jeremiah stared at the empty doorway. Had Bella actually walked out of the bedroom as if nothing just happened? As if they hadn't argued? As if her lies hadn't caught up with her?

He glanced around the room. The open drawers and clothing strewn on the floor confirmed he hadn't imagined the entire conversation—a conversation that left him with more questions than answers. Jeremiah aimed a kick at the cardboard box, which slammed into the wall and landed, spilling all of its contents.

Dammit! He would not chase after Bell again! This had become a thing with her. Anytime they got into some kind of argument, Bell stormed off, and then he apologized first. Not this time. This was not his fault! All she had to do was answer his questions. Instead, she'd walked away.

Jeremiah groaned. *Shit.* Throwing the pill bottle aside, he strode out of the bedroom and down the hallway, just as the front door opened and he heard his mother say, "Go on and get ready for bed. I'll be there to tuck you in shortly."

His younger brothers shuffled through the door and past him toward their bedroom without any argument. Their night must've been as exhausting as his, and his mother followed behind with the twins in her arms.

"Hey, Jeremiah. I wasn't expecting to see you home so soon," she said.

"Yeah, I. Uh ..." He paused. What could he say? Without revealing what he knew of Bell's situation.

"Hey, son," his father said, coming in carrying Jeremiah's younger sister, Natasha.

"Why don't you hand Nat over to Jeremiah and go get the boys settled?" his mother said, glancing toward his father.

"Sure."

Jeremiah collected his sister from his father's arms and followed his mother toward the bedroom Natasha shared with the twins. Holding his baby sister made his problems disappear for a moment. Too bad they would still be there when he put her down.

"So, do you want to tell me what's going on?" his mother asked, as she set each twin in their own crib.

"What do you mean?" Jeremiah laid Natasha on her bed and crossed to her dresser to get her a nightgown.

"I mean, why are you here? Or maybe you could explain why Bella ran out the door and peeled off like she was being chased."

Clutching his sister's nightgown, he dropped his head. He had no idea what to say. Bell had left him with more questions than he'd started with. Jeremiah sighed. "Honestly, I don't know."

"You don't know why you're home early? Or you don't know why Bella ran off?"

"We got into a fight." It was the simplest way to explain the situation. Without giving anything away. What would happen if he told his mother everything? She'd probably tell his father—or *he'd* be forced to tell his father. Would Bell get in trouble? There were the pills, which he assumed were drugs. Plus, the evidence in the box.

Jeremiah bent to change Natasha into her nightgown. Looking at her sleepy face, he thought, *Man, what I'd give to be that innocent again.*

"At the party?" his mother asked, continuing the discussion.

"No. Bell never showed up at the party." Well, that wasn't entirely true. According to Mandy, Bell showed up after everyone left.

"I see. Why don't I go put on some tea, and we can talk?"

As the screen door opened, Bella half glanced over her shoulder—she was more spooked than she wanted to admit. But her best friend had welcomed her with warm, loving arms—and now had emerged from the house with mugs of cocoa for them. It was nice, after the night she'd endured, and there was nowhere beside Alex's back porch she'd rather be right now. Although she still had to make a decision about the Gervasio situation.

Alex handed Bella her cocoa and sat beside her. "Do you want to talk about it?"

No, she didn't. Not really. The argument with Vick had been bad enough, but her fight with Miah made everything else seem meaningless. It wasn't just that he hadn't believed her about the pills. That she could've dealt with. But the ultimatum he laid out, what was she supposed to think about that? Had their relationship really reached its end? Bella stopped chewing on the inside of her cheek long enough to sip at the hot cocoa. "I think ... I think we're over."

"You and Jeremiah?"

For a moment, Bella said nothing. Maybe if she didn't say it, it wouldn't be true. She stared up at the night sky and tugged the light jacket tighter around her shoulders. She could *maybe* it all she wanted, but it wouldn't change what happened. If she had to let Miah go to keep him safe, then so be it. Her bottom lip trembled, and she wiped at the tear that rolled down her cheek. "Yes."

"I thought you guys were doing really good. What happened?"

"He found out ... some things and wanted an explanation. He told me if I didn't give him one, then that was it. And I ... I just couldn't give him what he wanted." More tears trickled down her face. Her world was crashing again, and she had no idea how to fix it.

"Okay. I'm confused. Why couldn't you just tell him?"

Bella wiped the tears away and inhaled a deep breath. How to answer that question? She didn't want to put Miah between her and his father. Or make him choose what was right. Not again. Hadn't she already put him through that choice when it came to her brother? Plus, knowing too much would put him in danger – and risking his life was not an option. "I wanted to protect him."

"Did you tell him that?"

"I couldn't. I just asked him to trust me. Even with everything he'd found ..." God, she was stupid. She'd asked him to trust her, and she couldn't trust him. Bella slammed her fist on the chair's wooden arm. Dammit. She could've told

Miah everything and given him a chance. Just a chance.

Alex reached over and gripped Bella's hand. "Hey. None of that. No matter what happened, Jeremiah loves you."

"He found the evidence I've been hiding. He found the pills I kept. I didn't take any, but I still had them. All that, after he found out I got fired because of these trips I've been taking with Heather; it's enough to test anyone's love." Bella blinked. The words had tumbled out and she couldn't stop them. Part of her felt better for getting it all out. Part of her despised the fact she dumped it all on her best friend.

"Okay. I get that he found out a lot of stuff at once. Even if it tests his love, though, it wouldn't make him stop loving you. You have to believe that."

Bella leaned her chin in her hands and sighed. "I want to, but what if I've put him through too much?"

"Think about everything he's already done, everything he's seen you through."

"But that's the problem, right? He's already been through too much. Then I go and hide all this from him. I don't deserve for him to stay."

Looking back, Bella realized that she'd never considered what chasing Gervasio would do to her relationship. The pain it would cause the people she loved most. She'd been so set on revenge, nothing else mattered.

"Do you remember when he broke up with you last year?"

Bella shifted her gaze to her best friend. How could she forget? The things he'd said to her had been awful. "Of course, I do. It was the worst feeling in the world."

"Right, but when you talked about it later, he told you he only did it because he thought he was protecting you, correct?"

"Yes." Miah had ended the relationship to keep her safe. And now she understood his reasoning. Bella looked out over the backyard. This time was different, though. She could just feel it. He meant what he said.

"Well, back then, did you think he was bullshitting?"

Bella had believed every word he said to her. The truth had been in his eyes. Those sparkling, emerald green eyes of his. "No, of course not."

"Then what makes this different?"

"I ... I don't know. I mean, he lied to protect me, right? But he doesn't know I'm trying to protect him. There's so much I haven't told him." Like about her hunt for Gervasio. Or that she'd bought a gun.

"Look," Alex said, with real compassion in her eyes. "I'm not saying turnabout is fair play. You've both lied to protect the other. It isn't great, but I also don't think it's the end for your relationship, either."

This was why she loved Alex. Not once had the girl asked her to explain anything. Not once had she indicated she didn't believe Bella. Alex accepted what Bella told her as truth and offered reassurance that it would all work out. The girl was a real friend. She was Bella's silver lining. "Maybe you're right. I just can't lose him over this. Not when I've been so stupid."

Alex grabbed Bella's hand and squeezed. "Then give him the night to cool down and go back in the morning. Talk to him. Tell him everything. He'll understand. He may not agree with what you've done, but he'll understand."

That's exactly what she would do. She'd also deal with the box full of evidence and do what she should've done when her brother first gave all that stuff to her.

Bella nodded. "Thanks Alex."

"So, you don't know where she's been all day?" Christine asked her son. Jeremiah made it a personal mission to know where Bella was at all times.

Jeremiah brushed the top of his head, nervously. "Not after she left work. I just know she'd been gone a couple of hours by the time I got there. According to Jamie, Bell got a phone call that pulled her away." Jeremiah looked stricken. "I just don't know what do about this, Mom."

Christine leaned back in the kitchen nook. It made no sense. She'd spoken to the group coordinator earlier that day and learned that Bella had finally opened up in group. The girl was getting better. Learning how to live a full life after the rape. Everything that had taken Christine an entire year to figure out after her own rape it seemed Bella was doing in just months.

She frowned and returned her attention to her son. It was time. God, she'd prayed this day would never come. "In the fight you guys had, you said Bella told you she'd explain it, not then, but that she would. Do you believe that?"

"I don't know. I want to. I mean, I know she's come to me with other stuff that's going on. Things she didn't have to tell me, but she did."

"Did she tell you those things when you first asked? Or later?"

She remembered that, right after she was raped, the last thing she wanted to do was talk about it. But then one night with Jamar, it all changed. Christine sipped at her tea. Yuck. Cold chamomile tea wasn't very tasty.

Jeremiah looked puzzled. "I guess mostly it would be a day or two after I asked."

Christine got up and walked over to the kitchen sink. She emptied her mug and rinsed it out. "If she's come to you before, then give her the chance to do so again. I'm sure she'll explain what's been going on."

"What if she doesn't?"

"I have faith she will."

"I don't know, Mom. It feels like this time is different."

Placing the mug in the drainer, Christine picked up the dish rag and wiped the counter. It didn't need to be cleaned, but she had no idea how to broach what she had to tell Jeremiah. She sighed. Then again, maybe she did. "Trust me on this. I know what Bella's going through."

"Mom, you know I trust your instincts, but you didn't see her."

"Jeremiah ... this has nothing to do with my instincts. I understand what Bella's going through because I've been there. I've gone through it, too." Christine draped the dish rag over the edge of the sink and leaned on it for support.

"What? What do you mean?"

Christine shifted her gaze back to her son. "I'm a rape survivor. So, I know what she's going through. I know how hard it is to trust people again when you've been raped."

"Mom! How? When?"

"The details aren't important. All you need to know is that I got through it, so I know Bella will get through it too."

"Does Dad know?"

Christine turned toward her son. "Yes. Your father knows everything that happened."

"Does Mandy?"

"She knows I'm a survivor, and that's all she needs to know." Like she'd just said, the details weren't important. Though from what Jamar had told her, her daughter knew more than she preferred.

"I don't ... I'm not exactly sure how I'm supposed to respond to this."

"Honestly, you don't have to say anything. I dealt with it a long time ago. I told you because I want you to understand why I say what I do when it comes to Bella. Okay?" That was the person who mattered right then.

"Okay. I'm gonna go to bed." With a nod, Jeremiah stood.

"All right. Good night."

Jeremiah stepped into the hallway, paused, and glanced back. "Mom ... for what it's worth, I'm sorry you had to go through that."

sixteen

His plan had been executed perfectly, and he owed it all to a map. Gervasio lifted the binoculars to his eyes and looked down the long, winding road. After puncturing the Beetle's tire, he hadn't hung around waiting for his girl to leave. Though he suspected she would—and right on time.

Yes! Gervasio grinned as the Beetle rounded the bend. At this range, the car was just a speck on the road, so he couldn't see how the tire was holding out. But Plan B had been set up, just in case. Though, unfortunately, the car would spin out more if that had to be utilized. Regardless, Plan A or Plan B, his girl would end up off the road. With few if any cars passing way out here, and at least ten miles from her friend's house—or any house for that matter—she'd be at his disposal.

He tossed the binoculars into his backpack and, stepping out from behind the tree line, climbed down into the ditch. Then, laying down the backpack, he dug out the syringe from its front pocket.

Sure enough, just as she approached Gervasio's hiding place, he heard the Beetle slow and ease to the side of the road. Then the ignition shut off, the door opened, and footsteps crunched over the gravel.

"Damn it," his girl said, and her footsteps clumped back to her car.

When he heard her pop the trunk, Gervasio crawled out of the ditch and snuck up behind her. He wrapped his bicep around Bella's throat and held tight for a few seconds, then slammed the needle into the side of her neck—and she drooped in his arms.

Lowering her to the ground, he released his grip, yanked a zip tie from his back pocket, and tied her wrists as she came around. Choker holds never lasted long, which was exactly why he brought along the Special-K. It might take a couple of minutes, but it would make her compliant. At least until he got her back to the warehouse.

"No ..." Bella mumbled.

"Save your strength," Gervasio said. Then he scooped his girl up and laid her down in the backseat of her own vehicle. When he had her safely tucked away, he closed the car door and the trunk. Then he jogged to a spot about twenty feet in front of the car and collected the spike strip he had laid out. No need to shred the tire. Plan A had worked beautifully.

Hoofing it back to the car, he set the spike strip and backpack in the passenger seat and climbed in behind the wheel. Before slowly easing the car forward, he glanced to backseat and grinned. His girl was a little out of it, but she wouldn't stay that way for long. "No worry. You awake for important part."

No need to repair the tire. His girl's car didn't have far to go. He drove less than half a mile up the road and grinned as he sighted his truck. Pulling the Beetle off to the side of the road, Gervasio shut the ignition off and climbed out. He grabbed his girl from the backseat and tossed the keys to the ground.

"Do you know what the fight was about?" Amanda held the phone against her ear with one hand and brushed her hair with the other.

"B told me some of it, but I don't think it's my place to tell. I just want Jeremiah to know she's going to talk to him about it," Alex said.

Damn. Amanda frowned. If Bella had talked to Alex about the fight, it had to be huge. Maybe it had something to do with why Bella missed the party last night. No wonder her brother didn't want to join them this morning. "Okay. I'll let him know."

"Thanks, Mandy."

"Don't mention it. I'll talk to you later." Amanda set her cell phone down and pulled her hair up in a ponytail. She grabbed the t-shirt off her bed and tugged it over her bikini—but a morning in the pool with her family could wait a few minutes. She walked across the hall and peeked into her brother's bedroom.

Jeremiah sat on the bed, attention focused on his laptop.

She couldn't tell for sure, but it appeared he was playing with music. Really? Shaking her head, she knocked on the door.

He looked up. "Hey, sis."

"Hey ..." Amanda paused. She didn't want to just toss out what Alex had asked her to share. She shoved her hands in the front pockets of her denim shorts. "Are you sure you don't want to go with us?"

Closing the laptop, Jeremiah nodded. "I need to be here when Bell gets back."

This gave her the in she needed. Amanda stepped into the bedroom. "Have you heard from her at all?"

"No, and honestly, it's driving me crazy." Jeremiah rubbed the top of his head.

"Do you want to talk about it?"

Jeremiah shrugged and then sighed. "I found out she's been keeping secrets from me, and I didn't handle it all that well."

"What do you mean?" Amanda walked over to the bed and sat down.

"I gave her an ultimatum. Either she tells me what's going on ... or we're done." He sagged a little more with each word.

Amanda's eyes widened. Well, she definitely didn't expect to hear that. Her brother was usually more level-headed. When did he become so dramatic? "I take it she didn't respond the way you thought she would."

"No. She apologized ... and walked out. I know, not one of my best moments. But what if it was Vick keeping secrets from you?" Jeremiah leaned back against the stacked pillows.

That was easy, she and Vick didn't have ... Well, that wasn't true. Amanda frowned. Vick's birthday present from Bella was a secret. And she hadn't told him the truth about her father. So, they had secrets. But this wasn't about her and Vick. Time to change the topic.

"Listen, Alex called me this morning. I guess Bella crashed at her place last night."

Jeremiah sat up. "She say anything else?"

"Just that Bella should be coming back to talk to you." Now she really wished she had pressed Alex for more details. Enough that she would have something to offer some kind of comfort to her brother. Amanda gripped the back of her ponytail.

"Did she say when?"

"No, but I would think soon. I can't imagine Bella would put something like that off. It sounds too important—"

"Hey, Mandy. Are you ready to go?" their mother asked from the doorway.

"Yeah. Give me a second, and I'll be right behind you." Amanda grinned.

With a quick nod their mother headed down the hallway.

"Go on. Have fun. I'll be okay," Jeremiah said.

Man, she was a horrible sister. Her brother could say he'd be okay until he went hoarse, but he obviously wasn't. Not that she could make him talk about whatever happened. Against her better judgment, Amanda relented. "All right, but if you need me, you know the drill."

"This should work." Using a pair of tweezers, Luis laid the latex fingerprint on top of Cristobal's finger. It was the last part of the puzzle. The code to the lockbox had been cracked a couple of days ago, but it also required a fingerprint scan.

"Why does it have to be my finger?" Cristobal asked.

Luis sighed. How many times had they gone over this? He might strangle Cristobal before they had a chance to test this out. "I told you; your hand is closest in size to Gervasio's."

"What happens if it does not work?" Luis's father asked.

"If the protocol Gervasio has in place is standard, then everything in the box disintegrates." Something this secure had to be important. Man, this had better work. Luis focused on getting the latex on Cristobal's finger perfectly.

Then, inhaling deeply, Luis set the tweezers aside. "Give it a go."

Cristobal nodded, input the eight-digit code and placed his finger over the scanner.

The lockbox beeped, and with a hiss it opened.

Luis exhaled the breath he'd been holding. "Holy shit. It worked." He looked to his father and grinned. Oh, yeah! Damn, he was good!

"Now let's see what required so much protection." Juan eased Cristobal to the side and lifted the lid. He stopped and went perfectly still.

"What is it?" His father didn't respond. Luis glanced past his father at the items inside. Lot of protection for a cassette tape and a small stack of Polaroids. He reached over and picked up one of the photographs. Then he blinked. No. This wasn't ... this couldn't ... no way this was his mother. Luis stared so hard at the photo, he barely heard his cell phone ring.

Forcing his gaze away from the horror in front of him, Luis dug his phone out of his pocket and checked the caller I.D. His sister. How could he talk to her at a moment like this? He had to find a way. Ignoring her wasn't an option. Taking a second to collect himself, he answered. "Hey, Gigi. What's going on?"

"Your sister not available. She ask me to call instead."

"Where the hell is my sister?" Luis growled. *Son of a bitch!* But he needed to get a hold of himself. Going off on Gervasio would not help his sister—wherever she was. Luis glanced at his father, who was clearly listening.

"No worry. She okay. For now."

Think, Luis, think. Getting his brain in gear, Luis turned the speaker phone on and walked across to his desk. "I want to talk to her."

Gervasio snarled. Then the phone shifted, and the man yelled, "Speak."

"Luis ... I need ..." Bella slurred the words.

Damn it! She'd been drugged. He had to find her, and now. Luis tapped a few commands on the keyboard.

Juan stormed over, snatched the phone, and spat, "What did you do to her?"

"Nothing yet, old man." Gervasio gave a surprisingly high-pitched cackle.

Shit! Luis grabbed the phone from his father and took it off speaker. The man hadn't dealt with Gervasio in years. The last thing they needed was for this storm to become a hurricane. "What do you want?"

"Good to know your father can come out of hiding."

"What do you want, Gervasio?" Luis repeated. He wasn't going into his father. Up until that moment, Juan had appeared to be useful. But he'd determine how useful his father truly was when he got his sister back safe and sound.

"It quite simple. You have something that belong to me. I certain you know what. I want them back."

"Fine. I'll get them to you. Then I get my sister." Not that he was going to give Gervasio anything, not without a back-up plan. Luis knew better. Gervasio was too obsessed with his sister to give her up for a lockbox and some records—no matter how incriminating.

"Of course. I sure by now you know where. You have one hour."

Luis glanced at the tracking system as the line disconnected. A nice red dot blipped at him. He snatched the camera off his desk and turned to Cristobal. "I need you to find a cassette player so you can copy that tape. Now!"

With a nod, Cristobal ran toward the back.

Getting the cops involved was only part of the solution. Luis scooped up all the photographs from the lockbox and laid them out, one by one. The story they painted was awful—and it fully supported his sister's theory that their mother had been murdered. Even told them who was responsible.

Juan pointed at the blip on the monitor. "Is this where he is?"

"Yes, but we can't go in half-cocked."

"I understand."

His father was the other part of the plan. The one that would leave Gervasio with no way to escape. Luis clapped his hand on the older man's shoulder. "Good, then let's get to work."

With the call ended, Gervasio yanked the back off the phone and removed the battery and microchip. His girl's cell phone had served its purpose. Then, he dug his burner phone out of his pocket and dialed. As much as he despised using the New Yorker, the guy came in handy when it came to money and information.

"El Silbón, three times in one month. I'm flattered."

There was no time to waste on the New Yorker's nonsense. "All accounts set?"

"Yes. You're ready to go. Everything you need is at the location, as requested."

"Excellent." Gervasio hung up. Tucking the phone away, he glanced at his girl and caressed her cheek. Money had been moved and their new home had been established.

"Please ... please let me ... let me go."

"We leave soon enough." With company on the way, he had to finish setting up the welcome he had planned for them. Four large plastic drums had been rigged throughout the warehouse, one in each corner. Gervasio double-checked the wiring and blasting caps on each. It had taken him weeks to get them filled with the appropriate proportions of ammonium nitrate and fuel. A timer would set off the primary explosion.

And that primary explosion would initiate the secondary explosion— the dynamite he'd rigged to the support beams. Between the two blasts, this warehouse would collapse. And burn. As would everything inside it. And. It. Would. Be. Beautiful.

"What ... what are you ... doing?"

All the components were in place. The only thing left was to review their exit strategy. "I make sure no one follow us. I all you need."

"What?"

"No worry. We be out before boom." Gervasio verified the door opened as it should. Good. He walked to the front of the warehouse and peered out the window. Everyone his girl loved would be taken out at one time.

"What if ... I go with you?"

Gervasio turned and studied his girl. Had she just volunteered to leave with him? It wouldn't stop anyone from coming after her, though. Plus, she was coming down from the Special-K. Still, she made the offer. "You not run? We marry. You carry my child?"

"Yes. Yes ..." Tears rolled down Bella's cheeks.

Of course. She might have convinced him, if she hadn't cried. But those tears, they weren't tears of joy. They were tears of loss. If she thought she was feeling pain now, she had no idea how bad it was about to get. Gervasio closed the distance between them and slapped her across the face. "You cannot protect them. They die today."

Jeremiah stared at the food inside the fridge. Nothing looked appetizing. But he really needed to eat. Breakfast was the most important meal of the day. What a crock of shit.

He grabbed an apple and closed the refrigerator. His mother and siblings had been gone over an hour and still no word from Bell. He hoped she'd show up while his family was still at the pool, so they could talk with no one around. Talk, and decide what to do about that box of hers.

Taking a bite of the apple, Jeremiah glanced at the kitchen phone. He should just call his father and let him know what he'd found. That was the right thing to do. But he desperately wanted to talk to Bell first. Find out why she had the stuff and how she'd come by it.

Then the doorbell rang.

Was it Bell? Maybe she'd forgotten her house keys last night. The bell rang a second time. Good Lord, somebody was in a hurry. He strode to the door and opened it—raising an eyebrow when he saw it was his girlfriend's brother. "What are you doing here?"

Luis pushed in past Jeremiah. "Where's Bella's room?"

"Hold on. You can't just shove your way in here." Jeremiah crossed his arms.

Bella's brother glared at him. "Dammit! I don't have time for this. She's been kidnapped. Now, where the hell is Bella's room?"

"What?" Kidnapped? But … why did it matter where her room was? While he digested this information, Luis was stalking down the hall, looking for Bella's door. Jeremiah sprinted by him and paused outside the room his girlfriend had used for the last couple of months, gesturing for Luis to enter.

Luis walked in and headed for the closet. He half glanced over his shoulder. "You haven't seen a brown box around here, have you?"

The box. Jeremiah should have known. He leaned against the door and took a deep breath. Flipping out over the news about Bell wouldn't do him or her any good. Instead, he'd try to get some much-needed information.

"How about you talk, and then I'll tell you where the box is."

Luis sighed and gripped the back of his neck. "I screwed up. I've been so busy trying to find Gervasio that I didn't bother keeping an eye on her—and now he has her. He's willing to exchange her for the evidence I gave her, along with a lockbox of his we found. But I only have twenty minutes to get to this damn warehouse. Any other questions?"

Well, yes, he did. So many questions, but now wasn't the time to ask. Jeremiah crossed to the closet, snagged a pair of shoes, and slid them on. Then he kneeled beside the bed and yanked the box out. He rose to his feet, box in hand, and headed toward the door. "Let's go."

"What are you doing?"

"What's it look like I'm doing? I'm going with you." Jeremiah continued down the hall, Luis trailing him.

"Oh, no, you're not."

"I don't think you get it. This is the love of my life we're talking about, and I'll be damned if I'm going to stand aside and do nothing." Fight or no fight, Jeremiah loved Bell with all his heart. She was the woman who one day would be the mother of his children. Protecting her was his duty.

"Yeah, and you're hers," Luis replied. "Which is exactly why you're staying put. Gigi will kill me if anything happens to you."

"Then I guess we're all going to have to come out of this in one piece, aren't we?" Jeremiah said. It wasn't like dying was on his agenda today. Neither was rescuing his girlfriend. But one thing at a time. Although, in fact, there was one other thing they needed.

Luis groaned. "Fine."

seventeen

"Slow down Ms. Grayson. Where did you find Miss Kynaston's car?" Detective Russell inquired, as he grabbed his keys. Something was going on, but the teenager's frantic ramblings weren't helping him understand the situation.

"Are you not listening?! It's on the side of the road, State Route 33, by mile marker 20. Something is seriously wrong! Her cell phone keeps telling me she's out of the service area and there's no way Bella would just abandon her car like this."

"I understand. I'll head out there now. Will you ..." His words trailed off as he spotted Cristobal Rodriguez walking in the door.

"Will I what?" he heard the Grayson girl ask.

"I'm sorry. Give me just a moment." Russell pulled the phone away from his ear as Cristobal stopped in front of his desk, carrying a small box.

"Inside is proof you need to arrest my brother for murder," the young man said. "And I can tell you exactly where he is." Cristobal set the box down on Russell's desk.

The detective glanced at the box and opened it. Inside were some graphic photos, Polaroids—but not of someone he recognized. Along with a cassette tape. Cassette tapes hadn't been used in, what, sixteen years or more? And with this the kid was going to tell him where to find Gervasio Rodriguez? "What's the catch?"

"You need to get a squad together, and you need to go now."

"Why?" It wasn't enough to know where to find Rodriguez. They had to strategize a plan of attack. Not to mention getting a warrant.

"Because if you don't, a whole lot of people could die, including Bella Kynaston."

Russell held up a finger and returned the phone to his ear. "Ms. Grayson, I'm going to send someone to you right now. Stay where you are."

"Okay. What's going on? Is—"

"Just stay where you are." Russell hung up and gestured for Cristobal to follow him as he headed toward the sheriff's office.

Sheriff Detrone looked up from a file he was reading. "Russell, what can I do for you?"

Russell tugged the kid into the sheriff's office. "Talk."

"Bella Kynaston's in trouble, sir. My brother kidnapped her. Her brother and boyfriend have gone to stall Gervasio, but we could really use your help," Cristobal said.

"What?" Sheriff Detrone jumped out of his chair.

"Please don't—" A swath of tape slapped across her mouth cut her off. Not that Bella had to say it again. She'd begged Gervasio over and over to simply take her away. But her captor refused to listen. He said there was no sincerity in her words. That it wasn't about being with him, but protecting her loved ones. Which, of course, it was.

Bella watched as Gervasio went to each drum one more time. He was doing something, but she couldn't tell what. *Damn it!* There had to be a way to stop this from happening. She scanned the warehouse, but saw a whole lot of nothing. Her only option was to free herself from the zip ties. How many videos had she seen online about how to get out of zip ties? Dozens. Not that she could remember a single trick right now.

Focus! Bella told herself. She dropped her gaze to the ties around her wrists. She had a little bit of wiggle room. There might be enough she could slip her hands out.

She looked up to see Gervasio walking toward her from the drum on the right wall.

Bella straightened. Time was ticking away, and her brother would be here soon. But she had to go slow, or risk getting caught—and that would help no one. She remained still until Gervasio passed her on his way to a drum in the back corner.

Moving her wrists back and forth, Bella glanced over her shoulder and noted Gervasio's progress. He was headed over to the next drum.

Then, she heard the car doors slam shut.

Shit! No way—

"Finally. Let the show begin." Gervasio grabbed Bella by the arm and yanked her to her feet. He tugged her closer to the back door and stopped with her in front of him.

Okay. Not good. Then there was a click. It was bad enough Gervasio was using her as a shield, but he had a gun, too. Things had just gotten worse. Way worse.

Collecting the brown box and the lockbox from the bed of his truck, Luis eyed the warehouse. It was smaller than he'd expected. Explained why Gervasio had been so difficult to track. The guy's hideout wasn't even on their radar. If the building hadn't already been condemned, it likely would be soon.

"Are you sure this is the right place?" Jeremiah asked.

"Yeah. I traced his call here, so it has to be." They were screwed if it wasn't. Not to mention what would happen to his sister. God, let this be the place. Luis glanced back at the other empty buildings, then at his sister's boyfriend. He was praying to a God he didn't believe in. He believed in luck. And if he was lucky, both plans would go off without a hitch. Because there was no time to come up with another one.

Sighing, Luis stepped forward. "Come on. Bella's counting on us."

They walked toward the front entrance. Jeremiah opened the door, and Luis entered, first cautiously scanning the dim warehouse. Most of what he could see came from the light being let in through the open door behind him. Then he saw them. Gervasio holding his sister at gun point.

"I brought what you wanted," he said, holding out the boxes.

"You also bring guest," Gervasio said.

"Yeah, well, your ledgers were at his house, so I didn't have much of a choice." Luis hoped bringing Jeremiah along would prove beneficial. For sure, the vest offered some protection.

"No matter. Walk forward until I say stop," Gervasio said.

Crap. He wasn't ready. His father was Plan A, but the police were Plan B, and for either to work, he had to stall. And maybe try to get Gervasio to come closer. As it was, no way his father had a clear shot, even with the height difference between Gervasio and his sister.

Hmm, maybe that was it. Luis shook his head. "What guarantee do I have that you won't just kill us after I set this stuff down?"

"I keep word."

"While I'd like to believe that, you're holding a gun to my sister. And the deal is we get her, and you get your stuff back. How about we both move forward?" Luis suggested. It wasn't the best idea, but he didn't have much to work with.

Gervasio pointed the gun at Jeremiah. "Or I could just kill him."

Luis didn't need to see his sister's face to know her reaction. Though if he had been looking at her closely, he might've realized his own forward steps were wasted. But the next sixty seconds happened so fast, Luis could hardly tell what caused what. Let alone how it all happened so quickly.

From the corner of her eye, Bella saw the gun's aim shift to Miah's head. Her heart stopped. No! She couldn't lose him. Not like this! She had to do something, but what? Her wrists were still bound. Gervasio still stood behind her with the gun. And her brother had nothing other than a couple of boxes.

Damn it! She was NOT helpless! Bella blinked … and everything went red. Before she had time to think, she had broken free of her restraints, elbowed Gervasio in the gut, and ripped the tape from her mouth.

But her actions didn't stop the gun from going off.

Miah didn't make a sound, save for the thud as he fell to the ground.

"NOOOOO!!!" Bella cried out. Another burst of rage flooded her body, and she stomped on Gervasio's foot and head-butted him, then ran across the concrete floor toward Jeremiah.

He has to be okay! He has to be okay! He has to be okay!

Her boyfriend had survived one gunshot wound, he could certainly survive another. After all they had been through together, God wouldn't take him away from her. Not like this. Not like this.

Juan stared through the scope of his rifle as his daughter broke free of her captor's hold. He smiled. But it didn't last a second. The way Bella's face was contorted in pain meant something bad had happened—although, from his vantage point, he couldn't see what. Clearing the possibilities out of his head, he focused on his target. As Bella flew out the way, the direct path he had waited for finally opened. An opportunity he'd had at only one other time in his life.

And this time, he wouldn't miss.

Juan squeezed the trigger and watched as the bullet hit his target right between the eyes.

Gervasio Rodriguez slumped to the ground. That man wouldn't hurt his family ever again. Or anyone else for that matter.

Holy shit, that hurt, Jeremiah thought. And the weight of his girlfriend on top of him didn't help. He groaned and blinked his eyes open.

Bella shifted and cupped Jeremiah's cheeks, tears pouring down her face. "You're okay? You're okay!"

Luis knelt on the other side of him. "Did you get hit?"

"Yeah …" Jeremiah moaned. The bullet may not have gone through his body, but it had hit the vest. Thank God, his father kept a couple in the trunk of the Dodge.

Luis unbuttoned Jeremiah's shirt enough that Bella could see the bullet-proof vest.

"Okay. Explains a lot." Bella paused and glanced over her shoulder for a moment, then turned her attention back to Jeremiah. "Can you stand?"

"I think so." Pressing his elbow into the ground, Jeremiah attempted to get up.

His ribcage hollered at him. Right. Nope. That's not happening.

Bella looked to Luis. "Help me get him up. We need to get out of here."

"I don't think he's—"

"You don't understand! This place is going to blow. We need to go. Now!"

Quickly, Bella and Luis each hooked an arm under Jeremiah's shoulders and helped him to his feet. They moved as fast as he could shuffle toward the warehouse entrance. His ribs continued to yell at him, but the impending explosion forced him to work through the pain.

Wait, he'd been shot by Gervasio. What happened to that asshole? Jeremiah peered over his shoulder toward the last place he'd seen the guy—and saw the man's body lying on the ground. He didn't have a chance to ask questions, because, they barely made it to the other side of Luis's truck, when the warehouse exploded and knocked all three of them to the ground.

eighteen

Jamar crossed his arms and stared at the remains of a warehouse. The bomb squad had yet to clear the area, and his own squad's investigation couldn't start until the bomb guys confirmed the explosion had been contained. But he still had to deal with the other half of this ordeal. He glanced over his shoulder to an ambulance parked behind him, then looked to Russell. "Come with me."

"Yes, sir."

With Russell trailing him, Jamar strode to the ambulance. He stopped and took in the sight of Bella focusing on the EMT's progress as he taped the bandage off that had been wrapped around Jeremiah's chest.

Jamar held in a sigh. This could've been so much worse. *God, however we managed to get here, thank you,* he thought. "How's it going over here?" he asked the EMT.

"Looks like some bruised ribs, but we're taking him in to be on the safe side," the emergency tech said.

"Okay. Bella, why don't you come down, and Russell can take you—"

"I'd like to ride with Miah, if that's okay," Bella said.

Jamar studied Bella, then Jeremiah. Disagreeing would be futile. The two were determined to stay together. As he rubbed at his face, he noticed the bomb squad leader exiting from what was left of the warehouse. "Fine, but I'm sending Detective Russell to the hospital. I expect you both to cooperate and answer all of his questions."

"We will, Dad." Jeremiah said, lacing his fingers with Bella's.

As the EMTs closed the back of the ambulance up and took off for the hospital, Russell gave him a sympathetic look. "Don't worry, sir. I'll take care of it," the detective said.

"Thanks. And take Ali with you."

One person had been taken into custody. If his son and Bella hadn't required medical attention, they would've been taken in as well. There was a lot that needed answering, and no time to waste – and Ali was good with an interview.

With that as handled as it could be, for the moment, Jamar turned and approached the bomb squad leader. "What's the verdict?"

"Sheriff, it's all clear. The scene is yours."

Bella squeezed Jeremiah's hand. She almost couldn't believe it. They were both still here. Luis, too. All still alive. "Is it really over? Is he really dead?" she asked, tears welling in her eyes.

"Yeah, I think so."

She had no idea what happened after she broke free and ran to Miah's side. The tears broke free and trickled down her cheeks. "I thought you were dead."

"It felt like it. And I'm not just talking about the bullet hitting the vest ... " Jeremiah paused. "But last night, too. When you left ... I didn't know ... I really thought it was the end."

"I'm so sorry. I shouldn't have walked out. I just figured the less you knew, the safer you'd be, but I was wrong." She understood now that even if she had told him everything, he wouldn't have been in any less danger. If she had told him, maybe she wouldn't have even been kidnapped. Or maybe she would have, but at another time. Bella wiped the tears from her face. Either way, she'd played right into Gervasio's hands and nearly gotten Miah and her brother killed.

"I understand. I felt the same way last year. I can't fault you for that. But I'm not blameless in all this. I flipped out when I found that box and the pills. I didn't handle it very well."

What? How could he say that? Everything that had happened had happened because of what she had done—on her own. Bella shook her head. "This is not your fault. This is on me. I was the one who hid the evidence. I was the one who went out and bought a gun. And I'm the one who ended up with the pills because of it. If I hadn't done any of that, none of this would've happened."

Jeremiah kissed the top of Bella's knuckles. "There's a lot we have to talk about—need to talk about. But maybe we should discuss it when we're alone."

"Absolutely." Bella glanced at the EMT who was sitting with them in the back of the ambulance. Her boyfriend had a point. She would tell him everything. Answer any questions he had. There would be no secrets between the two of them. She would do whatever was necessary to make their relationship work. But at a more appropriate time and place.

Was it really over? Could she truly return home? Milena listened to every word her daughter said, everything she had missed since her departure, from Bella's therapy sessions, to the girl's discovery that she had a brother, to this kidnapping.

Milena shook her head. Bella's biological father had been there, and still her daughter's life had been in danger. And even if Bella's rapist was actually dead, the okay for Milena to return home had not come from the one person she deemed most important.

"Mãe, are you there?"

Milena frowned. Had she been quiet for too long? There was so much to consider. "Yes, I'm here. You have been through a lot, my dear. I am quite glad it's over, and I would love to come home. I've missed you terribly, but—"

"I've missed you too, Mãe. So, you'll start ... Wait, did you say 'but'?"

How could she explain? The last thing she wanted to do was admit to her daughter the reason she'd left. Milena rubbed her now round belly. Especially with another little one on the way, about which Bella knew nothing. It was something the two of them needed to share, the last piece of DeWei that remained in their family. Well, she could wait for *that man* to give her permission, or she could verify what her daughter told her and go home. It seemed a phone call to the sheriff was in order. "But nothing, my darling. I will make the arrangements, immediately."

"I can't wait to see you, Mãe!"

"I'm excited to see you, too. There is something we will need to discuss when I return, but it can wait until then." Sharing the good news of this baby was not something to do over the phone. She would tell her daughter in person. Then ... then they would need to make a few decisions. Beginning with what to do with the house. It contained a lot of good memories, but a lot of bad ones, too. Maybe they should start over somewhere new.

"Of course, Mãe. *Eu te amo.*"

"*Eu também te amo.*" Milena smiled and hung up the phone. Good thing she was only six months along. She could still take the flight from Brazil to New Mexico.

"Thank you, Haylie. I appreciate your checking into it for me." Jamar, phone to his ear, looked up at the knock on his office door. The ADA. Given everything the investigation had turned up over the last few days, he hoped the guy's presence meant good news. Jamar waved the man into his office, as Haylie said, "Of course. I'm glad I was able to help. Let me know if you need anything else."

The call had put to rest his fears over the legality of Bella's adoption. Which, with Bella's mother returning to the country, had been important. Knowing now that the adoption was perfectly legal, Jamar raised his eyes and said a silent *Thank you, Lord*, and gestured for the ADA to sit.

The man got right to business. "Sheriff, after reviewing the evidence, the DA has decided not to pursue charges against Jeremiah Detrone or Luis Hernandez."

Jamar exhaled a deep breath and shot another quick *thank you* to God. Both Jeremiah and Bella had been through enough over the last year. They didn't need the stress of a trial—or even a plea deal. "What made him change his mind?"

"Honestly, I think it was the New York's DA that convinced him to let it go. With the evidence we provided on the death of Ileana Costa closing out a sixteen-year-old case, the guy was happy. He was even more thrilled when we confirmed the death of Gervasio Rodriguez, which saves them the time and cost of a trial."

Jamar nodded. He'd have laughed if it wouldn't have appeared inappropriate. The ADA had delivered the best news possible, not that he was entirely comfortable with the way Gervasio died. But there was no way to know what would've happened if the police had found Gervasio earlier, or if the evidence had been turned over to them when it was initially discovered. "You know what? I'll take it."

"Good. Just do me a favor," Perez said.

"You name it." With things having played out better than he could've hoped, the ADA could ask him for practically anything, and he'd probably agree.

"Tell your son to stay out of trouble. I do *not* want to see his name come up in any kind of investigation again."

"Done. I promise you, if he does get in trouble, I'll have him arrested myself." Funny, of all his kids, Jeremiah was the one Jamar believed he'd never have to worry about. Yet, inside of just one year, the boy had twice come close to landing in jail. Lord, he prayed his younger ones didn't give him this much hassle.

"Let's hope it doesn't come to that." Perez stood, the two shook hands across Jamar's desk, and the ADA left.

Jamar leaned back in his chair. Today had been full of good news. Once Bella's mother returned home tomorrow, things could get back to normal.

Then the file on Russell caught his eye. Well, almost normal.

Taking a couple of clean plates from the dishwasher, Jeremiah glanced over at Bell and smiled. The last few days had been long and had included a lot of talking, but they'd covered everything. She told him about her own hunt for her rapist— and he still couldn't believe Heather helped with that. Then of course there was the gun purchase. Scared the shit out of him when she told him about that. One time he was actually thankful for her brother. Talk about an intervention. As for the pills, he hadn't been sure what to think until she offered to let him talk to her dealer. But there was no need. He was convinced she was really done with them. Yeah, she struggled like any other addict, but he would be there by her side every step of the way to make sure she didn't relapse.

Bella smiled back. "What are you thinking about?"

"Everything it took for us to get where we are, and how happy I am that we made it through." And how much he loved her with all his heart.

"Me, too."

When Jeremiah reached up to return the plates to their proper place in the kitchen cabinet, his ribs throbbed. With a tiny wince, he grasped his side. "Ow."

"You okay?" Bella lifted a towel from the counter and dried her hands.

The bruise from the impact of the bullet against the bullet-proof vest reminded him how lucky he was that he still woke up every day. He'd happily deal with the pain as long as he got to see his girlfriend's exquisite face. A small smile tugged the corner of his lips, and he nodded. "Yeah, I'm good."

"Is it where you got hit?" She closed the short distance between them and placed her hand over his.

"Dad says it'll go away after a bit. Until then, I just have to live with the pain."

"Makes me wish I had killed him."

Jeremiah shook his head. He didn't know what to think about that. One bout of revenge had nearly ripped Bella apart. She wouldn't have survived a second. Whoever shot the guy in the head, he owed them. Jeremiah kissed her knuckles and held her hand against his chest. "I'm glad you didn't. That's not something I would've wanted for you to have to deal with."

"I know, but I just … I can't tell you what those minutes were like for me. I thought you were dead."

"I'm not. You feel my heart beating? It isn't going to stop any time soon. No matter what comes our way, as long as I have you, I'll always have something worth fighting for. I love you Bell, forever and always."

"I love you, too." Bella leaned up on her tiptoes and pressed a soft kiss to his lips.

He slipped a hand to the nape of her neck and held her lips against his. Urgency like he'd felt only a couple times before poured into the kiss. As their tongues touched, a spark of life exploded in his heart. He pulled her closer and wrapped his arm around her waist. Everything they'd faced together since the day they first met flooded through him, overwhelming him. He needed her in a way he'd fought for the past couple of months.

She slid her arms up beneath his t-shirt and gently dug her nails into his skin, sending little spikes of pleasure rippling through his back. Bella had to know he was ready. He lowered his hand down her back, and she pressed her breasts against his chest, encouraging him to keep going. He eased his other hand down and gripped her ass. It felt so good, so firm, he was unable to help himself, and he dropped his other hand and squeezed.

Bella moaned against his mouth and released their kiss. Biting her bottom lip, she looked up at him. "Miah ..."

That one word, as well as everything he felt from her body, told him all he needed to know. Jeremiah brushed a tender kiss against her lips, took Bell's hand, and led her toward her bedroom.

He paused outside her bedroom door—it was his way of letting her know she was in control. They had faced a lot in the last year. The rape. The first shooting. Bell's suicide attempt. The attack which resulted in her miscarriage. The death of her father. Her mother's departure. Bell's addiction and recovery. And the second shooting. Through it all, their love had remained intact. Not that it hadn't gone untested. Something that was bound to happen again, but even if it did, they would be okay, because they had each other.

Bella brushed a kiss against Jeremiah's lips and sashayed past him into the bedroom.

Taking his cue from her, he followed, closing the door behind them—and he pulled her flush against his body, and kissed her like she was his lifeline.

Bella released the kiss, stepped back, and lifted her t-shirt over her head.

"Beautiful," was the only word Jeremiah could manage to mumble, as he gripped her waist, nestled his fingers into her soft skin, and tugged her closer. Then he brushed some of her hair back and captured her lips with his own.

nineteen

"You're the sheriff. Couldn't you have gotten us to the gate?" Bella asked, turning to Miah's father. Yeah, okay, it was airport rules, and the sheriff had little power here, but it would've been nice to wait at the gate for her mother.

"You know as well as I do it doesn't work like that," Sheriff Detrone said.

"I know. I just wanted to make this really special for her." Bella tightened her grip on the bouquet of pink bitter dogbane she had selected as a welcome home gift. It was her mother's favorite flower and was part of a larger gift. She and Miah had spent yesterday cleaning the house, and they'd moved Bella's things from the Detrone's back to her old bedroom. She smiled at the thought of their time in her bedroom. Making a happy memory had been a great way to return home.

Miah draped an arm around Bella's shoulders and kissed her forehead. "I think this will be special for your mom, no matter where you greet her."

"You're right. It's about us coming back together as a ... family."

Just then, she saw her mother walking toward them. Bella blinked. She had to be seeing things. There was no possible way her mother was pregnant. And if the woman happened to be pregnant, no way she wouldn't have shared such news when they were on the phone the other day. Nope. Her mother had simply gained weight. A lot of weight.

"Bella? Oh, my darling, look at you." Her mother wrapped her in a hug, and Bella closed her eyes, as she inhaled the fresh, clean scent that belonged to her mother. How she had missed her. But hugging her mother tightly, she felt something move.

Bella released her hold and stepped back. "Mãe?"

Her mother patted Bella's cheek, gently, and sighed. "I know you're surprised to see me this way, but I simply didn't want you to worry."

"I'm, um, yes, surprised. I'm not exactly sure what to say." Had her mother known about the pregnancy before leaving? What about her father? Had he known? She had no clue what she had a right to ask.

"You don't have to say anything," her mother replied. "But we can certainly discuss it whenever you'd like. For now, why we don't go home?"

Miah placed a hand on Bella's shoulder and squeezed. "Right place, right time."

"Jeremiah's right. With all you and your mother have to talk about, it's something to be done in private," Miah's father said.

Bella glanced from her boyfriend's father to her boyfriend. Those words had applied to their recent discussion, and applied now, as well. The middle of the airport was not the place, nor was her mother's arrival after a long flight the time. Right then. She nodded. "Yeah. Let's go home."

Then, Bella remembered the flowers and held them out. "These are for you."

Her mother accepted the bouquet and lifted them to her nose. "Thank you," she said, with such love in her voice, that Bella knew, despite all they'd endured, all was right between them.

"Do you have any idea what they want?" David asked his sister. His parents had called a "family meeting," not that they could really be labeled a family. Whatever it was, he hoped it was over fast. He planned to hit the gym, then spend some time on the field before the upcoming championship game.

"No, but I hope it's just that they're leaving again," Heather said.

"Makes two of us."

Two sets of heels clacked across the floor. David turned to see his parents stepping through the foyer, looking prepared for travel. He glanced at his twin and smirked. Maybe their wish was coming true.

The butler came through the front door. "The car is ready, sir," he said, with a half-bow.

"Excellent," their father said.

"Heather, David, would you please come here?" their mother requested.

Huh? This wasn't the normal goodbye. Something was up. David raised an eyebrow at Heather, but she looked as confused as he felt. He headed to the foyer with his sister. "Will you be gone long, Mother?"

"Only a few weeks, my dear. Though that is not why we wanted to speak with you."

"Then what's going on?" Heather asked.

It was their father who replied. "There have been some changes to the business. While Amorte Cliffstone has been a wonderful base of operations, it no longer suits our needs. After our return, we will be moving to someplace more appropriate for our international base."

"What?! Are you serious? You want me to change schools right before my senior year? That's social suicide!" Heather exclaimed.

David blinked. He had no words. His parents planned to move after they returned home? Right after? "Dad, I have two months left before I graduate."

"I understand son, but it's business. It's what is needed for the company."

"And what? Screw your kids? Did you think about us at all?" David almost snickered as the question came out of his mouth. Nah. They hadn't thought about him or Heather. For his parents, a cohesive family unit was what looked great on a Christmas card—no matter how the members of the family treated one another.

"Of course, we factored you and your sister into the decision. That's why we've told you now," his father said.

"My dears," their mother said, "you're both eighteen, and you're welcome to stay here in Amorte Cliffstone. However, you will have to vacate the house. The new owners will be moving in at the end of the month. Now, we really must go. We don't want to miss our flight. Kiss, kiss." His mother smiled, hooked her arm in his father's and the two of them waltzed out the door.

New owners? Had their parents actually sold the house without his or his sister's knowledge? David gripped the back of his neck and turned to his twin. "What do we do now?"

"Still think getting a place of our own is a bad idea?" Heather asked.

"Are you nervous?" Luis glanced at his sister.

Bella was sitting in the passenger seat and twisting the bottom of her blouse into a knot. "Nervous? Why would I be nervous? I'm only about to meet my birth father for the first time in my life. No reason to be nervous."

Slowing the truck, Luis flicked on his blinker and turned right. His old truck had been destroyed in the explosion. Although he hadn't been thrilled with the idea, he'd used the money his father had set aside to buy a new F-150. A vehicle was necessary to get around Rescate County. "Technically, he was around for the first few months of your life."

"Fine. How about the first time I remember? Is that better?" Bella crossed her arms.

"It's certainly more accurate." Luis smiled. The question had been redundant, only asked to get his sister to relax. Maybe then she wouldn't—

"Why are you taking me *here*?"

He told their father the cemetery wasn't the best choice. Though Luis understood the spot had to be inconspicuous, why their father insisted on the cemetery was beyond his comprehension. "This is where we're meeting Dad."

"Are you kidding me? You want me to meet my biological father where *my* father is buried? Have you lost your fucking mind?" His sister looked like she wanted to jump out of the truck while it was still moving.

He'd been afraid she would react like this, which was why he'd spent the last few hours preparing responses. If he had to, he'd point out that her *father* was physically buried in China, but that was a last resort. Luis sighed. "Listen, I know it's not ideal, but the man is a fugitive. I suggested the cabin, but he thought this would be better. Easier for him to escape, if he needs to, and less likely we'd be noticed."

This seemed to calm Bella down, somewhat. She harrumphed and looked out her window. "You have a point. It doesn't mean I like it, but I get it."

Well, that was easy. So why did it feel like a setup? He glanced at his sister. Luis parked the truck alongside the huge oak tree their father had named as their meeting place—not that he saw the man. "Okay," he said. "We're here."

Bella peered through the windshield at the tree. Then she leaned back and eyed her brother. "Are you sure?"

"This is where he said to meet. At least ... I think—"

An olive-skinned man stepped out from behind the tree. "Is that him?" Bella asked. The guy's hair was dark, like hers, but she didn't immediately see any other traits they had in common. Anxiously, Bella bit the inside of her cheek.

"Yes. That's our father." Luis reached over and squeezed her shoulder. "You ready?"

No. She was so not ready, but this opportunity might not arise again. And she had questions—about him, about her mother. Plus, although her brother denied it, she suspected Gervasio had been killed by her father's hand. For that, she owed him.

Bella exhaled deeply. "I'm ready."

"All right. Come on."

Luis climbed out of the truck, and Bella followed. Walking with her brother toward the tree, she felt sweat bloom on her palms. She wiped her hands down the sides of her jeans and shoved them in her pockets. Why was she so nervous? She swallowed and took the final few steps to meet the man who had given her life.

"You look so much like your mother," their father said, when she stopped before him.

"Dad! You can't just open with that. I'm sorry, Bella," Luis said.

Her brother's protectiveness was sweet, but unnecessary. She liked the idea that she looked like her birth mother. She knew so little about the woman. And now, just maybe, since her relationship with her adoptive mother had sweetened so much since she had returned from Brazil, she could ask Mãe about Ileana Costa.

Bella smiled at her biological father. "It's okay. It's nice to know."

"I would bring her back if I could, so you both could understand the kind of woman she was. Unfortunately, I cannot change the past, but this does not mean you should not know where you came from." Their father stepped back behind the tree and returned holding two shoeboxes.

Bella glanced at Luis as they each accepted one of the boxes. Her brother's brow was furrowed. Why? Hadn't he arranged this whole thing? Evidently not this part.

She looked at her own box and lifted the lid. Inside were what looked like a dozen small notebooks. "What's this?" she asked.

At the same time, Luis pulled photographs from his box, asking, "Dad? Are these ...?"

"Pictures from before you were born, and after." Juan Castell replied to Luis. "As for your box, Bella, those are your mother's diaries. I know she would have wanted you both to have these things," their father said.

Bella shifted her gaze from her father to the box in her hand. These weren't just important to her mother, but to her father ... to their family. She closed the box, clutched it to her chest, and looked up. "Thank you."

"Yeah. Thanks, Dad. This really means a lot," Luis said.

"Yes, well, it seemed appropriate our memories remain with you both." Their father paused, then nodded toward the truck. "You should get going."

Luis and Juan exchanged a brief handshake, then Bella's brother squeezed her shoulder, and continued on to the truck.

But she, confused, didn't move. This had been the entire reason for the meeting? A fond farewell. Pictures, diaries? Was that all she got? She'd lost one father. Didn't she get to know the other? *This one's a fugitive*, she reminded herself. Then she surprised herself, by saying, "I know you can't stay, but I wish we had more time."

"As do I, but I promised your mother a long time ago I would ensure you stayed out of the kind of life I lead. And I intend to keep that promise."

"Can I ask you something?"

"Anything," her father said.

Suddenly, though, her mind went blank. There had been so much she'd longed to ask, and now she couldn't think of a single thing. Then one question popped into her head. She looked her father square in the eye. "Did you do it?"

His gaze, however, shifted from hers, as he said, "You and your brother are my world. And I will always do whatever is necessary to keep you both safe."

Her father spoke with such conviction, that, although he hadn't given her a definitive confirmation, she was certain that the man who stood before her had killed her rapist. And now, not only had he ensured she had a future, but he had also given her a piece of her past. Without second guessing herself, Bella stepped forward and hugged him.

"Thank you," she whispered, then released her hold and headed for the truck.

"I'm trying to get back to normal activities, but don't you think it's a little soon for me to take the tutor group back over?" Bella said to Vick, as she stopped at her locker and input her combination. They'd just come from a meeting with the principal—and, although it had been less than a week since her rapist's death, all they'd talked about was her retaking the head tutor position. And, yeah, with her mother's return, things had begun to feel normal, but she still had a lot to work through.

"There's only a couple of months left before I graduate, so why don't you rejoin us for these last few meetings, and see how you feel. If you do take the position, it won't be until next year, anyway," Vick said.

He had a good point. Opening her locker, she put the books up she didn't need and—What was that? Music flooded the hallway. Bella turned around. The choir was singing, which wasn't weird, but it sounded like the group was coming down the hall while doing it. She glanced at Vick. "Is that ... 5 Seconds of Summer?" One of her favorite groups.

Vick nodded. "Yeah. Sounds like 'She Looks So Perfect'."

The song got louder, like it was heading their way.

"What the heck?" her friend said.

She didn't immediately notice what Vick saw, then she turned her full attention to the end of the hallway—where her boyfriend was leading the choir, and doing some kind of amazing dance. A bunch of students followed after them, clapping and bopping along to the music.

As she watched, Miah danced closer, then out of nowhere did a back flip, and the crowd erupted into a cheer when he landed. Along with Bella.

Then Jeremiah dropped to his knees and slid across the floor until he stopped right in front of her. He grinned like he'd just won the lottery.

Which was contagious. She couldn't help herself. Bella returned her boyfriend's smile, then gestured to the choir. "What is all this?"

Jeremiah reached up and took her hand. "Bell, would you give me the honor of being my date to prom?"

"Really?" Her eyes widened. Jeremiah had done all this just to ask her to prom? With all that had gone on, prom had been the furthest thing from her mind. But not from Miah's, evidently. He was still waiting on an answer. Which was a no brainer.

Bella grinned. "Yes!"

Jeremiah jumped to his feet, wrapped his arms around her, and lifted her into the air.

Bella giggled and held on tight, as he spun her around. Holy shit! They were going to prom! They were going to prom! She needed a dress. A shopping trip was in order. Hmm, maybe this one she could do with her mom. That would be nice.

Setting her back on the ground, Jeremiah brushed a tender kiss against Bella's lips. "It'll the best prom ever."

Bella had no doubt.

"I think it's good you guys are moving," Jeremiah said, as he stacked books from Bella's bookcase into the box. He understood his girlfriend's mother's desire to start fresh, at least as fresh as a new house would let them. DeWei had been shot here, and the attack on Bell had occurred in this very bedroom.

"Yeah." Bella glanced out the window.

Jeremiah closed the space between them and cupped her cheek. "Hey. Are you okay with selling this house?"

"Yeah. I mean ... it doesn't change my memories. I guess ... when Mãe and I spoke about it a few days ago, I just ... I didn't expect it to sell so fast."

"I know what you mean." Jeremiah hugged Bella. He'd been through the same thing when his family left California. Except that move had been across the country. At least Bell was only moving across the county.

The doorbell rang.

"I should get that." Bell pulled out of his arms and headed toward the front door.

It was probably Mandy or Vick coming over to help. There was a lot to do and a short time to get it done. And with Mrs. Kynaston's pregnancy so far along, no one wanted her to be lifting stuff.

Jeremiah followed Bella, in case whoever it was needed help carrying boxes inside. But when she opened the door, he saw it was her brother. Jeremiah crossed his arms and leaned against the wall. Nothing had been mentioned about Luis joining their packing party.

"I had something in my mailbox this morning." He held out a newspaper.

Taking it, Bella scanned the paper, then glanced back to her brother. "I don't understand. Who is this guy? What does he have to do with us?"

"The lawyer who did our adoption papers," Luis said.

Okay. His curiosity was piqued. Jeremiah pushed off the wall and strode closer. He eyed the paper in Bella's hands. She was looking at an article on the death of a lawyer. What really caught his attention, though, were the two words scribbled at the top.

"What's over?" he asked. But no one answered him.

Bella glanced from Jeremiah to Luis. "Do you think he's responsible?"

"I do," her brother said.

"Who?" Jeremiah might regret the answer, but he and his girlfriend had agreed: no more secrets.

Turning to him. "Our father," she said.

Stepping out of the school gym, Aurora counted the cash in her wallet. Damn. Why hadn't she grabbed more on her way out this morning? Oh, well. It was too late to fix it now. All she could do was walk the five miles to her hotel. She stared at the dark sky. Or hitchhike. Which might not be recommended. Yeah, people seemed nice enough in this town, but it was hard to tell who could really be trusted.

Hiking her backpack over her shoulders, Aurora walked across the nearly empty parking lot. Among the few cars still there was a convertible BMW. Probably a straggler from the soccer game, she thought. Nice car, but not one she recognized. And for good reason. She didn't really know any of her classmates.

Aurora had a long walk ahead of her. Thank goodness it was Saturday. Meant she could sleep in tomorrow. Nice, especially given she probably wouldn't make it back to her hotel for a couple of hours. But then there was a flash of lightning, followed by the boom of thunder.

Oh, no. Please, please don't let it rain. Or, if it did, please let it wait a few … Aurora bent her head as the sky opened up. Great. Could this night get any worse?

A car pulled up alongside her, and the passenger window rolled down. A guy called out, "Do you need a ride?"

Aurora stopped. Of course, the night could get worse. She hadn't recognized his car in the lot, but she sure recognized him behind the Bimmer's wheel. Okay. Her choice was simple: walk five miles in the rain or get into his car.

"Come on. It's pouring. Get in, and I'll take you wherever you want to go."

Shit. Aurora groaned inwardly. This was a bad idea. A horrible idea. But, accepting her fate, she shrugged off her backpack and climbed in. "Thank you."

"Sure." The window rolled up, and David pulled back onto the road.

"I'm not going far. Just to the RC Motel. About five miles."

David nodded. "I know the place." Then he said, "Mind if I ask you a question?"

Thinking again what a bad idea this was, Aurora told herself that he was giving her a ride and saving her from possible pneumonia, so the least she could do was be nice. She glanced at him. Why did he have to be gorgeous? And smell so good, to boot? "Listen, I appreciate the ride, but I stand by what I said before. I'm not someone you should know."

"I just want to know your name. How can that hurt?"

That depended. His knowledge of her real name could prove dangerous. The people who were after her weren't particularly nice. And she had yet to find the one person who could help her. But … if she stuck with the name she used in school, it would likely be fine.

"Ari. I go by Ari."

"Ari. Not so hard, was it?" David turned into the parking lot of the single-story motel, one of the cheaper places in town, and shut off the ignition.

Aurora scooped up her backpack, grateful it had been a short drive. Less chance he'd get information out of her. "Thanks for the ride."

"Wait a second. This isn't exactly the best neighborhood. I wouldn't feel right if I didn't at least walk you up."

"It isn't—" Aurora watched as David climbed out of the car. Well, nothing she could do to stop it now. She got out as David came around with an open umbrella.

This guy was almost too good to be true. Standing so close to him, her body warmed from the inside out. Sweat bloomed on her forehead, as, shielded from the rain, they walked side by side toward her motel room. Aurora swallowed. She felt as if she had stepped into a sauna.

Thankfully, her room wasn't far. Aurora dug her key out of her pocket—then stopped. The door to her room was open a crack.

David looked at the door, then back to Aurora. "Don't suppose you left your door unlocked?" he asked.

"No. I didn't." Oh shit. Not good. She pushed the door open all the way and eyed the mess. Her stuff—the few clothes she had, a couple of notebooks for school—had been strewn all over the floor. Someone had been looking for something. Not good.

Panicked, she ran to the connecting door—she'd rented two rooms for this exact reason. Had the other room been ransacked? Please let the other room be untouched. She yanked it open. "Damn it!"

The other room had been tossed, too.

"What?" David asked.

Aurora couldn't speak. Shaking, she made her way through the extra room into the bathroom. *Shit.* The lid had been removed from the toilet tank. Her money. It was all gone. Aurora punched the wall. What the hell was she going to do, now?

David rushed in and slid to a stop in the doorway. "Are you okay?"

"No." Aurora choked on tears and anger. "My money was in there, and it's gone. I don't know what I'm going to do or where I'm going to stay." The words came out before she could stop them. Getting this guy involved in her problems was the last thing she should do. She shook her hand. *Fuck.* Her knuckles stung like a bitch.

Shoving his hands in pockets, David nodded. "Um, if you want ... we have spare bedrooms at my house. You could crash there while you figure things out."

He had to be joking. This guy knew nothing about her. Aside from the few times they'd run into one another and she'd warned him away. Or *tried* to warn him away.

Any minute, he would laugh or take it back.

When he didn't, Aurora blinked. "You're serious?"

"Yeah. I mean, why not? You need a place, and we've got plenty of space. Seems logical to accept."

Aurora stared at David.

On the one hand, if she went with him, she would be putting his life at risk to save her own. On other hand, if she stayed put and prayed the break-in was random … No. Xavier had obviously found her.

But what to do? Neither solution was right, but she had to pick one.

But which one?

To be continued ...

David despises Bella, but still can't stop loving her. He'd do anything to let her go. Even help a girl who is dangerous for both his health and his heart.

Rescate County is supposed to be the perfect place for Aurora to hide from her past. But one moment, one decision, and one guy changes all that. As her past bubbles to the surface, she unexpectedly finds herself losing her heart to someone she'd be better off without.

Can Aurora escape her past and safely fall into David's arms? Can David allow himself to love someone so close to the fire? Or will they both get burned by the flames?

Look for

b u r n e d

Summer 2020

URBAN FANTASY SERIES

Awakened
Released May 2019

Disillusion
Released June 2019

For FREE sneak peeks, giveaways, upcoming events, and more,
sign up for Krys Fenner's monthly newsletter.

https://mailchi.mp/ded3a6cb847f/krysfenner

A u t h o r   N o t e

I hope you enjoyed *Avenged: Dark Road Three*. I have to tell you, I really loved rebuilding the relationship between Bella and Jeremiah, while still testing the limits. Recovery isn't easy for anyone to deal with, even loved ones of the addict. Although this concluded a lot of things for Bella and Jeremiah, doors opened for other characters. Some of my readers have asked about David and Heather. Others have inquired on Aurora. No worries, these characters will return in the next book *Burned* due to release Spring 2020.

Making the books what they have become today has all been based on the feedback I've received. As an author, I found it useful and insightful. I love receiving feedback! There are so many characters to explore in this series. I'd love to hear about what you liked, what you loved, even what you hated. You can write me at **krysfenner@gmail.com** and visit me on the web at **www.krysfenner.co/**.

Finally, I need to ask a favor. If you're up for it I'd love a review of *Avenged*. Loved it, hated it—I'd just enjoy your feedback.

As you may have figured out from my books, reviews can be hard to come by these days. You, the reader, have the power to make or break a book. If you have the time, here's a link to my author page on Amazon. You can find all my books at **amazon.com/author/krysfenner**.

Thank you so much for reading Avenged and for spending time with me.

In gratitude,
Krys Fenner

www.ingramcontent.com/pod-product-compliance
Lightning Source LLC
Chambersburg PA
CBHW071602110726
47908CB00007B/2209